MURDER HAS A PRETTY FACE

MURDER HAS
A PRETTY FACE

Jennie Melville

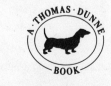

St. Martin's Press
New York

Library of Congress Cataloging-in-Publication Data

Melville, Jennie
        Murder has a pretty face / Jennie Melville.
                p.   cm.
        "A Thomas Dunne Book."
        ISBN 0-312-03405-9
        I. Title.
    PR6063.E44M8   1989
    823'.914—dc20   89-35327
                                                            CIP

First published in Great Britain 1981 by Macmillan London Ltd.

First U.S. Edition

10 9 8 7 6 5 4 3 2 1

MURDER HAS A PRETTY FACE

Chapter One

When the woman first came into town nobody knew what to do about her. Certainly not the police. She was standing watching a large parked van in which a group of doctors and nurses were conducting a mass screening of women for cervical cancer. She watched the other women go in and come out, but never tried to go in herself.

'As far as I hear, she just stands and looks,' said Inspector Charmian Daniels of the Deerham Hills C I D. 'We can't arrest her for *that*.'

She added: 'And she can't have anything to do with all the other problems we have on our plate.' She totted them up: 'One dead man, unknown, probably murdered; one robbery of a local furrier's, stripped bare; one pedigree dog, stolen. Problems in descending order of importance.' Even then she knew the woman stood for something. Disorder, maybe.

The robbery of the furrier was specifically Charmian's job. She was supposed to be something of an expert at break-ins. The murdered man was her boss's task at the moment. (Her boss was Chief Inspector Walter Wing.) Everyone took an interest in the murder. Anyone who had an idea was offering it. Nobody had an idea about the dog.

And a spate of small, relatively trivial incidents, violence, break-ins, assaults. Many more than the average in Deerham Hills. Nastier.

'No, the woman has nothing to do with all that,' said Charmian.

She got up and looked out of her window. She had a room in the newest part of the newish police station in the

5

centre of Deerham Hills, and from her window on the third floor she could see the pleasant town, through which ran a slow-flowing river, bordered by gardens. The town's profile was dominated by the spire of the fifteenth-century church and the tower of the twentieth-century polytechnic: old town and new town happily blending.

'I ought to go down and look at her myself,' she said absently. 'When I've got through some of this paperwork on my table.' Even more absently she added: 'We ought to know about the death of the man found in the river. Perhaps we'll be lucky and he drowned himself.'

'Having first tried to weight his feet?' said her sergeant, Adam Lily, whose name annoyed him very much. 'There are patches of cement on his socks.'

'Were,' said Charmian. 'The pre-mixed sort, too. Perhaps he was a builder. Joke,' she said hastily to Sergeant Adam Lily's blank face. She looked at her watch. 'The shops are still open; the woman might still be there. I think I'll go down and have a look myself. Also, I have an appointment.'

When she'd gone, the sergeant turned to the woman police constable seated at the typewriter. 'Getting over it, is she, then?'

The constable shrugged. 'If you ever really do. It's been a year.' Agnes considered the year, and her life during it. 'Lousy year, really.'

'I *do* agree. What's gone right? For me, nothing.'

'One or two things,' suggested Agnes.

They looked at each other. 'Yes,' agreed Adam. 'Not as often as I'd like, though.'

'Got your car back yet?'

Adam scowled. 'Yes, and a bill with it. Don't know how I'm going to pay it.'

'You shouldn't gamble, but save.'

Adam shrugged. 'Only way I'm ever going to make money, I reckon. I'll never earn it, that's for sure.'

6

'No, nor me.' Agnes looked at her hands. 'Money, money, money.'

She didn't sound amused.

'Well, I'm off.' Adam moved away. 'See you later?'

Agnes barely muttered her answer.

Inside the van where cervical smears and breast-scanning were taking place in curtained alcoves was a small waiting-area. Comfortable seats and magazines were provided: sometimes the wait was long. At lunch-time there had even been a queue, but it was now early afternoon. Four women were seated there, each with her head buried in a magazine. No one was talking. There was something about the clinical air that discouraged conversation, although the atmosphere was friendly enough.

A tall, strong-featured, fair-haired woman was reading *Vogue*. She was thin, but looked as if she could have been a heavy well-built woman if rigorous dieting had not kept her weight under control. Her breasts were tightly laced inside an expensive brassière that was going to be hell to get out of, and she would probably have to ask the nurse to hook her back in. As for the other test, well, her uterus had never been a welcoming one, and she could already feel her muscles tightening.

'Can I have that *Harper's* if you've finished reading it?' she asked her neighbour. In her left hand she clutched a card to hand to the doctor, with her name, Diana King, written on it.

Her neighbour, small, pretty and blonde, politely handed over the magazine she was reading and accepted *Vogue* in return. She was an elegantly boned creature with huge hungry blue eyes and a constant smile.

Next to her was seated a tall spare woman in jeans and a check shirt. She wasn't reading at all but was obstinately smoking a cigarette in defiance of a large notice request-

7

ing no smoking. She carried the cards for herself and her companion: Phyllis Ladbury and Beryl Andrea Barker.

'Whichever of us is called, *you* can go first, Baby,' she said tolerantly. 'I can see you're on the twitch.'

The other woman present was using the time to check her bank statement. Baby tried to read it upside down, but found it difficult. She could read the name, though, and it matched that on the card in the woman's lap, which vaguely surprised Baby's suspicious little mind. She was always on the look-out for discrepancies, and enjoyed them. 'Beatrice Dawson,' she read, on bank statement and card.

She whispered to her friend: 'It's the cold steel going inside me that gets me. That's what I can't stand.'

Presently, Charmian Daniels came in and sat down. No words passed.

They all sat there quietly. It was an hour in a day in their lives.

Kitty Morley, having recently had a child, had not been summoned to the mass screening of Woman. Nature had just cleared out her system magnificently, and she was well. She went home from her weekly 'big' shop in the Bonanza Supermarket in Deerham Hills, drove the car into the garage, scraping the paintwork again, and unpacked the frozen goods first, then the baby and last of all the bags of groceries. She had worked out her priorities weeks ago. Presently, when the baby began to sit up and grab things, she would have to move *him* first, but for the moment he could only lie there and stare and wave his hands.

At dinner she said to her husband, Ben: 'There was such a funny woman outside the freezer-shop today.' She waited hopefully for him to make some response, but he only chewed on. So she tried again. 'Really *queer*. Just stood there and stared.'

'At you specially? Or everyone?' He was still young enough, and newly married enough, to think his wife well worth staring at.

'No, not just me. Everyone.'

'Ah.' And he went back to chewing his steak, which was tough.

'She had such heavy make-up on. Thick black eyebrows, and a great red Cupid's bow of a mouth. It looked all wrong.'

'So she was ugly, then?'

'No, not ugly,' said Kitty thoughtfully. 'More grotesque. I was sorry for her.'

'Oh well, you won't see her again, so why worry? Is there any pudding?'

'You haven't finished the steak yet.'

'Only thinking ahead,' observed her husband mildly. 'You're always telling me to.'

'Yes, but I meant about cutting the grass, and decorating the living-room, and planning our holiday, not food, not eating,' said Kitty with deep conviction. 'Important things.'

'Food's important,' said her husband rather sadly. It was not always important to his Kitty. Hence, no doubt, the toughness of the steak. 'Anyway, to me. And to *him*,' he said as there was an angry roar from upstairs. 'How's he getting on?'

'About the same as he was when you last saw him this morning. Not much change from that. What do you expect?'

'You feel as though they should be advancing every minute when they're as small as that,' said Ben. 'They've got so much to get in.'

'I don't think he's very bright,' observed Kitty appraisingly. 'It's disappointing. He should be reaching out to grab things – bright things – with his hands by now, and

9

he's not. About ten weeks, he should be doing at least that.'

'But that's the *average*. It's the average for that sort of thing. Doesn't mean any more. It's not a law.' Ben stopped eating to make his point.

'Oh, of course, I know that. But naturally I thought he'd be better than average.'

'He'll catch up.'

'I don't want him catching up. He ought to be right out there, leading,' said Kitty.

Ben tried to read her expression. He was never quite sure when she was joking. Because she was clever he was never sure of her at all. Possibly she was joking now.

'However, he was very intelligent this afternoon,' she went on. 'I give him full marks for it.'

'You *were* joking then,' said Ben with relief.

'When that woman looked at him, he *glared* back.'

'I don't like to think she even looked at him,' said Ben nervously. He was very protective of his son. 'You don't suppose that she was . . . . No, I suppose not. Still keep an eye on the baby, Kitty, when you're out.'

'Oh, I always do,' said his wife placidly. 'I don't think she was looking at him hungrily. No, not at all. It was just a stare. Not much expression was in it behind the mascara.' She got up.

'Where are you going? He's stopped crying.'

'I'm not going up to him. I'm going to telephone my friend Charmian and tell her about the woman. I think she ought to know.'

'She probably knows already,' observed Ben. 'You don't suppose you were the only one who noticed the woman, do you?'

'No,' said Kitty thoughtfully. 'Now you mention it, I don't. There must have been others today. Wonder if she'll be there tomorrow.'

10

Next day it rained; but there was a covered-in promenade around the new market, where it was possible to stop and stay dry. Also to stand and stare.

'Baby, have you seen the way she *looks*?' said Phil, returning to her car where her friend was waiting. 'I went back to see again. Face like a mask and a stare on her that'd frighten a horse.'

'She's creepy,' said Baby. Gleefully, she shuddered: 'Her hands!'

'Did she touch you?'

'No, Phil. Never came near me. Don't be so fierce. It frightens Baby.'

'Not you,' said Phil with conviction. 'You love it. What about her hands, then?'

'Red nail-varnish and ragged cuticles. Ugh!'

'Everyone can't spend the hours on their hands that you do.'

'Don't be spiteful, Phil. After all, it's my *job*.'

'I'll drive you back to work,' said Phil, changing the subject. 'You're going to be late. Got all the shopping you want?'

'Enough till the weekend. Thanks for carrying the heavy stuff.'

Phil grunted. 'That's what I'm for.'

'Not *only*.' Baby put out a little hand, the nails a delicate pearly pink. 'You know that.'

Phil grunted again. 'It's that woman. Got under my skin somehow.'

As they drove past the corner, they both turned to look.

'She's still there.'

'Poor soul,' said Baby. 'It's sad, really.'

The car stopped outside *Charm and Chic* hair salon, and Baby got out, waved goodbye and went in. She was nearly, but not quite, late; and Diana King, her employer, was standing in the window of the shop, looking out.

11

'Your two o'clock's just come in,' she said to Baby.

'Sorry if I'm late.'

'No, you aren't. She's early.' In Diana's eyes it was as great a sin for a customer to come early as to come late. Not to come at all was worst; but *Charm and Chic* charged for that.

'I'll just get my things together.' Baby was putting on a pink overall and gathering up a large pink cushion on which were disposed a small bowl of scented water in which to soak the client's fingertips and a tray of lotions and varnishes. Baby floated a rose petal in the bowl and was ready.

'You might change the water.'

'It's perfectly fresh. Mrs Driscoll before lunch wouldn't use it. Said the bowl reminded her of her dog. And I can't keep splashing out on scent to put in it. Too pricey.'

'You're as mean as Old Nick, really,' said Diana. 'She's never got her dog back, then?'

'No. I don't think she ever will now.'

Diana continued to look out of the window. 'Big girl, your friend,' she said. 'Nice car she drives. Good driver, is she?'

'It's her life,' said Baby earnestly.

'Introduce me some time.'

'Oh, I will,' said Baby. 'She's a dream.'

Charmian Daniels had weathered the first week of the woman's coming into town, and was now having a few hours off duty. It had been her intention to spend the time gardening, but the rain prevented that. Instead she decided to clear out some cupboards. Charmian was no housewife; the house was tidy and clean because she would have despised living in a mess, but she paid someone else to clean it for her. This job, however, was special, and she had to do it herself. She had left it long enough as it was.

Charmian's house had the anonymous look of all houses not loved by their owners. Everything in it was in immaculate order but was neglected. If a house could be bored, this house was bored. Only Charmian's bedroom had any character, with the clothes she had just taken off hanging up to air, her shoes on special trees, and on the air the faint breath of a very fresh, light toilet water. The big bed with its pleated chintz quilt was placed squarely in the middle of the room, reflecting, perhaps, the character of the man who had once shared it with her. Charmian had moved her pillows into the centre of the bed. This was the only sign of change.

She opened a cupboard door. Inside, it was full of men's clothes. She stared for a moment, then deliberately closed the door.

It was over a year now since her husband had died. The first numbing shock had been lived through and had lifted. Time now to deal with all the tasks she had pushed aside. She opened the cupboard door again. 'These first,' she said aloud.

By her side she had placed two large empty cardboard boxes, into which she methodically tumbled the clothes. She went through the pockets of jackets and trousers as each garment came off its hanger, deliberately suppressing all emotion as she did so. All the pockets were empty, for her husband had been a careful foreseeing man.

All except one outfit, the suit in which he had died. Died suddenly and painlessly (or so the doctors had assured her) of a massive myocardial infarction. His police identification-card and his cheque-book and similar papers had been removed with his wallet, as she knew, but in the jacket some objects might still remain.

Even after this length of time Charmian disliked digging

13

through his pockets, prying. She and Rupert had treated each other with dignity and reserve.

Not the foundation perhaps for the very happiest and closest of marriages. 'And, as a matter of fact,' said Charmian, as if she had only just discovered it, and was surprised, 'it wasn't.'

Her husband had been fifteen years her senior, and already a distinguished policeman when they married. He had been even more distinguished when he died. Charmian, too, had been steadily ascending the career-ladder, her ambitions unchanged by marriage; indeed, stimulated by it. Her husband's career had shown her what *could* be done.

'I'm not as clever as he was, but I sometimes have flashes of insight which make up for it. And I'm very thorough,' she said.

The top pockets of the jacket were empty. It was good tweed, and well tailored; he had had excellent taste, better than Charmian's, as she acknowledged.

All the clothes could be cleaned and sent to Oxfam.

Now, *my* clothes, if I drop dead, won't be worth a penny, thought Charmian. Shan't drop dead, of course. Go plodding on, dogged and indomitable and very, very irritating. Just like my mother.

She could feel something in a small inner breast-pocket.

She felt carefully with her fingers, and then drew something out.

At that moment the door-bell rang: a busy little chime which had irritated Charmian for the ten years of her marriage without her ever doing anything about it.

Holding what she had extracted from the pocket, she went to the front door and opened it. Outside was her friend Kitty, with her infant son.

'I don't like that door-bell. I never have.' She held the

door open wider. 'Come on in. I think I'll move from this house.'

'It is too big,' agreed Kitty, dragging baby and push-chair into the hall and chipping Charmian's paint as she did so. 'I'm afraid I've put mud on your nice carpet.' She looked about her in a distracted way. 'Oh dear, quite a lot, really. It'll dry, though. It's clean mud. Why are you holding that photograph?'

'I've been going through my husband's clothes.'

'At *last*. You've got round to it at last. I *knew* you needed me. I got that feeling,' declared Kitty dramatically. 'That's why I came.' She paused.

Something seemed necessary, so Charmian said it: 'Thank you, Kitty.'

'You know, when my sister said, "Do look up my old college chum, Charmian Daniels; she works in Deerham Hills," I nearly said, "Not likely". Well, Fiona is so bossy it's a pleasure to deny her. And working on the *Deerham Hills Herald* was my first proper job. But when I met you I was bowled over. I thought: There's a real woman, with a real job, and a real husband. It's why I married Ben. He's *very* real. What's it like being a policewoman, Charmian? I never asked you before.'

'Kitty, you're talking too much.'

'I know. I'm excited. I've just had a row with Ben. That's why I came.'

'I thought it was to help me,' said Charmian.

'That, too. What's the photograph of?'

Charmian held it out, and they both looked. It was the snapshot of a young man. He was smiling into the camera, screwing up his eyes faintly against the sun.

'Is it your husband?'

Charmian shook her head. 'No.'

'Looks like him a bit.'

'Yes.' Charmian nodded, and put the photograph down carefully on a table. 'So it should. His son, Tom.'

15

Kitty bent her head over the picture. 'Oh, yes, of course. His first wife died, didn't she? Good-looking boy. Where is he?'

'I don't know,' Charmian said. 'Dead, probably. Certainly missing. His father was looking for him.'

After a moment of shocked silence, Kitty said: 'I'm so sorry. I had no idea.'

'It's why he died, I think. Emotional excess, you could call it.' Her tone was hard and dry. 'After Tom disappeared Rupert spent all his time trying to find out what had happened. There was a body, never absolutely identified. But even after that he went on looking. He couldn't stop. He went on and on till it killed him.'

'I can understand that,' said Kitty. 'Can't you?'

'Oh, yes, I understand.'

'But it doesn't stop you minding?'

'How could it?'

'No, how could it? Silly question.' Kitty gave Charmian a push. 'I'll make some coffee. I suppose you've got some. Your housekeeping!' She had the door of the refrigerator open and was looking inside. A bottle of milk, a piece of stale cheese and one egg were all that greeted her.

'It's gone from bad to worse, I know,' said Charmian. 'I don't eat here much. But there is coffee and I'll make it myself. Your coffee shows your youth: it's too weak.'

'You're feeling better,' said Kitty philosophically, and sat down at the kitchen table. 'Fancy you keeping this to yourself all this time.'

'I didn't keep it to myself. Plenty of people knew. You didn't, that's all.' Charmian started making the coffee. 'It wasn't something I wanted to talk about much.'

Kitty watched her pour boiling water on to the coffee grounds. 'Did you know Tom well? That's another thing you've never talked about.'

16

'He lived and worked in London. Our lives didn't touch very often. But I knew him well enough to grieve that he's gone.'

She poured the coffee into cups and pushed the sugar forward.

Kitty shook her head. 'No sugar. I'm dieting. How did Tom disappear?'

'He was working on a case. Under cover. One day he went off, saying he'd report back in two days. He never did.'

'That's terrible.' Kitty was horrified at the story.

'His father thought he could find him.'

'Did he discover anything?'

'I don't think so. If he did, he never told me of it. We didn't talk much those last weeks. When he was home he used to sit in a chair, just staring at nothing.'

'I suppose he was thinking,' said Kitty.

Charmian wrenched herself back to the present. 'Yes, I suppose so. Shall I tell you something I did? I am a bit ashamed of it now. Six months ago I had advertisements put in a range of newspapers – here and abroad, in the States and Australia.'

'Sort of "Tom, come home, all is forgiven"?' asked Kitty with interest.

'Asking him to get in touch. No answer, of course. Now I feel I was a fool to do it.'

'No, I don't think you were,' said Kitty. 'If you hadn't done it, you'd hate yourself.'

'I hate myself anyway. Well, on and off.' Charmian grinned, trying to take the edge off her remark, which had come out with unexpected bitterness.

Kitty finished her coffee. 'Come on. I'll help you with those clothes.' She stood up. 'Come on.'

'What about the baby?'

'He can look on. Give him something to think about.'

17

She frowned at him. 'He needs stimulating.' But the baby was asleep.

The two women worked hard and silently. Charmian took the clothes from the cupboard, and checked through them, then handed them to Kitty, who folded them and put them in the cardboard boxes.

'In the end it didn't take so long, did it?' said Kitty, when they had finished.

'A few more things in these drawers,' said Charmian, 'and then it really is finished. Help me carry the boxes to the car and I'll take them to the Oxfam shop tomorrow.'

'I'll do something better,' panted Kitty, as they carried the boxes out (they were surprisingly heavy). 'Put them in my car and I'll take them for you.'

'Yes. Thanks,' said Charmian, and then, after a pause, 'Do something else, will you?'

Kitty paused at the door of her car. 'What?' Her eye caught something. 'Fancy, I've scraped the paint.' The air emanating from the boxes smelt sour and heavy. She didn't like the smell.

'Take the boxes to the shop in Feverley, not in Deerham Hills.'

'Of course. You don't want to meet the clothes walking around Deerham Hills.'

'I don't want to see them again,' said Charmian so fiercely that Kitty blinked. Her husband called it 'Kitty's protective blink, when she doesn't like what she sees'.

'Clothes are quite anonymous, Charmian,' she said gently, trying to correct the balance.

'No, by God, they're not. That's something I've learnt this last year. Clothes pick up character like scent. A cupboardful of clothes like that have a life of their own. A half-life, maybe, but a long one.'

Kitty said with conviction: 'You should never have shut this up inside you for a whole year. Any more than you

18

should have let those clothes stay there. And you sleeping in the same room.'

'Don't go into that,' said Charmian harshly. 'The cupboards are empty now. What did you quarrel with your husband about?'

'Oh, that.' Kitty was getting the baby into the car and herself in after it. Already she was planning how she would unload the car when she got home. First the baby, because those clothes had death in them if ever she smelled it, and then the clothes, and then she would put the car away. That was the order of priorities this time. The rest of her mind dealt with Charmian's question. 'Oh, it was about the woman, the woman who's been standing about Deerham Hills, staring at other women. Remember, I phoned you about her. Ben says I'm getting too interested in her.'

'Oh, her,' said Charmian. 'I went and looked at her myself. But she wouldn't look at me. What that means I don't know.'

'She knew you were police, I expect.'

'Oh, no, she didn't,' said Charmian. 'I took care of that. Unless you think it's a brand one can't efface.'

'You're vicious tonight,' said Kitty sadly. 'That woman – you don't think she's dangerous?'

'I have no idea,' said Charmian patiently. 'But she'll bear watching.'

She watched Kitty drive away, then went back into the house.

The photograph was still looking at her from the table where she had placed it. It wouldn't get up and walk away. Almost she wished it would: a young, intelligent, self-contained face with a quality which had always puzzled her.

She laid a finger across the eyes, and studied the mouth and chin. No, the quality did not come from there. Then

19

she covered the lower half of the face. Yes, it was the eyes.

They were her husband's eyes, young, as she had never seen them.

Charmian put the photograph away in a drawer in the table and went into her bedroom. She closed the cupboard doors firmly on their ghosts.

She could see her reflection in a wall mirror. 'Ten years of my life,' she said to her reflection. 'And now I'm not even sure if I liked him.'

The room was very stuffy and smelt of old clothes.

She opened the window to let in some fresh air. The rain had stopped, and a warm sweet early-summer breeze blew into the room.

Charmian enjoyed it for a moment. Then a breath of air that smelled like groceries floated across to her. It was still early evening and the big supermarket down in the shopping-precinct did not close until ten o'clock.

I wonder if the woman's still there, thought Charmian. Still standing there watching. And what exactly is she watching? And why?

A few miles away the woman, who did not live in Deerham Hills, but on a convenient bus-route into it, was seated in the room she rented, making a display-card.

It was a large card, on which she had stuck pieces of newspaper. She meant to wear it round her neck. She was now attaching lengths of white tape, sewing them on with large clumsy stitches, using an outsize darning-needle. She was no needlewoman.

Her first card announced its message, unreadable, as she now decided, with underlined words on newsprint. She still continued to use pieces of newspaper, but now she wrote on them with a felt-tipped pen in red and black ink. She found this deeply satisfying. It worried her that it was still sometimes difficult to read what she wanted to say, but a cloud often descended between her and her message and made her work difficult.

'I am the message, really,' she said aloud.

To make the display hers, indubitably hers (and so little *was* in this world), she wrote her name on the back of it: Glory, Gloria.

It looked good, so she wrote a whole line of Glorias along the bottom of the card which none but she would ever see.

Unlike her sewing, her handwriting was small and neat.

This done, to Gloria's satisfaction, she stumped over to the bed and lay down on it. She was worn out. Standing, and especially wearing high-heeled shoes with pointed toes (winklepickers were back in Gloria's circle), was very hard on the legs.

Down below, her landlady's husband heard her progress across the floor.

'She's heavy-footed, that one,' he commented. 'The whole room shakes when she moves.'

'Not her fault,' said his wife.

'Is she going to get a job?' Gloria had been living with them for over a month now, and for the first few weeks had spent her days sitting in her room, reading. She did go out occasionally, but certainly not to work. It made her landlord uneasy, especially as when she first came she had said she was a nurse. Not adding that she was an unemployed nurse.

'I think she's got one now; she's out all day,' said his wife uneasily.

'Doing what?' he asked.

'I don't know.'

'She's not a nurse,' he said with conviction.

'But she might have been one once,' said his wife. On principle, she rarely agreed completely with her husband. In any case, she had better opportunities for observation

21

than he and had seen a book about nursing in her lodger's room.

It rained again next day, which was Saturday, and it rained again on Sunday: a wet weekend. On Monday, Charmian, although by no means in a good mood, felt better able to tackle her problems. Not that they were her problems alone: they were shared by the entire police force of Deerham Hills, which was badly stretched by the rising crime-rate.

'It's a crime-wave,' said Charmian's immediate boss, Chief Inspector Walter Wing, a tall sweet-tempered man, who always kept his voice low. 'Every tiresome silly little crook in town seems determined to do his thing.'

'Perhaps some of them are from out of town, out of Deerham Hills,' said Charmian. She reached out her hand for the telephone. 'Get me the local paper,' she said to the switchboard operator.

'No, I recognise their silly little faces.' Walter Wing stared down at the clipboard of papers he carried. 'Jimmy Jones, Larry Bell – beauties, both of them, with long records. What are you doing with the *Deerham Hills Herald*? Getting yourself some publicity?'

'No, putting in an advertisement,' said Charmian, studying her nails, which were badly in need of some attention. Pale polish? she thought. Perhaps a professional job. 'I'm selling my wardrobe.'

Walter Wing did not answer. Charmian's domestic arrangements puzzled him without interesting him. He did not really like working with women, but he had adapted himself to a mixed profession by ignoring anything they said which seemed to reflect their sex, although he liked them to respond to anything which reflected his.

'I'm off, then,' he said. 'Glad the rain's stopped, but it's helped my roses.' And he departed.

'He always goes away when you mention anything like

wardrobes,' observed Charmian without rancour. 'It might be beds next.' She was perfectly well aware how he felt.

Her typist, Policewoman Agnes Ryan, laughed. 'He's not a bad sort. Always polite.' Between the two women there was a relaxed friendly relationship which allowed of such comment on colleagues and superiors. Quite simply, they were two women who were friends. But they were careful not to let this show too much when others were present. Professional good manners demanded a certain distance then, but the underground alliance was probably felt by the men and was perhaps what prompted Walter's instinctive feeling that it was difficult working with women. No doubt he sensed that they had ways of communicating not open to men. 'I like him. Where's he going? Not driving that terrible car, I hope?'

'I think there's a meeting in London,' said Charmian. 'I'm going to get a manicure.'

'Are you?'

'Don't you think I need one?' And she held out her hands.

Agnes looked at the ten fingers, immaculately clean but with torn irregular fingernails. 'You certainly do. But it's not like you.'

'You think I don't care how I look?'

'I know you care. But you haven't gone in for decoration much lately.'

'Now I've changed,' said Charmian.

'Where will you go? To your hairdresser's?'

'I do my hair at home,' said Charmian. 'Set it on rollers and blow-dry, you know. No, I'm going to *Charm and Chic*.'

'Oh, yes. I've been there. I've tried everywhere. Wasn't bad. Run by a tall fair blonde. But I decided she wasn't really interested in hair.'

23

'Perhaps she'll do better with nails,' said Charmian with a tiny secretive smile.

The two women worked on in silence for a few minutes. The silence was relative, as the new police building was a noisy place. They could hear doors banging, the constant coming and going of the lift from floor to floor, and, through the open window, the steady drone of the traffic in the crowded street below.

Papers passed backwards and forwards between the two women, typescripts were checked, notes on cases initialled and passed up for consideration to the office of Walter Wing, who, of course, was not there. He, for his part, had sent down a file of papers on the murdered man for Charmian's consideration. Of all his colleagues, he trusted her perceptiveness most. She saw into things, he said.

Charmian read everything in the file carefully, and the upshot of it was nothing, as Walter Wing had remarked in an attached note, written in his small neat hand. 'May be some illumination when we get the pathologist's detailed report,' he said.

Her sergeant, Adam Lily, came in and leant against the desk; he looked as though he had something to say.

'Any more sightings of the woman?' asked Charmian, raising her eyes from Walter Wing's file.

He didn't ask what woman. 'No reports,' he said. 'But that doesn't mean she isn't there. Probably is.'

Charmian looked at him. 'So what is it? I can tell by your face there is something.'

'It's admiration,' he said.

'Of me?' said Agnes hopefully from her corner.

He ignored her. In public he always did so. 'There's been a raid on another fur-shop. This time they left the poor-quality furs and took only the best. They're learning.'

24

Charmian stared at him silently. Then she raised one eyebrow.

He nodded. 'Yes. Sometime over the weekend. Same mode of entry. No sign of a break-in; they just unlocked the door and walked in.'

'Or that's what it looks like,' agreed Charmian.

'Think of another explanation if you can.'

She got up. 'Where's the shop? I'm coming to look for myself.'

'Arden Avenue, off Hillingdon Road.'

Charmian looked surprised. The Hillingdon Road district was in the less prosperous area of Deerham Hills, not where you'd expect to find a shop selling expensive furs.

'That area is going up in the world, isn't it? I noticed the other day. I suppose it's because the houses there are good, solid and old-fashioned. It must be quite a new shop.'

'Yes, it is. Selling mostly what they call "fun" furs, although the prices aren't funny. And they carried a few really good pieces – mink and fox.'

'And those are the furs stolen?'

Adam nodded. 'Together with a few of the choicer "fun" furs.' He grinned. 'One was a striped pale blue and pink knee-length fur smock. That should be easy to recognise.'

'If we ever see it again.' Charmian led the way to the door. 'We ought to be able to put a name to the fur fancier, oughtn't we? But no faces seem to fit.'

'We'll find one.' Adam followed her down the stairs.

'You're an optimist.'

'No, I'm not. No one with a name like mine is an optimist. You bring out the worst in people when you're a man called Lily. Do you know, my grandfather had a perfectly decent name, L-i-l-l-e-y' – he spelt it out for her – 'and then he changed it to Lily.'

25

Charmian laughed. 'So you say.'

'No, it's true. And he did it because he was a lazy man. Lily is easier to write. Anyway, my mother called me Adam to make up for it.'

Charmian drove her own car. Usually she drove much too fast, but today as they went through the town centre she slowed to a crawl, her eyes studying the crowds.

'Busy today,' said Adam.

'Yes, for a Monday. Some of the shops are closed, of course.' She was still scanning the crowds. Then she looked away. 'There she is. Over there, by the Baby Care shop.'

'Who?' But he knew who she meant: the new arrival in Deerham Hills, the woman who stood and stared.

'She's chosen her spot well, hasn't she? Where else would you get more women passing than by a baby-shop?' Charmian was braking the car; she found a parking-spot and drove into it. 'Wait here. I won't be long.'

She got out of the car and hurried, with long strides, across the wide stretch of pavement to where the woman stood.

As she got closer, she could see that a large length of cardboard hung from the woman's neck, rather like an apron. Pieces of newspaper, some of their headlines scored under with thick black pencil, were stuck to the cardboard. Charmian wasn't close enough to read what their message was, if any.

Before she got any closer, a uniformed policeman appeared round the corner of the block; he strolled in the direction of the Baby Care shop, mildly but purposefully making his way towards the woman. As soon as the woman saw him, she swung on her heel and marched briskly away.

'Damn,' said Charmian. She returned to the car.

Adam looked at her. 'She got away.'

'I didn't want to catch her. Only to look at her face.

26

Still, I saw something. Did you notice the way she walked?'

'No.'

'You should have.' Charmian started the car.

'She's only just gone round the corner,' said Adam lazily. 'She'll come back when you and the constable have gone.'

'No, she didn't see me.' And Charmian drove away, very quickly this time.

At *Prettifurs,* the fur-shop in Arden Avenue, they were met by the indignant owner. She introduced herself: 'Jane Pretty. I came here because it was a good town. I could have stayed in Whitechapel Road and been robbed.' She had a pile of brightly coloured furs bundled in her arms, striped black and yellow, red and green.

No, you didn't, thought Charmian. You came here because it was a prosperous town where women had money to spend on coloured furs. And you were right.

She looked round the shop, which appeared prosperous, and thought: They have been buying them. And now someone has stolen them. 'Will you get them back?' Jane Pretty was a tall, plump lady with dyed red hair.

Charmian did not answer.

'Ah, well, everything's insured,' said Jane Pretty philosophically.

'Have you lent your keys to anyone, Miss Pretty?'

'Mrs Pretty. No, I have *not* lent anyone my keys. What do you take me for?' She sounded indignant again.

I take you for a very alert, sharp lady, thought Charmian, with a keen eye to what is good for you and for *Prettifurs.*

'Those keys never leave my possession.' And she brandished her handbag.

'At night?'

'Under my pillow,' she said. 'And don't ask: these are the *only* keys to the shop, and I have never lost them.'

27

And Charmian believed her. But someone, somewhere, had been able to make a copy of her keys.

It had been exactly the same with the owner of the other furrier's which had been robbed. 'I always keep my keys safe,' the elderly owner had protested. 'And when I have to be away – I have another business in Manchester – I leave my wife in charge, and she is even more careful.' His wife was a carefully groomed lady with hawk-like eyes under blue-grey hair, and Charmian believed in her competence. Still, someone had used their keys.

So it would be necessary to check the firms that had installed their security systems. Two separate firms, she noted.

'I do regret that pink and blue tabard,' said the owner of *Prettifurs.* 'I was going to wear it myself.'

'Oh, is that what it was, a tabard?' said Adam. 'I thought it was a smock.'

'No one wears smocks now,' said Mrs Pretty dismissively. 'No, it's a tabard.' She looked in their faces and read the signs.

'You two off, then? Will I be seeing anyone else? Or is this all that happens?'

Charmian said nothing, but Adam said: 'You might get someone else in, asking a few questions. And, if we get any news of your property, of course we will let you know.'

'Oh, you won't get anything back. Don't know why you bother. *If* you are bothering. Don't even know why you came just now.'

On the way back, Adam said: 'Are we going to tour the town looking for the woman?'

Charmian shook her head. 'No, I know where she is.'

He was surprised. 'Where?'

'As you said: she went straight back to where she had been before, outside the Baby Care shop. That's her place for today.'

28

'I thought you wanted to see her face?'

'I'll go back at the end of the day,' said Charmian.

'You put a lot of faith in her predictability.'

'Oh, no,' said Charmian seriously. 'No, I don't. I think she is totally predictable in some things, such as her hanging on at one place, and totally unpredictable in others, such as her future behaviour. That's what makes her alarming.'

She drove rapidly back to the Central Police Station, and parked. Then she sat back and looked up at the building.

'Does it strike you that something is up?' she asked after a moment.

'No.' Adam was surprised. He thought: She's getting imaginative. 'Why? All looks quiet.'

'That's just it: everything's *too* quiet. Not the normal pattern of behaviour for this hour of the day.' She looked at her watch: twelve noon. 'And there's a group standing talking in the front lobby.'

Adam looked at her doubtfully. He knew those colleagues of his, and they very often stood in a group talking. He wanted to say, 'That's a bit elaborate, isn't it?' but he was never quite sure when she was joking. Also, he was just a little bit afraid of her – more so than he really liked to admit to himself. And, finally, she had an unnerving trick (surely it was no more than a trick?) of being right.

Then one of the talkers, a man called Harvey, caught sight of them sitting in the car, and came to the door and waved.

When they got into the hall, someone else, not Harvey but a woman police constable, Edith Baughan, said loudly to Charmian: 'Walter Wing's crashed his car on the M1.'

Charmian hurried up to her own room, a question on her lips.

'It's all right,' said Agnes, as soon as Charmian opened

29

the door. 'He's not dead. But bad. I knew that old Jag was no good.' She was almost in tears. 'I've had his wife on the phone. She wants you to ring her. She's frightfully angry. Or that's how she sounds.'

'I don't suppose she is, really,' said Charmian. 'It's just how it takes you at first.'

'She wants you to ring her.'

'Later,' said Charmian, who did not fancy making the call. She could not yet help bind anyone else's wounds when her own skin still bore scars. 'How did it happen?'

Agnes shrugged. 'No details, just the bare message from the hospital. No other car involved. He managed it all on his own. Just like Walter.'

'And you know what it lands on your plate, don't you?' said Adam, sitting down at his own desk, and looking at the two women.

'Yes,' said Charmian. 'The man in the river. Since I was the chief recipient of Walter's thoughts.'

'He fancies you, you know,' said Agnes.

'You're hysterical,' said Charmian coldly. 'But it will certainly be assumed that I knew most of Walter's thoughts on the subject of the man in the river. Which I don't.'

'You'd better start thinking your own, then,' said Adam.

'On one other point there is something I want done,' said Charmian crisply. 'Go round to all the principal jewellers, fur-shops, and high-class dress-shops – there aren't so many in a town like this – and get them to tell you what their security arrangements are. In detail, please. And then I want to see them.'

'Including the shops that have already been done, I suppose.'

'You suppose right. One of your nice neat lists, Adam.'

30

'And I'll type it for you,' offered Agnes.

'Don't bother. I'll do it myself. With two fingers.' And he stumped out.

Charmian and Agnes watched him depart. 'He didn't want that job,' commented Agnes.

'But he does lovely lists,' said Charmian absently.

Later that day, with Walter Wing undergoing surgery and with shock and anaesthesia wiping like a damp towel over all his ratiocinations on the dead man, Charmian received the pathologist's report on the murdered man found in the river.

It was delivered by Dr Matthew Scobie, a huge Scotsman.

'The subject was a man aged between thirty-five and forty-five, so I would judge. In life he was probably about sixty-eight inches tall, and weighed about one hundred and twenty-six pounds. Thin, but muscular. No scars, no obvious signs of identification. Dressed in a shirt and grey trousers, socks which had been slightly weighted with cement, as you know. The stuff set round his ankles and feet.'

'Cause of death?'

'He was not drowned, but strangled by a ligature.'

'With what ligature?'

'We don't know. The marks indicate something with the texture of a towel.'

He hesitated, then drew out a photograph taken on the mortuary slab. 'But there's something else.'

'What?'

'A bruise here, and another one here.' He pointed with delicate fingers, as if touching the dead body itself. 'The foreskin is torn, and there is bruising internally at the radix of the penis. And a scraping of the skin in the groin.' He looked at Charmian. 'Unmistakable signs of force, you know. And spermatogenesis was taking place.'

31

Charmian blinked. 'You aren't telling me he was raped?'

Dr Scobie shrugged. 'Call it what you like.'

'Could he have done it himself? To himself?'

'Well,' he hesitated. 'Anything can happen – but this time, no. There were bruises on his wrists and ankles: he was tied. In fact, some of the cord which tied the ankles still remains. Bruises on his back, too, as if he was beaten.'

Charmian sat there thinking. Finally, she said bluntly: 'Were the sexual injuries done manually?'

'I thought you'd ask that.'

'It makes a difference to picturing the scene.' She hesitated. 'It's bizarre.'

'I'm going to make it even more bizarre for you. I think not manually – I found tiny traces of plastic. Minute but identifiable.'

'You mean that, well – a kind of gadget, a contrivance, was used on him?'

Dr Scobie nodded.

'He seems to have had a bad time,' said Charmian.

'Ach, I'm afraid he may have had, puir wee fellow.'

The subject had been five feet eight inches tall, but Dr Scobie was at least ten inches taller.

The news spread around the station instantly and subterraneously.

'Of course, he could be wrong,' said Agnes sagely. 'The old boy's imaginative on the subject. I've noticed.'

Charmian's reaction was enigmatic, or so her colleagues thought, and her tone neutral. 'It's an interesting idea,' she said. But she trusted Dr Scobie, and she did not think him imaginative. Far from it, in fact. I find what is suggested bizarre, she thought. And the woman hanging about in Deerham Hills is bizarre, too. That makes two of them.

But later that day she went down into the centre of

32

Deerham Hills, and took up an observation-spot. The woman had moved a few yards but was still more or less where she had been that morning.

From where she now stood Charmian could see that the cardboard display-card hung around her neck was covered with newspaper cuttings, each heavily underlined here and there, usually beneath words in headlines, with a black felt-tipped pen.

Carefully, unobtrusively, Charmian moved up closer until she could read the headlines. But the words underlined seemed to make no sense. To Charmian they were just a meaningless collection of newspaper cuttings. She was trying to get a better look to make something of them when the woman moved away smartly, as if alarmed.

Charmian stared after her. It was impossible for her not to see the woman as a symptom of something wrong in Deerham Hills. Perhaps even a warning.

Chapter Two

The girls were having a meeting. Just a cosy little domestic sociability, all four of them on their own, almost a party.

'Champagne or tea?' asked Diana. Baby gave a happy giggle. Diana looked towards the table. 'Or coffee or whisky?'

'Champagne,' said Baby.

'Whisky,' said Phil. 'Give me a fag, Baby.'

'My hair's wet,' protested Baby.

'Well, I'm under the dryer,' pointed out Phil. 'You're mobile.'

Baby teetered over on her four-inch high heels.

'Honestly, those shoes,' said Diana. 'What those heels are doing to my carpet!'

'Well, light it!' said Phil to Baby, cigarette in her lips. 'Light it for me.'

Baby obliged.

'I do deplore the return of stiletto heels,' said Diana.

'I wasn't old enough to wear them first time round,' said Baby.

'That's a lie,' said Phil, but she said it without malice.

'High heels suit me. I need the extra inch or two. Otherwise, I'm such a little thing.'

'Dry your hair,' said her employer. 'You're dripping all over my floor.'

'You're besotted about that floor. Don't keep on about it.'

They were all seated in the open-plan ground floor of Diana's hairdressing salon among the basins and hair-dryers and potted plants, with the blinds drawn over the windows against the gaze of passers-by. The salon was closed for the day. Phil was actually sitting under a dryer with her hair in rollers; Baby was blow-drying her hair by means of a little hand-held machine; and Diana was halfway through the new cut she was giving herself.

'Sure these rollers will give me a casual wave?' asked Phil, leaning forward and studying herself with a worried look.

'You're quite right to worry over that carpet, Diana,' said Bee Dawson, the fourth member of the party, going back to an earlier subject. She was usually a sentence or two behind everyone else; she liked to think things over before she spoke. 'But you need more cleaning help here.' She looked around the littered floor.

'I did have a cleaner, but she was always taking time off to visit her sick son in hospital, so I gave her the push.'

'Help costs,' said Bee seriously. On money she was usually prompter to speak.

'I call Bee my accountant,' said Diana fondly. 'My little accountant.'

'I bet she's six feet if she's an inch,' said Phil, turning round in her chair and peering from under her dryer. 'And thin with it. Not so little.'

'It's a term of affection.'

'Oh, good,' said Phil. 'Now we know.'

'I *am* an accountant,' said Bee, once again picking up a dropped stitch. 'Your accountant. And I don't know where you'd be without me.' She had a thin, serious, bespectacled face.

'In prison, I expect,' said Phil, leaning forward and studying her hair in the mirror. 'And we might end up there anyway.'

'*No,*' said Diana. She stood up, a tall, striking figure, one side of her hair cropped short, and the other flowing. 'I'd die first.'

Bee groaned. 'Oh, Di.'

35

Phil looked up at Diana. 'You know, except for your height, you'd never know you two were sisters. I mean, you're a beautiful woman, Diana.'

Diana was dismissive. 'Half-sisters. Different dads. But it's mothers that count.'

'Oh, that's true,' said Baby. 'My mum's lovely.'

'When did you last see her?' demanded Phil. 'Three years ago, I'd say.'

'But I *think* about her,' said Baby.

'We've still got the old place where we lived as kids,' said Bee, coming in late, as so often. 'Bit of a barn, full of outhouses and old sheds, but I'm used to it. I tried to fix it up a bit. Needs a new path. I made a start. Lonely since Mum died. I don't live there, but Di and I pop in. Still seems sometimes as if Mum's still there. She was on pain-killing drugs for ages before she died, poor love. I feel as if she's there. But Di doesn't. Di, we ought to get rid of some of those drugs. Get rid of the house, too, I suppose.'

'It's useful,' said Diana. The eyes of the two sisters met. 'But of course we both have our own little places, too.'

'Aren't you lonely?' asked Baby with sympathy. 'I can't bear being on my own. I'm sensitive that way.'

'Not really,' said Bee. 'I read a lot.'

'Oh, I love reading,' said Baby. 'I've always got a book going. I belong to the Reading and Criticism Circle. We all read a book and then talk it over.'

From under Phil's dryer came a derisive snort.

'I have to get my culture from somewhere,' said Baby. 'Don't get much from *you*. I'm reading a lovely book now – all about a haunted house and a possessed family.' She gave a happy shiver.

'See what I mean?' said Phil.

'Oh, you be quiet and think about your hair.'

36

But Bee wanted to clear up an earlier point, and at last she got it out.

'And I'm not,' said Bee to Phil. 'Beautiful, I mean.'

'You look very clever,' answered Phil with sincerity.

'I'd need to be with you lot. And remember, I keep the books. Profit and loss, that's my job. And so far,' Bee paused, and added heavily: 'There's not been a lot of profit.'

'Go and bring us all a mug of coffee. If we are going to have business talk, we'll need it,' ordered Diana to Baby, whose hair was dry and frothed over her head in tight curls. 'I can smell it's ready. I left it dripping through.' Diana took her coffee seriously.

'Yes, I can't stand that quick muck. You don't get the uplift. Oh, I use it when I have to, but only then.'

Baby came back into the room bearing a tray of coffee, the steam rising fragrantly around her. A pretty blue and pink fur jerkin hung from her shoulders.

'I just love this one,' she said. 'Do you think I could keep it? As my share? It's my colour.' She took a look in the mirror. 'Matches the shop, too.'

Without looking at her, Diana ordered: 'Put it back.'

'Are you crazy?' said Phil.

'But it's beautiful.'

'And very recognisable.'

'Well, I wouldn't wear it round here,' protested Baby. 'I'd save it up for my holiday. Majorca, this year.'

'No,' said Diana, without raising her voice. 'Put it back.'

Baby pouted, but she tripped off and replaced the fur among the others in the back room, saying as she went: 'It would have been quite safe. And I chose that one specially for myself. I made sure you'd let me have it.'

'Then you made sure wrong.' Diana turned to Phil. 'When are you taking the whole consignment off? The sooner the better.'

37

Phil came out from under the dryer. 'Brush me out and I'll be off. Who's coming with me?'

'Bee. She knows the way. And she'll see we get the right prices.'

Diana picked up a brush and began on Phil's hair with long sweeping movements of her hand.

'*And* you don't trust me on my own. I mean, I might make off with the proceeds, mightn't I?' Phil leant back luxuriously and gave herself up to the pleasure of the brush. 'Oh, do go on. It's lovely.' She wriggled her shoulders. 'Slow, slow, slower.'

'Well, you might. But I've got Baby here, and I don't think you'd leave her behind.'

Phil laughed. 'Ah, well, it's an academic point, because I'm not going to do it.'

'Very wise of you,' said Diana.

'I'm enjoying myself too much. Besides, this is all chicken-feed, isn't it?'

Diana looked at her without speaking.

'We're still training for the big stuff. I mean, I hope so.'

Still Diana did not speak.

'I don't want to waste my time,' Phil went on, 'or sacrifice my spotless reputation, which I've had for thirty-five years, just for peanuts.'

Diana sucked in her breath with excitement. 'I knew I was right to get you in,' she said. 'Bee was against it.' Bee opened her mouth, then shut it again. 'But I knew it was right. You've got it in you. I could feel it.'

'I am ambitious, yes,' drawled Phil. 'You'd say that, wouldn't you, Baby?'

Baby nodded energetically. 'Oh, yes, Phil. I absolutely agree. You're full of it.'

'I must admit that Baby had me sizzling when she first told me what was going on. I would never have believed it. Nor that she could have kept it from me so long. Clever little Baby.' She looked briefly at the girl.

'I'm not in your pocket,' announced Baby triumphantly. 'I'm not in anyone's pocket. I'm a free girl.'

'Well, that's a declaration of faith, I suppose,' said Phil.

'Sizzling?' asked Bee. 'What's sizzling?'

'Hot. Burning with interest. Excited.'

'Oh, I see. You mean you were keen to come in?'

Phil laughed. 'Once I knew about it, I was. Apart from anything else, someone's got to look after Baby. *She* can't do it.'

Diana gave a short laugh, as if she knew something about *that*. 'And *you* certainly needed a driver. And a better-looking car,' added Bee.

'Those other jobs were just rehearsals,' said Diana. 'I wanted to play myself in. I wanted to know what I could do. I had to find that out.'

'And you have done?'

'Oh, yes. Now I can clean out the town.'

Phil stood up and seized her mug of coffee; she took a deep gulp of it. 'You can't have made much out of the jobs you've told me about – the Curio Shop, then *Prettifurs*. Is that the lot?'

'More or less,' said Diana. 'All that's worth talking about.' She dropped her eyes. 'I was practising.'

'And I've always liked furs,' said Baby.

'Yes, I thought I detected your tiny hand,' said Phil, half turning to look at her. 'I'm surprised you let her in,' she said to Diana.

'Oh, she's essential. Her job's important.'

Baby smiled smugly. A dimple appeared in her cheek. Her hair had dried beautifully. the new 'streaking' effect she was trying out was a superb success. With the curls blowing about her head she looked like an angel who was going very slightly grey.

'I'm essential,' she said. 'And it's because I'm essential that furs came first. Work that one out.' She looked mischievous.

'Yes, I know there're things I've not been told,' said Phil. 'How long have you been in Deerham Hills?' she asked Diana.

'Three months. When I opened the shop.'

'I've lived here twenty years. It's changed a lot. What made you come here?'

Diana said coolly, 'I looked it over and it seemed suitable for my business.'

'And where were you before you came here?'

Diana and Bee exchanged looks.

'Never you mind,' said Diana.

'Prison, I should think,' said Phil.

'Oh, no, I've never been in prison,' said Diana quickly.

'Something's marked you, then,' said Phil. 'Oh, well, never mind. You don't tell me things and I don't tell *you* things. That's fair. I won't ask questions.'

'About cleaning out the town,' said Bee uneasily. 'I wonder if Deerham Hills knows.'

Diana threw her arms open wide. 'It will. Believe me, it will.'

Bee said: 'I mean, does it know now? I don't know why, I feel worried.' She stood up. 'Come on, Phil. Let's get going.'

Next evening, after a visit to the local cinema and a Chinese meal, Baby and Phil drove home together to the maisonette on the outskirts of Deerham Hills which they shared (and Phil saw to it that Baby paid her way: she was rather naughty about it). It was still before nine o'clock in the evening. Phil had popped into *Charm and Chic* to have a word with Diana about yesterday's delivery and to collect her reward. She had interrupted Baby in the

40

middle of a manicure upon a tall, rather striking young woman at whom Phil had looked more than once. After waiting for Baby to finish they had decided on a mild celebration. Now they were at home.

'Wish I could drive,' said Baby.

'Well, you can't.'

'Think I'll learn.'

'For God's sake, don't try,' said Phil. She put her foot on the brake, hard, and Baby jerked forward and screamed. That would show her.

They passed through the square in Deerham Hills from which all the buses started.

'Oh, look,' said Baby, pointing. 'There's that woman again.'

'What woman?' Phil was looking at the traffic behind her in the driving-mirror.

'The one I told you about. The one who stands and stares. She's getting on a bus. Going home, I suppose. Funny to think of her having a home.'

Gloria had got on a number 43 country bus and had disappeared from view.

'I'm more interested in that car behind us. Seems to have stuck with us for a long time. Wonder if it's been following us?'

'Oh, no, it couldn't have been,' said Baby.

'No, probably not. It's turning left now, anyway.'

'Who was driving it?'

'Some woman,' said Phil, more or less indifferently. 'I've never liked that shade of red hair.' She belched. 'Oh, God, I hate Chinese food; it always gives me indigestion.'

How funny to see the woman getting on a bus, thought Charmian. The sight of Gloria decided her. She would not go the way she had planned to go tonight. Instead she would follow the woman. One should always follow a sign

41

from the gods, she thought, and this surely was her sign. It had been a hard, tough, boring day and she wanted something interesting to happen. However, she had had her nails manicured, and they looked good.

The bus-route ran through the suburbs of Deerham Hills and then out into the country. Not that the district around Deerham Hills was deeply rural; rather, it was a kind of modified suburbia, with plantations of small houses here and there. Very soon the outskirts of the industrial town of Midford began to appear.

The bus stopped several times but, although some people got off and others got on, the woman was not among them. Charmian followed the bus right to the garage where it ended its run, but by this time it was empty except for the conductor and driver.

Somehow she had missed the woman. Perplexed and out of temper, she drove back to Deerham Hills. It was raining again.

Gloria walked home. (She didn't really think of her room as home. She was as near homeless as was consistent with keeping a roof over her head, and this was how she wanted it to be.) Inside the bus she had put on an old raincoat left over from a former life, a protection against the approaching rain.

She had no idea how it changed her appearance. If she had, she wouldn't have put it on. Whatever Charmian might have thought, Gloria *valued* the way she looked.

When Charmian got home she found a package. She took it indoors. It was a cake, neatly wrapped in silver foil. With it was a note from Kitty. 'I know you're in a rotten mood. I saw your face as you drove off this morning. Do you know what expressive eyes you have? I thought this might make you feel more cheerful.'

It was a rich fruit cake, and on it in thick icing were the words 'Happy Birthday'.

'Damn,' said Charmian. 'I didn't know anyone knew it

was my birthday. My horrid, dreadful, hateful, thirty-eighth birthday.' In another year she would be practically forty. Also husbandless, loverless and childless. No accident, she thought. Long, long ago, you took the choice that brought you here. Kitty had dragged that out into the open, soon after their first meeting. 'You always do exactly what you want,' she had said. 'And so you have to pay for it. Everyone does, but you pay more than most.'

As if to underline her importance in Charmian's life (which was actually strong, even crucial), Kitty herself appeared at the door, waving a jug.

'I've run out of milk. Can you let me have some?'

'You shouldn't run out of milk with a baby,' said Charmian absently.

'I'm not a *cow*.' There was only mild protest in Kitty's voice. 'Besides, he was weaned ages ago.'

'I didn't mean that. I meant you should always keep some by you.'

'You know, you're severe,' said Kitty. 'Have you got the milk or haven't you? Never mind the lecture. And what about the cake?'

Charmian opened the refrigerator and got a bottle and gave it to her friend. 'Here's the milk. And the cake's lovely, and I deplore my birthday.'

Kitty sat down at the table. 'You know, I'm always in your kitchen. You never invite me anywhere else. I think there's something significant in that. I wonder what it is.'

Kitty was always looking for significance in everyday things. Charmian never was; she had too much of that to do professionally.

She ignored it now. 'I'm just making some coffee. Have some with me and I'll cut the cake.'

Kitty studied her face. 'You're tired. You look exhausted.'

43

'The town's gone mad. Everything's happened. And it's not that I *mind* my birthday, but I'm getting to the age when you ask yourself what you've done wrong and what you've done right.'

'I think you've done a lot that's right,' said Kitty gently. 'And you're a very attractive woman. Very.' Ben had said so, and on this subject, if no other, Kitty trusted his judgement.

Charmian shrugged. She poured the coffee and cut into the cake. 'Won't your husband wonder where you are?' she said.

'No. Ben never wonders. Anyway, he knows. Happy birthday. What's it like being a policewoman?'

Charmian shrugged. 'A job. Like any other.'

'Not *quite* like any other, I should have thought,' said Kitty, considering. 'Why did you choose to become one?'

'I wanted a career.'

'You could have had a career in the Civil Service. Or the Foreign Service. You'd have made a good diplomat.' Charmian gave a tiny incredulous hoot of laughter. Kitty pressed on: 'Or you could have taught. Or become a journalist.'

'I had a second-class Honours degree in history from a Scottish university. My special subject was Sir Robert Peel and penal reform. The police force seemed indicated,' said Charmian drily.

She might also have added that a certain arrogance and energy pushed her that way, too.

'You've silenced me,' said Kitty, getting to her feet. 'But I don't know if you've told me the truth, or even if you know it.'

'Oh, Kitty, you're being profound again,' complained Charmian. 'I'm too tired for it. Go home.'

'Yes, I'm off.' Clutching her bottle of milk and her jug (which had never been more than a symbol to her, since she had always expected Charmian to give her a bottle), Kitty rose to leave. At the door she suddenly stopped short and said: 'Do you know what? This morning the telephone rang, and when I answered there was no one there; only the sound of music. But it was *Chinese* music, all tinkling and little bells. Wasn't that funny?' She giggled. 'Do you think I've got an anonymous Chinese admirer?'

'Oh, go away home,' said Charmian, giving her friend a little push, and closing the door behind her. She leant against it and drew her first quiet breath of the day.

She was alone in her house, shut up with the ghosts of her husband and his son. 'I wish I could have saved something for you,' she said sadly to his memory. 'Supposing your son deliberately got lost, ran off, or even made away with himself. I know you thought of all these possibilities. Well, it wasn't my fault, was it?'

There was his son. She could try again there. Perhaps he was alive, somewhere.

Meanwhile, she had a murdered man, who might or might not have been raped, more or less on her hands. And several robberies, and a general feeling of casual violence breaking out.

'If anything else happens, I shall scream,' she said as she got into bed.

She was just dropping off to sleep when her telephone rang.

When she picked up the receiver there was nothing to be heard except the sound of tinkling bells and strange little rattles and a high, thin, piping tune: Chinese music.

The next day the best jeweller's in Deerham Hills was entered and robbed. Benton's was an old-established firm, which still retained a few of the airs and graces of

45

a jeweller's shop in the county town, which was what Deerham Hills had been in the eighteenth century, before decline had robbed it of that status, and then transmogrification into a 'New Town' had revived its fortunes.

Benton's always closed for an abnormally long luncheon hour. The implication was that none of Benton's customers, people of substance and leisure, would dream of shopping except in the morning or afternoon. So the doors would close and the iron grille go across the windows where just a few trays of small ornaments would remain visible for the passers-by to feast their eyes upon.

Deerham Hills being Deerham Hills, Benton's was not, and never had been, the country equivalent of Asprey's or Cartier. But it sported trays of deliciously pretty and good-quality rings and brooches, even though the stones themselves were not very valuable nor the whole pieces what jewellers like to call 'important'. The most highly priced ornament in Benton's was a brooch valued at five thousand pounds. It was a square Brazilian aquamarine set with brilliants in white gold.

Charmian admired this jewel greatly, and sometimes would stand looking at it in the window, imagining circumstances in which she might buy it and wear it. She had never in her life had five thousand pounds to spend.

I'd settle for that black opal ring if I couldn't get the brooch, she thought. Relatively cheap, a gift really, only five hundred pounds. She had never had five hundred pounds to spare, either. At the present moment she was probably as well off as she had ever been. But there was nothing much over at the end of each month.

She had never set foot inside Benton's in all her years in Deerham Hills, but she knew, because of her job, a good deal of what went on within its elegant walls.

As the doors were locked in the lunch-hour, the grilles drawn across the windows and locked, and the alarm

46

system set, the trays of jewellery were left on view, with the exception of the odd specially valuable piece like the aquamarine and the opal. These were removed and placed in a locked cupboard in the manager's office. Benton's strong-room and safe were in the basement and only used at night.

An eccentric arrangement perhaps, but it suited Benton's because the manager hardly ever went out to lunch except when she got her hair washed and set or had her nails manicured. She had beautiful hands.

That lunch-time, however, she was working quietly away at the VAT papers in her office, and pausing to drink some coffee from a Thermos flask and nibble a sandwich with her strong white teeth which she looked after so regularly, when she heard a noise. She raised her head to listen. It sounded like a door being opened.

Impossible, she thought, remembering that she had set the alarm system herself. One step in the wrong spot, and bells would ring in the Deerham Hills police station. She knew they worked, as she had tried them out herself. You had to know where to put your foot or what to touch with your hand, or you were in trouble. She knew it to a hair's breadth, and she had mapped out the path on a plan to the nice young detectives who came to enquire.

Presently she got up and went out to the small cloakroom next door to her office.

'Thank God for weak bladders,' said a light whisper. Like a breath of wind, it was anonymous.

'Jam that door and don't let her out until I say when,' said a muffled, unrecognisable voice, adding with anger: 'I thought this was the day she was supposed to go to the dentist.'

A soft giggle came in reply. 'I can't be expected to learn *everything.*' Another little giggle, and then the giggler said: 'Also I don't seem to have the advanced powers of

47

persuasion you seem to have. A proper inimitable horror, you are.'

The manager trapped in the lavatory heard these words. Later she reported them to the police and they remained in the police records. Later still, Charmian remembered them.

When Charmian got to work that morning, before the robbery had taken place, she was greeted by an anxious face.

'Well, what do you want?' she demanded of Adam Lily. 'I can see by your look you want something.'

'Something's come in that you ought to see.'

'Ha!' said Charmian.

Adam pushed a folder of papers across to her. He flipped it open. 'Lab report on the clothes found on the strangled man.'

The strangled, drowned, raped man.

'Tell me,' said Charmian impatiently.

'You know, at first they couldn't find much. Sort of anonymous chap, that one. But in an inside pocket there was a card, some four inches by three, about the size of an old-fashioned visiting-card. The lining of the pocket had preserved it from the water. It was well soaked, of course.'

'Of course,' said Charmian, still impatiently. 'So?'

'But they worked on it – new technique – and something came up. *Your* name. Your surname.'

Charmian looked at him.

'Married name,' he said. 'So, of course, it could have been a reference to your husband. Your surname, Ascham, and your home telephone number.'

'Oh,' said Charmian, pondering.

'So, all in all, they wonder down there at the laboratory if you wouldn't come and have another look to see what

48

you can identify. Not the body,' he said quickly. 'No visual identification is possible. Just the possessions.'

'I'll do it now,' said Charmian.

Silently, grimly, she drove them across the town to where the police forensic laboratory skulked on the edge of habitation. Perhaps she kept a weather eye out for the woman as she drove but, if so, she said nothing.

Without speaking, she studied the objects spread out on the table before her. A tweed jacket, once a ginger tan, now stained and faded to no colour, blue jeans, a check shirt, and the remains of a pair of suede shoes. Beside them a meagre heap of personal possessions: a leather wallet, which was empty, a pencil, and a handkerchief. The handkerchief had some individuality left, as the bright pattern of dots and stars of blue and red had survived. The pencil had been chewed and was well worn down.

With relief, Charmian said: 'No, not a thing. I've never seen these things before. They couldn't have been my stepson's. That was what you thought, wasn't it?'

'Not even if he was playing a part?' said Adam.

'He'd still keep the same wallet. Use a pencil the same way. That's not his wallet. His father gave him one of morocco leather, and that's pigskin. Also, he never chewed a pencil.'

'Good,' said Adam. 'It leaves him still alive.'

'Perhaps,' said Charmian.

Somehow the card caught her attention. It reminded her of something. To the attendant technician in charge of the laboratory, she said:

'That card – I'd like you to see if you can get anything more out of it. It looks to me as if there might have been some lettering on the other side once.'

Later that day the laboratory rang through to Charmian and said, Yes, they were getting something positive on the

49

card obverse, and if it looked like being anything legible they'd let her know.

And later still they rang again and said, No, they were dead sorry, and they'd tried their best, but nothing readable had come through. They'd send her a photograph. Yes, by special messenger, straight away, she'd get it within the hour, if she liked.

Charmian did like, and when it came she stared long and hard at a faint shadow of something on the back of that card.

It did seem to say something to her, just the shape of it, but she couldn't say what. And, in any case, she was alarmed and startled that the card had her name and telephone-number on it. She wondered if she would be right to catch the faintest whiff of trouble to come here, but decided she was being neurotic.

Still, she looked long and hard at what the roughly scrawled words said: *Ascham. Deerham Hills 9337.*

The telephone ring and Charmian picked it up.

'Hello? Speaking. What, Benton's? Benton's in the High Street? Yes, as old as the hills and as respectable. I know it well. Tell me.' She sat listening, nodding and making notes. 'Oh, I'll come round and look myself.'

She put the receiver down and sat thinking.

'What is it?' asked Agnes in a tense voice. 'I heard a bit, but couldn't quite make it out.'

'Benton's.'

'A raid?' Agnes sounded frightened.

'No. Or not the way you mean. The shop was entered by someone using a key while the manager was at work there. It was the lunch hour. She was on her own.'

'Was she hurt?'

'No, shut in the lavatory. She shouldn't have been in the shop at all; by rights, she should have been at the dentist's. But her dentist had a heart attack yesterday and her appointment was cancelled.'

50

'I suppose the shop was cleared?'

'All the most valuable stuff, apparently. I don't know the details yet.' I bet that opal and the lovely aquamarine went, thought Charmian. 'But guess what – the thieves took the trouble to lock the door behind them when they left.'

'Cool,' said Agnes.

'And sensible. Because it took the staff returning from lunch some time to realise anything was wrong. They just thought the manageress was late back from somewhere. And then they had to get a key from one of the Benton directors to get in at all.'

She sat thinking for a few minutes. 'And there's something else, too: the alarm didn't go off as it should have done. And that means the raiders knew exactly where to tread and what switches to turn off. That takes some thinking about.'

'Information from inside the shop, one of the assistants?' suggested Agnes.

'Perhaps, perhaps,' said Charmian.

The days ticked away, and she worked hard, but she never seemed to get closer to the heart of her problem.

Or so she thought, but unconsciously, deep inside her, she was putting together a picture – an exercise in lateral thinking, if there ever was one.

Chapter Three

What are the institutions in a small town like Deerham Hills, part old, part new, through which information is passed? How does gossip get around?

Through the shopping complex, where housewives meet; the library, where schoolchildren and the retired mingle and listen to one another; the health centre, where everyone goes.

These were places to keep your eye on, and Charmian knew it. She had her contacts at all of them. In addition, she had a secret informer of her own.

Self-recruited, or very nearly, elderly Mrs Buck had cleaned house for Charmian in her early married life. She had regarded it as her duty to pass on all she knew (and, one way and another, she knew a lot) to her employer. Since she was a woman who continually changed her jobs, she had worked for many before Charmian and many since; and when their working relationship ended Mrs Buck continued to keep in touch. She required nothing for her services except an occasional cup of tea with Charmian.

Sometimes, in her dreams, Charmian imagined herself as having contact with mysterious underworld links, phoning her with vital information in husky frightened voices, but her life had never been like that, and nothing could have been more ordinary than Jessie Buck; but she seemed to know a good deal for all that.

'I keep my eyes and ears open, dear,' she said. 'And, living on the estate as I do, there's plenty going on to hear.'

The estate was the large estate of houses built and

owned by the Housing Department of Deerham Hills District Council and let at subsidised rents to the workers in all the light industries that clustered on the outskirts of the growing town. The whole area was beautifully landscaped, sturdily built, and a bubbling pot of crime and passion, if Mrs Buck was to be believed.

'A voyeuse extraordinary,' Charmian's late husband had called his employee, accurately and characteristically getting the gender of the noun right. 'Have you ever thought what she passes on about you, about us?'

'Of course,' said Charmian. 'She'd need some sort of coin to repay the people who tell *her* tales, and information about us could be it. And I don't care.' It was her first gesture of defiance to the rules of discretion by which her husband ruled his life.

On the day after her visit to the police laboratory, when she was still puzzling over the fact that her married surname and telephone-number had been found on a card in the strangled man's pocket, and still mulling over her *own* speculations about that card, she had a call from Mrs Buck.

'What about a cuppa, dear?' It was the usual summons to a parley. 'It's ages since we met.'

Charmian looked at her watch. The day's work was nearly done. She was conscious of her typist's curious eyes on her (Mrs Buck's voice did carry) and of the fact that Adam Lily had just come into the room. 'In about an hour, then,' she said. 'Where?'

'The Old Adelphi. Then I can pop into my bingo afterwards.'

The Old Adelphi was a former cinema, now used as a bingo hall. On the ground floor was a bar where a remarkable assortment of drinks could be had. Charmian knew it well from earlier occasions; she never felt at ease in it. Jessie Buck slotted in there, but Charmian did not.

'What's it all about, Jessie?' She fitted her long legs into

53

the plastic booth where Jessie was already seated. 'What are you drinking?' Informality had long ago set in; they were not employed and employer, but 'Jessie' and 'luv'.

'Tea, luv.' Charmian felt just as uneasy with 'luv' as she did with the Old Adelphi. 'I felt I *had* to see you, dear. There's something I must talk to you about.'

'What is it?' Charmian decided to skip drinking the Old Adelphi's tea, which was a pale fawn liquid, nasty to taste. No need, surely, to immolate herself on two altars at once.

'Well, my dear, it's about where I live – the estate, you know – it's gone from bad to worse.'

'What is it this time?'

'Now, don't sound like that, dear. Anything I've told you, any little bit of information I've been able to let you have, has always been good, you know. Now, this time it's *me*. I've been robbed. The whole street was done over.' She sounded outraged. 'Would you believe it?'

'I'd believe anything,' said Charmian.

'I lost twenty pounds and two bottles of milk. Gold top.'

'Any idea who did it?'

'I could make a good guess.' And she leant forward and whispered in Charmian's ear.

'Oh, them again.' The name was familiar to Charmian. 'You'll have to cut your losses there, I expect. I don't suppose you'll get anything back. You've reported it, of course.'

'What's the good?'

Charmian sighed. 'Not much, I admit. But we'll watch the Jones clan.'

'I'm watching them,' said Mrs Buck. 'If there's anything you can get them on, I'll let you know, don't worry.'

'Well, then, Jessie,' began Charmian.

'But I mean it's getting rotten where I live. Violent,

54

nasty. A bad feel. Crackling with malice, the place is. Goodness knows, we're no angels on the estate, and I've never said we were. You'll bear me out in that?' Charmian nodded. 'But there was neighbourliness. Now we're all worried, as if anything might happen. It's just a feeling. I don't count the burglaries – just a pair of kids, that was – but, still, it's a sign.' And she leant back triumphantly. For her, it had been a long speech. 'I feel better now I've told you, dear.'

'I can't help,' said Charmian. 'I agree with all you've said. I've felt it myself in the town. And I don't understand.' She stood up. 'I think I *will* have that cup of tea.'

When she came back she could see that Jessie was about to produce the real point of the meeting.

'I think I know where it's coming from,' she said suddenly.

Charmian looked expectant.

'Or why, anyway. I've heard a rumour or two. It's something about women or a woman. I think it's got a connection with that woman that's come into the town. You know who I mean?'

'Yes,' said Charmian. 'So what's the connection with her and what's going on in the town?'

'Dunno. She's not doing it, but she's causing it.'

'Is she?' said Charmian. 'Or is she a symptom like the rest?'

But even as she said it she knew the woman was more than a symptom; she was more like a summer insect attracted to a light that was flaring. She was significant in her own way.

Jessie was obstinate. 'I've heard her mentioned.'

'You don't know where she comes from?'

'Arrives in the bus,' said Jessie.

'I know that myself,' said Charmian. 'But where from? I followed the bus one night and still missed her.'

55

'I don't know where from,' said Jessie. 'But you know that big notice she had hung round her neck? Just rubbish it was. A jumble of words about *Women*. You couldn't make anything of it. I went right up to her and said, "What are you protesting about, dear?" and she just ran away. But the way she had the words written in big black letters on newspaper reminded me of the open market in Midford. Quite a few of the stalls there use notices like that. Perhaps she comes from there.'

'A living woman and a dead man are my problems at the moment,' said Charmian.

'Oh, yes. I've heard about him. Strangled, wasn't he?'

'Anything to tell me about him?'

Jessie shook her head. 'No. Nothing's come my way. I'll let you know if it does. Don't think he was known. Not on the estate. From out of town, I'd say. Anything else?'

Charmian thought for a minute. 'About this woman. Perhaps you'd better tell me exactly what you know and where you heard it. Word for word, if you can.'

'I was cleaning out the bar at the Bofors Gun. You know I work there part-time? This was a couple of evenings ago.'

'Are you there in the evenings?'

'Not usually, but the guv'nor's wife had been poorly and I was helping out. In the back room was a group of his friends. *You* know.' Charmian knew. She knew all about the Bofors Gun and the guv'nor's friends. 'And I could hear there was angry talk. Sounded like men who had had their noses pushed in.' She gave a dry chuckle. 'You know what men are like when their pride's scratched. *That* sort of voice. And someone said, quite loudly: "That bitch's come down from London to do us on purpose. They want to muscle in."'

She looked hopefully at Charmian.

'Is that all you heard?'

'I had to leave then. The missus was calling from upstairs. She thinks her husband is poisoning her.'

'And is he?' asked Charmian, momentarily diverted from her main track.

'Don't think so. She's just a greedy eater. And then she drinks a bit. Well, that's it for now, then,' said Jessie, her eye on the clock. 'Got to get off for my bingo now.'

'Thanks. You've told me a lot.' Charmian stood up.

But, in spite of her professed keenness to get to her bingo, Jessie did not rise but still sat there, her hands fidgeting with her purse.

'You want to watch yourself, dear. You might be in trouble yourself.' She sounded serious.

'Oh, go on, Jessie,' said Charmian sceptically. 'What sort of trouble? Got an enemy, have I?'

Jessie stood up. Reluctantly she said: 'Well, I heard that lot talking in the Bofors. Not my favourite men, dear, but on your account I listened, 'cos I heard your name.'

Charmian stared at her.

' "She don't know what she's sitting her arse in," he said. Forgive the language, but I know you like it word for word. "She's sitting in shit right up to her — " Well, I *won't* tell you what he said then.' Jessie put on a virtuous look.

'Thanks,' observed Charmian mildly. 'Well, all right, Jess. I'll bear it in mind and watch out. Especially among my friends.'

'He's a horrid man, dear,' said Jessie, waddling off. 'But you can usually trust what he knows. Not that "trust" is a word to employ with him.'

Sitting in her car, Charmian thought: 'Yes, Jessie, you've told me a lot. More than you know. The men in the Bofors Gun were not talking about the woman who stands watching: she is not the aggressor, but another woman. It's another woman who's brought anger to the town.

Perhaps more than one. A group of women? And how do I identify them? And what are they into.

Well, what except crime?

And what have we got in Deerham Hills except a crime-wave?

On an impulse Charmian telephoned her friend Kitty the moment she got back home. She could hear the bell ringing in the house, but it took Kitty longer than usual to pick up the receiver. Usually she rushed to it like a greyhound; she was always on the look-out for something to happen.

Then she answered: 'Hello? Oh, Charmian, you. Sorry to be so slow. I had to take the baby away from the cat's milk.'

'Is he all right?'

'Oh, yes. But he gets terribly angry and scratches everything.'

'Goodness. Does he?'

'The cat, idiot. Not the baby. He's just got milk on his face. The thing is, I'm trying to get him off milk on to solids and I'm afraid he resents it. Still, it shows —'

'Kitty,' Charmian interrupted her. 'If you decided to embark on a criminal life – say, burglary – where would you start?'

'What a fascinating question. Oh, a jeweller's or a fur-shop first, I think. Yes, I'd really enjoy that. Or I might go for antiques. Little ones that I could carry.'

'I thought you might say that,' said Charmian. 'Interesting. We've had some break-ins just like that.'

'But I shouldn't stay in that small league,' said Kitty. 'No, pretty soon I'd go for real money. A bank, or something of that sort.'

'Thanks, Kitty. You've given me something to think about.'

'Any time,' said Kitty, with a giggle of pleasure. 'I love helping you. What's it all about, anyway?'

58

'Just throwing ideas around. We've had a series of robberies, all similar in character, two fur-shops, a small jeweller's and a curio-shop – you couldn't call it antiques they sold, but valuable enough. Must all be the work of the same gang.'

'And you think they are women? How gorgeous. Clever things,' said Kitty admiringly.

'Is that your reaction?'

'Oh, yes. It's what we've wanted for a long time – isn't it? – the really emancipated woman criminal.'

'It's creating hell among the criminal fraternity on the estate over in the new town,' said Charmian gloomily. 'Or that's what I think.'

'Oh, it would,' agreed Kitty. 'Their male *machismo* and all that. Poor little things, how they'd hate it. More power to the girls, I say.'

'I've got to catch them,' said Charmian.

'So you have.' Kitty had a thought. 'Charmian, do you think the woman – you know the one I mean, the one who stands looking – do you think she's one of them?'

'I've been wondering about that myself,' said Charmian. 'But I don't think so. I don't know what she is. Some sort of natural phenomenon, perhaps, but angry, different. Yes, different.'

'I saw that woman again today,' said Baby as she cooked supper. She was a clever cook. Phil could feed herself, if she had to, but felt it was 'woman's work'. So did Baby; she put on a frilly apron and big red rubber gloves and enjoyed the sight of herself. 'For a moment I thought she was going to talk to me.'

'I hope she didn't,' said Phil quickly.

'Oh, no. It was just a look. She wanted to, though. I could *feel* it. You know how one can.'

'No, I don't,' said Phil.

'Oh, you've got no sensitivity. Anyway, I know what I'd have said to her if she had spoken.'

'What, then?'

'I'd have said, "My dear girl, get your hands fixed; they are awful."' She gave the lettuce she was drying a particularly vigorous shake.

'Salad again for supper,' complained Phil.

'I have to think of my waistline. I'm not a great big brawny thing like you.' And she looked at Phil provocatively from under her eyelashes.

'I can't keep my strength up on salad,' said Phil.

'I'm doing you a nourishing steak.' And Baby from the refrigerator produced a thick piece of sirloin which she began to whack with a rolling-pin.

Phil got up. 'Here, let me do that. You'll break your wrist.' Baby handed over the rolling-pin and sat watching. She seemed to enjoy what she saw. 'Oh, I love to see you do that. It's really brutal.'

Phil threw aside the rolling-pin. 'There you are, tender as a baby's bottom.'

'Ooh, I don't think this baby would like it,' said Baby.

'Don't you?' Phil reached out and picked up the rolling-pin.

When they were eating their supper, Baby said: 'Remember that ginger-haired woman who came in for a manicure the day you popped in to talk to Di? We saw her in a car later.' To herself, she added: I saw you watching her.

'I wouldn't have called her ginger,' said Phil. 'More red-haired. Titian.'

'You said you didn't like the colour of her hair the first time.'

'I can change my mind, can't I?'

'She's a policewoman, I think,' continued Baby uneas-

60

ily, deciding to ignore the comment about the hair. No point in going for trouble.

'What of it?'

Baby didn't answer, but she gave a nervous little shrug.

'A good-looking woman, I thought,' said Phil. She gave a piercing giggle. 'I thought she might have been following us with some ulterior motive in mind.'

'Oh, you would,' said Baby petulantly. She remained thoughtful during the rest of the meal.

'How do you know she's a policewoman?' demanded Phil suddenly.

'What?' Baby was roused from her own abstractions. 'Oh, another client told me. I saw her_out walking with her baby – oh, he's a little doll. Phil, I wonder if we could....'

'No,' said Phil.

'Just adopt,' said Baby. 'Just adopt .... I didn't mean .... Or I believe you *can* ....' She looked sideways at Phil. 'It's a new technique.'

'*No,*' said Phil. 'Go on about what this other girl told you.'

'Oh, just that her friend had come in to have a manicure from me and how good it looked. Then she said about the police.'

'Well, it can't matter,' said Phil.

'No,' agreed Baby. 'Only, well, you know that lovely blue fur? The one striped pink?'

'Safely away out of your clutches,' said Phil.

'Mmm. I *do* regret it. If there's one thing I regret, that's it,' said Baby. 'But the thing is, I tried it on once more. I simply had to, Phil. You know what I'm like when I simply have to do something.'

'Well, I don't suppose she saw you,' said Phil grimly. 'I suppose you had that much sense.'

'Oh, yes, I was quite on my own. But a bit of the fur

61

got stuck in my bracelet.' Baby held out a delicate wrist well weighed down with bangles and bracelets of gold and ivory and enamel. 'I didn't realise, but she saw it when I was doing her nails. She said what a pretty colour it was. I wish we could have kept some of that lovely jewellery, but it wasn't to be.'

'You silly bitch,' said Phil.

'I told her it was from my cat.'

'She'd believe that.'

'I said it was a white cat and that I'd given it a blue rinse,' said Baby defiantly. 'I had to think of something quick.'

'You didn't have to think of anything. You didn't have to *wear* the fur, that's what you didn't have to do.'

'Oh, you are in a paddy,' said Baby, eyeing her fearfully. 'I could get a white cat and dye it.'

'Oh, shut up.' Phil got up and stared to walk. 'Let me think. Well, to begin with, don't tell Diana.'

'No, I won't,' said Baby with conviction.

'I'm glad you've told me, but, my God, you are stupid sometimes. If she knows about those furs – but, on the other hand, perhaps she doesn't. Why should it be her case? And, if it isn't, the significance of the blue fur will be lost on her. Maybe, anyway. Probably she's forgotten already. Oh, God, that sounds like you talking, not me. Living with you all these years has affected my brain.' Phil kicked at the table leg. 'No, we've got to assume she does know about the furs. And we ought to assume that she will connect it with what she saw on your arm. We must take the worst view.'

'Yes,' said Baby.

'But she can't prove anything. Did anyone else hear you two?' Baby shook her head.

'And you've destroyed that tuft of fur?'

'Oh, yes.'

'Then it's your word against hers. And you can deny it ever happened.'

'Oh, I will,' said Baby.

'With any luck, she'll never come into your place again. She's not a regular, is she? Well, then.'

'But what will I do if she does come?'

'Act normal. If possible. And certainly don't tell Diana. We've got to watch our step there.'

'Yes,' said Baby, who knew that Charmian had an appointment for a pedicure and leg massage the next day. It can't mean anything, she thought. Policewomen have to look after their feet.

Nor did she feel inclined to tell Phil that the blue and pink fur tabard had not gone off, but had been quietly abstracted by Baby and hidden.

When Charmian arrived for her pedicure the next day she was wearing soft tan leather sandals and no stockings. Her feet didn't appear to be giving her any trouble.

Diana saw her coming through a kind of spy-hole she had in the back room: she could sit at her desk and look straight into a mirror which reflected the reception area.

She saw Charmian come in and frowned. Baby, who had her own reasons for disquiet, saw the frown.

'She's soon back, isn't she?'

'Come for a pedicure,' said Baby nervously. 'I booked it myself.'

Diana grunted.

'You don't usually mind if clients come back soon.'

'They're not usually the Fuzz.'

'Oh.' Baby considered. 'So you know that?'

'Of course. As you do, too, obviously. Get rid of her as speedily as you can.'

'Oh, I will,' said Baby fervently.

Baby had an instinctive cunning, and almost without conscious thought she proceeded to do a job on Charmian's toes sufficiently professional to provoke no criticism, but not so good as to bring her customer back for more of the same. People like Baby learn little quiet ways of self-defence.

'I don't really like that colour,' said Charmian, looking at the enamel that now decorated her toes.

'No,' said Baby appraisingly, putting her head on one side. 'Perhaps it is a bit bright.' (It was a wild orange.) 'Oh, look, now I've smudged it. I'll do that big toe again.'

'No, don't bother.' Charmian withdrew her foot. 'I like it that way. How's your cat?'

For one wild moment Baby thought of saying that it was dead, but a flash of good sense saved her. 'It's all right. Fine. Dear little thing.'

'What's its name?'

There was a pause. 'Bluey,' said Baby hoarsely.

'Descriptive.' Charmian smiled.

'Yes, isn't it?' Baby's hands trembled as she put her manicure things together and placed the bowl of water for the soaking of hands on the pink velvet cushion for the massage and painting of nails. Water slopped on the velvet. Charmian saw it, but she didn't say anything. Baby was almost sure she was baiting her.

She hurried into the inner room, hardly waiting for Charmian to go.

'Gawd, I must have a fag,' she said, imitating Phil. They did talk like each other occasionally.

'You've done her, then?' said Diana from behind her desk. She was wearing a pair of spectacles with huge round pale-brown lenses; behind them her eyes looked tense and worried.

'Yes,' said Baby, taking a deep and desperate drag on her cigarette.

'She hasn't gone, though,' said Diana.

The salon was now full of customers in various stages

64

of hair repair, change and modification. Bleaches, streak-ings, tints and frizzes were in full progress.

'She's only paying,' said Baby. 'Now she's gone back to leave a tip. I can see her putting it down on my pink velvet cushion.'

'She's looking at something, too,' said Diana. 'And she's got something in her hand. What's she doing, sniffing it?'

Baby's head jerked round. No, surely it wasn't poss-ible. A hair of fur couldn't have stuck to that velvet cushion surely. For a moment she could just see it, delicately blue against the pink. No, it couldn't be.

'Sniffing around,' commented Diana bitterly. 'Typical of the police. It's what makes them so disliked.'

'I think she was just looking at something,' said Baby, feeling sick.

'I wouldn't mind so much, but she's a nice-looking woman. Needs grooming, but I could help there. It'd be a pleasure. In other circumstances.'

'Don't care for that sort of look myself,' said Baby, finishing her cigarette. 'A hard look, I think.'

Diana opened a drawer in her desk and took out a mirror and studied her face. 'Suppose you could say that of me.'

'Oh, no,' said Baby, although she had said so often, and with knobs on, as she put it to herself.

Diana went over to the reception desk and checked the book. 'She's made another appointment. With you. For a manicure. Find out what you can about her. I want to know.'

'Why?' asked Baby quickly.

'Oh, don't worry, she's not a sex object to me.'

'I wasn't thinking of that.'

'Weren't you? You usually are. No, I want to know about her. What she does with herself. What she's interested in. What her weakness is. There'll be one. You find out.'

'I don't think I'm very good at that sort of thing,' said Baby in a soft little voice.

'Oh, I think you are. I think you're very good at it. I've watched you doing it.'

'I'm just interested in people, that's all.'

'And I'm one of the people you've interested yourself in.'

Baby just shrugged.

'And what is it you've found out about me, then?'

'I know you were married once,' said Baby. 'But you haven't got a husband now. I don't know if you're divorced or widowed.'

'There's no tragedy about me to find out,' said Diana. 'I may have caused one or two but I haven't been one. That's not my style at all.'

'If you say so,' agreed Baby politely, not anxious for trouble.

'And what else do you know about me?'

'Not much. I know you came here from London, and that you haven't got many friends. I haven't got many, but you have even fewer.'

'It's the way I've wanted it,' said Diana. 'For what I'm after, it's an advantage! Anonymity, that's what I've chosen. But you only know what I've let you know. There is more to me than that.'

'Well, naturally, I didn't think you came out of an egg,' said Baby, thinking to herself it would be a pretty tough egg. 'I have to go now. My eleven o'clock's just come in and she hates to be kept waiting.'

'Right. By the way, tell Phil she's booked for a hair appointment at six here tomorrow. Last appointment of the day. We'll have a drink afterwards. Satisfied with the profits from the last time, was she?'

'Very,' said Baby, edging towards the door. 'I was, too.'

'And no flashing the money around, remember; that's dangerous.'

'Wouldn't dream of it,' said Baby. 'Have I ever?'

Diana's expression softened slightly. 'No. You're a loyal little thing,' she said.

'Yes, I am,' said Baby and, as a matter of fact, within her limits, it was true.

When she had gone, Diana sat for a moment at her desk in thought. 'A woman is only as strong as the instruments she uses,' she said, half aloud. 'I wonder how strong that makes me?'

She picked up the telephone and spoke to her sister. 'Tomorrow evening. I've told the others. I'll spell it out to them then.'

'I hope you know what you're doing.'

'Listen, I'm doing it and I'm doing it my way, and I'm doing it right.'

There was a pause while her sister gathered her thoughts. 'Others have tried. There was that woman in Germany. Look what happened there: killed herself. Hanged in her cell.'

'Don't go comparing me with that mentally unbalanced woman. A rank amateur, that's what she was. If I'm anything at all, I'm a professional,' said Diana sharply.

'All the same, you keep a collection of cuttings about her. Articles, pictures, bits you've cut from magazines. I've seen it. The Ulrika Meinhoff Collection.'

'For information only,' snapped Diana. 'Clues, that's all. You have to learn as you go. And how you can.'

After a longish pause, her sister muttered something like 'Aiming high'. That was what it came out like, anyway. Diana continued sharp. 'I have to choose my helpers and make what I can of them. They don't come fully trained, you know. Not in our sex.'

Bee muttered something again.

'Oh, plenty of that,' said Diana. 'Shoplifters, look-outs, or experts, but always with men. Or nearly always. On the edge. Not planning and doing. Not the big jobs.'

'Well, don't count me in on this lot,' said Bee. 'Remember, I'm strictly neutral. I just balance the books.'

'Oh, you're nothing but a walking pocket calculator, I know that,' said Diana. 'But that's how it should be. I have to know the percentages.'

'You think I'm very stupid,' said Bee. 'Clever with figures, but sexless and stupid otherwise. You can't have everything, I know, but you really haven't left me with much.'

'That's rubbish. You're my own sister. I've fought for you, haven't I? Done my best for you. Can I help it I'm the elder and have had to take the decisions?'

'You have, and I'm grateful. But don't think I don't know there's something in this for you other than sheer profit.'

'What do you mean by that?' said Diana sharply.

'I'm not quite sure. I'm thinking it over. But the signs are there.'

'Such as?' asked Diana smartly.

'Such as that suddenly you're like a stranger I'm trying to be polite to; we were never like that. The change isn't in me, so it has to be in you. So there's something you haven't told me. It's logical.'

'Rubbish.'

'No, not rubbish. Nor imagination. I haven't got an ounce of that and you've often said so. I'm a slow thinker, but I do think. Go down to that woman who stands about staring and look her straight in the face and ask yourself what you have in common.'

Diana put the receiver down without answering. 'She's trying to make out there's something wrong with me,' she

68

said angrily to herself. 'But between me and such as that woman down by the shops there is nothing in common.'

Nevertheless, she did drive down and try to locate the watching woman. When she found her outside Marks & Spencer's she got out of the car and walked right past her, going quite close.

But the woman turned her face to the window and would not look at her.

'She's got thick ankles,' muttered Diana, and drove herself back to the shop. 'Damn it, we haven't got anything in common, we haven't, we haven't.'

Back in her office, before the shop closed for the night, she sorted through the papers on her desk. She had a small pile of her own trade-cards in front of her and she picked one up to study it. She was thinking of getting it redesigned. '*Charm and Chic*,' it read in gothic characters. 'Unisex Hair Styling for Women and Men.' But in fact she was giving up the unisex idea, and men were not any longer booked as customers. There had never been many.

Suddenly she pushed the whole lot from her with a gesture of impatience. 'Oh, fiddle,' she said. 'I know what I'm doing.'

When Charmian arrived in the Deerham Hills police station, having made a diversion to her own home to cover her painted toes, she took the delicate pale hair from her purse where she had secreted it and put it in an envelope with a hastily scribbled letter.

'Please tell me if this hair is cat or mink,' she wrote.

Then she addressed the letter to the police laboratories and got back to the affairs of the day.

'You look pleased with yourself,' said Agnes from behind her typewriter. She took up the letter Charmian had just dropped in the 'Out' tray and said: 'Send one, get one.'

'What's that mean?'

'*They've* just sent you a missive. About the card in the strangled man's jacket.' In spite of her professionalism, Agnes managed to get a certain amount of feeling into the word 'strangled', so that Charmian frowned. 'They can't get any farther with it. There *was* lettering on it, but it's beyond picking up now. Here, read for yourself.'

Charmian, still frowning, read the letter. 'That was another good idea,' she said. 'But I haven't given up on it yet. I'm sure there's something to be got from it.'

She stared at the blown-up photograph of the card. Just a faint, faint shadow showed itself.

'How's Walter?' she asked, putting it down.

'Coming on nicely. Threatening to get up and come back and start work.'

'I wish he would,' said Charmian absently, not really meaning it. 'He can have the drowned, strangled, raped man.'

'At least we've got his name now,' Adam Lily said from the door. 'They finally got his fingerprints to mean something, and we made a match. Or the computer did. I love that machine, the work it saves me.'

'So who is he?'

'Name: Terry Jarvis. Aged thirty-nine, said in life to look younger. Served two and a half prison sentences for armed robbery: seven, ten and fifteen years – all quite long; he was lucky to get them in, but he started young,' said Adam Lily briskly.

'What do you mean, two and a *half* sentences?'

'He escaped. The escape wasn't engineered by him or for him, it was for Rocky Roller.'

'Oh, him.' Rocky Roller had been for a little while the king of violent crime in London.

'Yes, him; his mates sprang him, and Terry just joined in. Then he got lucky and really got clean away, and we picked up Rocky within twenty-four hours.' When Adam said 'we', he was using the term royally. In person he had never set eyes on more than a photograph of Rocky Roller.

'And then he died, anyway.'

'Yes. He had cancer. I suppose he knew and that's why he wanted out. One last fling. But he died inside, just as he should have done.'

'And Terry Jarvis stayed out. I wonder where he hid?'

'Here, perhaps. Perhaps all this time we had him in Deerham Hills.' The royal 'we' again from Adam. 'He died here. That must mean something.'

'Not necessarily,' said Charmian. 'Supposing he was just dumped in the river.'

'But by someone who knew of the river here, and knew there are quiet stretches where you could put a body in unobserved.'

'That's true,' said Charmian. 'And the ground slopes from the belt of trees on Ringmill Hill. You wouldn't need help. Just a shove and the weight of the body would carry it down into the river, rolypoly.'

Unconsciously, she had built up a vivid word-picture, and all three of them, Charmian, Agnes and Adam, were silent for a moment in tribute to it.

'Is he known to have any friends here? Any contacts in Deerham Hills?'

Adam shook his head. 'None that can be traced.'

'Was he married?'

'Yes.' He consulted some notes. 'Married in 1970. A girl called Olive Francis. Half-Italian. Mother from Milan. But the marriage broke up. They seem to have been separated for years.'

'Other women?'

Adam shrugged. 'No names. There must be some, though; he wasn't a natural monk.'

'And certainly sex comes into it.' Charmian got up. 'It

seems to me that sex comes into everything at Deerham Hills at the moment. That woman who just stands and stares at other women; this sudden wave of violence – it's not just the hot weather.'

The other two were silent, watching her.

'Do you know what I'm going to do? I'm going out for a walk to think about it.'

When the door had closed behind her, Adam Lily said: 'Is she all right?'

'Of course,' said Agnes loyally.

'I mean, saying that, though. Putting it like that.'

'Oh, don't be silly.' Agnes was angry, whether with Adam, herself, or Charmian, she did not quite know. 'You know the way she meant it.'

'No, I don't.' He was looking out of the window. 'She isn't walking, you know. She's taken her car.'

'It's the same thing,' said Agnes, still loyal.

But she came over, and they stared out together at Charmian's car disappearing.

In fact Charmian drove a quick tour round the town centre to get rid of the unnerving mood she found herself in: a state of mind which seemed to say that something was about to happen, that something ought to happen, but that, if she wasn't careful, she was going to fail to understand what it was all about.

Then she headed the car towards the police laboratories. Every time she saw them she thought they needed a new building. As it was, they were housed in an old disused school which did not do justice to the professionalism of the work done there.

They were surprised to see her, but welcoming. They didn't get many visitors. Not live ones, anyway. Hunks of bone, drying skin, gobbets of flesh and scraps of cloth were what usually came their way.

'That card,' said Charmian, introducing her business

72

without preamble. 'From the photograph you sent me I can't pretend to guess, but could you make out what colour it once was? It's pale grey now.'

The technician to whom she was sent was thoughtful. 'I *might* find a trace of the dye. I really doubt it, though.' He looked at Charmian. 'What colour do you think it was?'

'I wondered if it might be pink.'

'If it is, then you shall be the first to know.' And he grinned. 'But I think the answer's going to be, I don't know; but I can tell you here and now about that hair.'

'Oh, it's arrived?'

'By pigeon post,' he said solemnly. 'And it didn't need more than a look. That's no common old moggy that parted with that hair. It's the mink. The best-quality Canadian mutation mink. Nature turned it out greyish-white, but it has been dyed a pretty blue. Very chic, and very expensive.'

'Oh, that's good,' said Charmian. 'That's very good. Thanks.'

The girls were making plans. In the inner sanctum behind the salon, where few were admitted, they were seated round a table. Diana had poured out drinks and handed round cigarettes. Diana didn't smoke, but it gave her satisfaction to supply others with cigarettes. Her sister Bee called it her Borgia complex.

Diana had a map on the table. A street-map of Deerham Hills.

After a pause, Bee said: 'That map's out of date. Six years old.'

'For our purposes it's all right.'

'You can't be quite sure. I like to be a hundred per cent accurate.'

'I've been there and looked. For myself. With my own eyes.'

73

'Still, you can't be sure of everything,' Bee said doggedly.

'I don't think it matters,' said Baby, with the air of a peacemaker. 'Not for this.'

'I agree,' said Phil. 'Come on, get on with it.'

Diana picked up a pencil to use as a pointer. 'Well, we've agreed that now we must go for real money. We've had our trial runs, and very satisfactory they've been in their way. And here we've had Baby's special services to thank.'

Baby smiled and gave a little bow.

'Thank you, Baby. But what we've got so far has been chicken-feed. And we're all agreed that's not what we're after.'

'Hear, hear,' said Phil.

'So we're moving into a new bracket. And here again I think Baby might be able to help us.'

Baby gave another little bow.

'We've agreed on the idea that it's straight cash we want. Notes and plenty of them. Baby has so far helped us by taking the keys from the handbags of some of our wealthier customers, so that we could get copies done.'

Baby smiled. 'The one thing women *can't* do while they are having a manicure is hold on to their purse. They don't want to see it. Psychological, I suppose.'

'I've added a bit of psychology myself,' said Diana.

'You have. My clients always sit for their manicure in a special armchair. There's really nowhere to *put* their bags except on the floor. And when I'm sitting close to them, with my head bent over my lovely pink cushion, blocking the view, about all they can see is their nails and me; and of course I keep up a stream of conversation. I'd do that anyway; it's part of the job. "Never mind what you say," they told me when I trained, "as long as you say something."'

'You have natural talent, Baby,' said Phil.

74

Bee said: 'Could we get on with it?' And she looked at her watch.

'Got an appointment?' asked Phil.

'No, I just like to check up on the time.'

'In case it runs out on you like money?'

'Oh, leave her be,' said Diana. 'She's quite right to watch the time. It's a commodity like anything else. Come on, Baby. It's for you to say.'

Baby sipped her drink, and stroked one ankle with the prettiest hand in Deerham Hills. 'Do you think I could learn to shoot?' she said. 'I've got a very good eye. One of us ought to have a gun. I don't see why it shouldn't be me. It must be touch that counts and not brute force, and there I'd score. I have a delicate touch.'

'Baby, get on with it,' said Phil.

'Well, now, I have a new client. She's only just come to Deerham Hills. In fact her arrival represents a new departure. Just wait till I tell you.'

'We are waiting,' said Diana. '*I* know, mind you,' she said, turning to Bee and Phil, 'but she's certainly spinning it out.'

'She's called Brown. Not a very memorable name, is it? But she's very fussy about the way her hands look. Angela Brown: she's the manager of the new branch of Grimbly & Hughes Bank in Bridge Street in Deerham Hills.'

'Interesting,' said Phil.

'Yes, and you haven't heard the best yet. It's really made for us.' Baby's voice rose with excitement. 'The branch is going to concentrate on women customers. That's the policy. It's going to be a branch for women.'

'It's our duty to rob that bank,' said Phil.

'Duty be damned,' said Diana. 'It's going to be a pleasure.' She stood up and started to walk up and down the room. 'Do you think you can get the keys, Baby?'

'Well, I can have a jolly good try.'

75

'Can I have another drink?' said Phil. 'This needs thinking over. I see what you mean about the gun, Baby.'

'Oh, they don't have armed guards there. I'd just feel safer.'

Diana went round, pouring out drinks.

Bee said: 'There's still the safe and its lock, and the strong-room. All you will get are the keys to the front door and the side door.'

'Yes, there's all the details to be worked out,' said Diana.

'But the keys to the bank and where she lives above it, if we can get them, make a good beginning. We ought to think about it. I mean, we can get *in*.'

'I agree,' said Phil.

'There's still the safe,' said Bee obstinately. 'And the strong-room.'

'She lives above the bank. In a flat that's provided. Part of the job. We could take her down and make her open the whole apparatus.'

'So she could identify us?' asked Phil. 'Be your age.'

Diana sat down at the table and looked at the map. 'There's one way round that.'

'Dress up, you mean? Disguise ourselves?'

Bee was looking at her sister's face. 'No, she doesn't mean that.'

'The river is close by,' said Diana, pointing with her finger at the map.

'Kill her, you mean? And dump her in the river?'

There was a moment of silence. Then Diana said: 'It's only a suggestion. We have to consider everything. I don't know that I consider it the best suggestion.'

'I'm sure I don't,' said Phil.

'You are savage, Di,' said Baby uneasily. 'And a woman, too. I don't think women ought to kill women.'

'My dear, one way and another they do it all the time,' said Diana. 'And this is business, not a crusade.'

'I'm not so sure,' muttered Bee.

'How many times do I have to tell you I am not sexist about anything?' shouted Diana. 'This is strictly business.'

'*If* I believe you,' murmured Bee. Baby heard, and her eyes grew round with interest.

'There'll be a lot of money in that bank,' said Diana, 'and I'd like, at least, to try to get it.'

'Hear, hear,' said Phil again, puffing at her fag and reaching out a tentative hand for the whisky-bottle.

'And don't you get drunk,' said Baby sharply. 'That won't help anyone.' She raised her voice and addressed the room. 'You haven't heard yet about my other client. The prospect there might be better than at the bank.'

Diana sat down. 'Speak up, then. We're listening.'

'You already know, of course, Diana, so I'm not really talking to you. I've got a new client who works in the Deerham Hills Hospital in the Treasurer's Office.'

Bee stirred.

'She's only been in here once, but she's going to be a regular. She's said so – and, anyway, I can always tell. She's got a problem, you see. She's been let down and thinks having her hands done will help her out.'

'A man, I suppose,' said Diana.

'I fear so,' said Baby with delight. 'Terrible hands she's got, too, poor Mrs Sims, all red and square.' Baby gave a little shudder. 'Nothing I can do to them, really, but she deceives herself about their appearance. You'd be surprised how some women do. Natural, but stupid.'

Phil gave her a sharp look. It always gave her a funny feeling to see little Baby perform. A side of Beryl Andrea Barker showed then that she didn't see often, and sometimes found hard to believe existed. 'Hurry up,' she growled.

77

'All *right,* Phil, let me do this my way. She'll be a regular because she really hates her hands, but kids herself they're beautiful.'

'A contradiction,' said Phil, as if she never had any contradictions inside or outside herself.

'But she has the keys to the office where she works,' went on Baby unperturbed. 'I've seen them already, and read the name-tag.'

Bee said: 'Hospitals are always swarming with people. We'd never do it.'

'At *night,*' said Baby. 'At night they are *not* swarming. She tells me that the corridor where her office is situated is like Piccadilly Circus tube station in the day-time. At night it's like a tomb. It *is* underground.'

'I don't like that for a start,' broke in Phil.

'There is a way out, a door on to a flight of steps,' said Baby.

'I've been to that hospital,' said Bee. 'And there's a whacking great notice up saying "Guard Dogs Patrol This Area at Night".'

'There are no dogs,' said Baby simply. 'Only a notice.'

'I don't know,' said Bee.

'You never do,' said Phil. 'And I can see you never will. Or, anyway, not until the opportunity is long past. But, for once, I'm with you. Better be safe than sorry.'

'Oh, platitudes,' said Diana.

'I'm your driver not your thinker,' said Phil. 'Your sister sees to that. Only she's a bit slow.'

'No, we all have to decide,' said Diana. 'And take our share of the responsibility. I shall take most because I shall take more of the money.'

'Oh, will you?'

'Naturally. I'm putting more in. This shop is mine. The contacts are mine. I pay Baby's wages.'

'The car is mine,' said Phil significantly.

'We'll work out the proportions properly,' said Diana. 'Once we see what we get. As we did before with the furs. Bee will do that. All will be agreed to beforehand.'

'Splendid,' said Phil. 'Because I'm a fast driver and I just might drive far away with whatever I'd got.'

'Ah, but there'd be Baby there with her little gun.'

'Oh, good, I am going to have one, then?' said Baby.

'She'd never turn it on me,' answered Phil. 'Would you, Baby?'

'No, I don't think so,' said Baby, considering.

Bee broke into this sparring with: 'There would be much more cash in the bank than in the hospital safe, where I imagine they only keep the money for the wages on pay-day and for running expenses.'

'The branch of the bank is for women,' said Diana thoughtfully. 'I want to do it. Call it my ambition if you like. I'd like to do a bank. Any bank would be good. But this one would be special.'

Baby said, raising her head from a careful survey of her nails to see if one was chipped (it wasn't – what a relief), 'Know what they call this place down in the town? "Cheap and Cheek", that's what they call us.'

'What?' Diana was quick and sharp.

'It's a joke,' explained Baby. She held out one hand so that she could see it in the mirror she was facing. What she saw seemed to satisfy her. Hands were so important.

'We're not cheap,' said Diana with mounting indignation.

'No, we certainly are *not.* Your latest price increase, Di – I suppose that's what they mean. That and style. In the end it comes down to a matter of style,' said Baby, with a faint smile.

'You're being clever,' said Diana. 'Don't be clever. I don't like it.'

The gentle smile did not move from Baby's face. A tiny

feeling of disquiet stirred within Phil. Could it be her friend was cleverer than she looked?

Baby shrugged. 'All I'm saying is: Do you want to stay here for the rest of your lives or don't you? Bank or hospital? One or the other it's got to be.'

'Yes, you're right,' said Diana quietly. 'In some ways you've got a lot of sense, Baby.'

'Thank you.' Baby gave a little bow.

'But why shouldn't we do both?'

Bee said: 'She certainly knows how to manage you.'

At this point the outside bell rang.

It sounded through the suddenly quietened room like an alarm.

Diana stood up.

'Expecting anyone?' said Phil.

'No.' Diana was breathing quickly.

'Don't go to the door, then.'

'I think I will.' She had her breathing under control. 'After all, why not?' She walked towards the main door of thick glass which opened out of the salon area of Diana's establishment. There was a small pink and white foyer where a girl normally received customers, and took their coats and made them feel at home if that could ever be said to be true of Diana's salon, which was a grinding mixture of the fashionable and the gimcrack. 'But you keep out of sight. Probably better not to be seen together as a group.'

The bell sounded again. Just once. Not a determined sound.

'That person will go away if you ignore the bell,' said Phil.

'I don't think so,' said Baby. 'I can see in the mirror through to the door and through the door to the person at the bell. It's that client of mine.'

'The bank manager?'

'No,' said Baby with a dry little note in her voice. 'The

80

one that's a police detective. Daniels, she's called.' She didn't look at Phil, and Phil said nothing.

'I shall open the door,' said Diana calmly. 'She's a customer and I shall treat her as one.'

What you might call a suspicious customer, thought Phil.

The two women confronted each other on the doorstep.

'Good evening,' said Charmian to Diana. 'I saw your light on and thought you wouldn't mind me ringing.'

'Always glad to see a customer,' said Diana. 'Of course, we're really closed.'

'You do have one late night, don't you? When you stay open until nine in the evening?' Charmian managed to get herself inside.

'This isn't it, though,' observed Diana, unable to prevent Charmian inserting herself.

'No, my mistake. I do apologise. But I want to cancel my appointment for my next manicure.'

Baby, listening, all ears, breathed a deep sigh of relief, as Phil heard.

'Well, not really cancel,' said Charmian. 'But can I rearrange it?'

'Damn her,' said Baby under her breath.

'Of course. I'll be glad to rearrange it for you,' said Diana. 'It was lucky you caught me here.' She drew the appointment-book towards her. 'Let me see. Tomorrow, was it to be? When would you prefer?'

'The day after? Could I have an early-morning appointment?'

Charmian's nose wrinkled slightly, and Diana knew she had smelt Phil's cigarette. Neither party said anything, but it was perfectly apparent to Diana that Charmian was looking around, taking in what she saw and unobtrusively listening. Mercifully, the trio in the back room were quiet, and as far as Diana was concerned they could even stop breathing temporarily if they liked.

'Oh, yes, early will be fine. Say nine-fifteen?'

'Your manicurist will be in so early?'

Diana smiled and nodded. 'Certainly. Even earlier, if you like.'

'She must live on the premises!'

'Oh, no,' said Diana. 'In the town, though. Nine-fifteen, then?'

'Goodbye,' said Charmian. 'Sorry to have disturbed you. I just blew in on impulse.' And she smiled. 'Silly of me. I ought to have used the phone. But I didn't have your number to hand.'

'Oh, I'll give you our card,' said Diana, reaching out and handing one to her.

When Charmian had gone, she went back to her silent listening colleagues.

'She only came to rearrange her appointment,' she reported.

'Do you believe that?' said Phil.

'Not really.'

'She came for a look round,' announced Baby, with conviction. But naturally she did not pass on the reason for her conviction to her employer.

'I think so, too. You get an instinct about these things, and my instinct tells me she was looking me over. But I can't think how she got on to me.' Diana was frowning. '*If* she has. We mustn't overreact.'

'Do we give up planning ahead?'

'No, certainly not.' Diana was sharp. 'If it so happens that we've got to get out, then we've got to get out with money. No, we go on. Only faster. And there may be nothing in her visit.' She turned to Baby. 'You'll be able to judge when you do her treatment.'

'Oh, yes,' said Baby in a hollow voice. She looked

round for her gloves and handbag. It was obviously time to say goodbye and leave.

On the way home, she said to Phil: 'That woman was asking after me. Wasn't she?'

Phil did not bother to answer.

Bee had remained with her sister. At last she decided to speak. 'You can always surprise me, Di. You've done it just now.'

'What do you mean?'

'You weren't as upset by all the implications of that Daniels woman's visit as I'd have expected.'

Diana was silent as she emptied the ash-tray filled up by Phil.

'I should have been worried. It *is* worrying. I'll probably wake up in the night in a cold sweat.' She gave a laugh. 'But all the time I was talking to her I could sense something about her. I've developed that power with women, you know I have, Bee. I sense things.'

'I think you have in a way,' admitted Bee. 'It's not one I share. People are enigmas to me, the whole lot of them.'

'I felt a sort of question inside her,' went on Di. 'There's a basic insecurity about that woman that I think I could use.'

'Now you've surprised me again,' said Bee after a pause.

Charmian went home and spent a quiet evening writing letters to her family in Scotland. Initially she had trained as a policewoman in a sober Scottish town on the North Sea coast, transferring to England later, from motives made up about equally of ambition and restlessness. But she still had friends there as well as family, and she kept in touch.

She slept well and got up cheerfully. Unlike Baby, who rose grumbling and unrefreshed, complaining of the routine. Phil, too, was morose; her head ached. Bee went off to her post in the offices of the big Trading Box Company in Midford where she worked in the accounts department. She never said much to anyone, anyway, but she did just telephone her sister that morning to see how she was. Diana said she was all right.

And that day for Charmian there was the relentless regular course of a policewoman's life.

In the early morning she saw her letters and scribbled answers to those which needed reply. She made several reports, and took several telephone calls.

Agnes watched her with sympathy as she put down the receiver. 'And, on top of it all, you've got to have some unladdered tights to put on tomorrow, and remember to pay the milkman.'

'I expect some men have to do that, too,' said Charmian, pressing her hand against her forehead. 'Although probably with not so much conviction. Do you know, I think I'm getting a temperature.'

'No, it's just anger,' said Agnes. 'You've been angry all morning, I've noticed.'

'Have I?' Charmian was surprised. 'I thought I felt good.'

'Anger often makes you feel good,' said Agnes. 'I've noticed that, too.'

'You know what my real problem is?' and Charmian stood up.

'I have a dead man and a walking woman, and between the two of them they are driving me mad.'

'Nothing new on the man?'

'Half and half,' said Charmian ambiguously. 'That is, there's an idea. Unacceptable. And as for the woman – what can we do? We haven't got the sort of force here to send someone to follow her. And she hasn't done anything. She just moves on when anyone official appears.'

The Deerham Hills force was small, undermanned and relatively without sophisticated equipment. It made up for that, so they all believed, by the high IQ of all the members and their good relationship with the people of the town. But it lacked the spare officer, man or woman, to send after the walking woman as a full-time task.

'What can I do?' said Charmian. 'I'm sure there's a connection somewhere between this woman and the murdered man. It may not be a real physical connection. Perhaps they never met.'

'What is it, then?' asked Agnes.

'It's what you might call a psychic link,' said Charmian.

Agnes gave a hoot of laughter. 'Oh, go on,' she said.

'Well, I'm fumbling for a thought,' said Charmian. 'And it's hard.'

She didn't tell Agnes about her conversation with Jessie, because that was her secret.

But the observation about the blue mink hair was not secret and she left a memo for Adam Lily, who was out (interviewing a lady who thought she had seen a white Mercedes car parked outside the *Prettifurs* shop), telling him, and asking for some unobtrusive investigation of Baby. 'Because this must be done.'

And Diana? She said to Agnes: 'You know, yesterday I met a woman who interested me. As soon as I saw her I thought she might be capable of almost anything. And yet I have absolutely no evidence of it. Call it intuition, if you like.' Perhaps there was some evidence, but no need to mention it now. 'A fascinating woman in a terrible kind of way. I thought, when I looked at her: There's a big problem hanging over you, and I can solve it.'

Agnes listened. It's women, women, all the way, she thought. She leant forward. 'I'm going to say something you might not like. Don't you think you need a man?'

She and Charmian had a quiet deep friendship, all the

stronger for not being much in evidence. It was on her shoulder that Charmian had wept her painful tears when her husband died. It was to Charmian that Agnes had confessed her early abortion.

A deep flush rose upwards from Charmian's neck, finally reaching her cheeks before ebbing away. She bent her eyes downward.

'I'll answer that in the spirit it's offered. Yes, probably yes. In many ways, yes. But in this matter I am not obsessed, nor about to become so.'

Oh well, thought Agnes, another friendship down the drain. Sorry I spoke.

But to her surprise, as both of them prepared to leave, Charmian smiled. 'Don't worry, Agnes. I've seen you and Adam Lily watching me. It was a shock, Rupert's dying when he did, and I have missed him in all the ways you imply, and more.'

'Sorry,' muttered Agnes.

'And there is something still left about our life together that worries me. A problem left uncleared.'

'His son?' speculated Agnes.

Charmian didn't answer, but went on: 'But I am on my own now, and I like it. I feel good. I told you that. You should believe me.'

But that doesn't rule out memories of affection, mourning and a feeling of guilt, she thought, as she closed the door behind her and ran towards her car.

She drove towards Midford, hoping to find the market in full swing still, in spite of evening coming on. Jessie had pointed out that some of the stalls in Midford market displayed notices proclaiming their bargains by printing on newspapers in big black or red letters, in the manner of the banner hung round the strange woman's neck.

Charmian parked her car and walked through the market. The stalls were roughly grouped according to what they sold: fish-stalls in one area, meat and bacon in

86

another, clothing in yet another, and, at the heart of it all, stalls laden with vegetables and fruit.

Almost at once, she saw the notices Jessie had mentioned. They were in use among three or, yes, it was four of the stalls. And these four stalls were all bunched together as if owned by a family group. *Furnivall's Fruit Bazaar,* the name blazoned above one stall, the largest, seemed to belong to them all.

And when you had a close look at the people serving on the stalls or moving mysteriously in the background, carrying crates of bananas and boxes of apples, they had a family resemblance. Long noses, blue eyes, firmly defined eyebrows, and the same loud carrying voice marked them all. Now she thought about it she remembered hearing about such a family group, but they weren't called Furnivall; that was a name assumed for business only. Their own was much humbler: Biddle or Bumble or Beadle or something similar.

Charmian walked back through the crowds and drove away, passing, had she but known it, Gloria in the homeward bus.

As she drove, she totted up the score.

She was one up on the walking, staring, standing woman; she had a clue now to her provenance.

She had a lead on the robbery at *Prettifurs.* Somehow or other, the blue-eyed fair-haired manicurist with the face of a Botticelli Venus had been in contact with one of the stolen furs.

And, finally, at the back of her mind, she had a tremendous idea about the dead man, whom he had known in town, and even why he might have had her surname and telephone number on a card in his pocket.

When Charmian got home she garaged her car and let herself into the house. There were a couple of letters – bills, by the look of them – and a small card from a man offering his professional services as window-cleaner and sweep. Charmian's home, being newish, had no chimneys, and she couldn't remember what she did about her windows. Probably she didn't clean them.

She went into her living-room and stared out through the big glass windows. Ten years, she thought, and haven't they been cleaned once?

Not much to her surprise, Kitty appeared in her own garden, grimacing and waving to Charmian.

Now what's up? thought Charmian. She opened her window and called out.

'Kitty, what do I do about my windows being cleaned? I don't think they ever have been. I can't remember ever doing anything about it.'

'Of course you do, you idiot,' said Kitty. 'The man comes once a month, does mine and yours and I pay him, then you pay me.'

'Oh, that's what the money is for?' said Charmian, who regularly handed over one pound fifty pence to Kitty. 'Do you know, I thought it was a subscription for the church?'

'I'm coming over,' said Kitty. She gave a peremptory wave, ordering obedience from her friend, and disappeared from view.

When she arrived, breathless, she said: 'You had a visitor.'

Charmian was surprised. 'I never have visitors.' Which was true enough. She always arranged to meet her friends elsewhere, and discouraged casual dropping in.

'Well, you had one today!'

The two women went into the house, into the kitchen, as usual.

'I saw the car from the garden when I was putting out the baby. I wouldn't have known it was connected with you, if I hadn't seen a movement at your front door.' Kitty never made much secret of the strong curiosity which was such a splendid feature of her character.

'Who was it?' asked Charmian.

'Couldn't see through the shrubbery. And when I went round to have a look I saw the car drive off. I put two and two together.'

After a pause for thought, Charmian said: 'Man or woman?'

Kitty shook her head. 'Couldn't say.' Then she said: 'Does it matter?'

'Why do you ask?' said Charmian vigorously.

Kitty hesitated. 'No reason. Except that I thought that to you, at this moment, it did.'

Charmian stood up and went to the window, looking out, so that her face was hidden from her friend. 'The roses need pruning,' she said absently. 'And they've got mildew or foot rot or something. God, what a lousy cruel world it can be.'

'You're in the business to know,' said Kitty, as lightly as she could. There was a terrible tension in Charmian.

'I mean trouble you fall into without ever meaning to, without noticing it's happened. The first time I saw Tom I didn't even like him. He stayed away most of the first year of my marriage with Rupert. Then he came back once or twice, and, bingo, there we were, in love. Rotten, wasn't it?'

'I don't think so,' said Kitty gravely. 'Sad, perhaps, or even joyful. It depends what you made of it.'

'We made nothing. Not even a one-night stand.'

'Oh, Charmian.'

'Don't be so sorry for me. It was my own fault. I was quite adult. I could have handled the situation how I liked. As it was, I handled it in the worst possible way and let my husband find out. There was nothing much to find out, but that was hard for him to believe. He wanted to trust me, he did trust me, but it ate into him a little bit further each day. I could see it. In the end he quarrelled with Tom. It was inevitable.'

89

'I suppose,' agreed Kitty.

'Oh, not over me. Not ostensibly. But I think both of them knew what the real reason was. Things were said. . . .' She paused, as if reliving that scene in her memory. 'I tried to stop them, but it was no good. Tom went off. He didn't say anything to either of us. He just went. Then Rupert got a telephone call from him saying he'd taken this under-cover job and would be out of circulation for a bit, and not to worry. We never saw him again.'

'That bit I know,' said Kitty with sympathy.

'Well, you know more than anyone else. Because I've never spoken about Tom to anyone at all. I think now he took this particular secret operation on so that he could disappear. He didn't invent it. Rupert checked that. But I guess he took the chance to go.'

'Isn't it surprising he didn't come back when his father died?'

'If he knows. If he ever heard he died. He could be on the other side of the world. Or he could be dead.'

'Do you think that?' Kitty watched her friend's face.

'Rupert thought so, I believe. But just lately I have come to believe Rupert discovered something, found out some fact, picked up some story that triggered off his heart attack. So perhaps Tom isn't dead. I don't know where he is, but he may not be dead.'

'Oh, I do hope not,' said Kitty.

'My colleagues, who know far more than I wish, think he may be,' said Charmian in a cold voice. 'They got me down to the forensic laboratory to look at something they found in the pocket of a dead man they had down there.'

'The one found in the river?'

'Yes, that one. He had a card in his pocket with the name Ascham and the telephone number here scribbled on it. I don't know what the card meant. The funny thing

90

is, the card did say something to me, only it wasn't "Tom Ascham" it said. I don't know what it was, yet; I'm still thinking about it.'

'But it wasn't Tom?'

'No. And once my colleagues had thought of it, they could check the fingerprints, of course.'

'They did that?' Kitty was curious.

Charmian nodded. 'They didn't tell me. Too tactful, I suppose. Nothing's ever been said openly on the subject. But I found out. I see all the reports; I read for myself.'

'Well, anyway, you know he's not dead.'

'He's not *that* dead man,' said Charmian, still troubled. 'And sometimes, like today, he seems very near and close. So, when you said someone was calling, I wondered, could it be Tom that came calling?'

She shook her head angrily. 'Stupid, stupid thought. How could it be?'

'I wish I'd seen,' said Kitty with regret.

'But Tom would have come in,' said Charmian. 'He had a key.'

'But *would* he?' said Kitty. 'Knowing his father was dead, and you were on your own, would he come in? Wouldn't it be a mite insensitive? I don't believe he'd do it.'

'If he knew.'

Kitty was decisive. 'You look worn out. Take a sleeping-tablet and go to bed.'

'Yes, I will.'

Charmian saw her friend out, locked up the house, and prepared for bed. It was still early, but Kitty was right; she felt exhausted, hollow inside and stupid with it.

When she looked at her dressing-table, she thought it looked more untidy than she remembered, but it was only an idle passing thought, to which she gave no weight.

As she slept, lightly drugged, a key was turned in the

91

front door of her house, and the door pushed open slightly.

The intruder stood there in thought, and then quietly opened the door farther, and crept upstairs to the room where Charmian was asleep. For a moment the intruder studied her, then turned round and went out.

Charmian slept on, heedless and unknowing.

Chapter Four

It was on the day following that Gloria had her metamorphosis. There was nothing surprising about it, of course; the only odd thing was that it hadn't happened sooner. But the truth was that none of the principals concerned in the police force and in Deerham Hills had really been giving their minds to Gloria. They were looking at her, but looking at her, so to speak, out of the corner of their eyes. A good look was really needed at Gloria. It was what she wanted. A cry for help walking on two legs was what Gloria was, as her landlady's husband more or less suspected.

'She worries me,' he said more than once to his wife. 'There's something very wrong there.' He was a rather shy man who never liked to stare at his lodger. So his looks at her were indirect, and as often as not at her reflection in the mirror as she passed their living-room on her way out of the house. This did not give a true image of Gloria. It cut her short at the waist.

His wife gave him a short wry look. Could any man be so dense as he sometimes seemed? 'I made a mistake letting that room. It's all my fault.'

'You mean you're going to get rid of her?' His mouth dropped open in a gape.

'It'll end naturally. That one will always move on. A real wanderer – haven't you noticed?'

'I think she'd like to stay,' he said, almost to himself. 'If she could.' He shook his head.

'It's more a mystery why she *came*, rather than why she may go,' murmured his wife. It was a comment with which Charmian would have wholeheartedly agreed.

93

But, at that particular moment, when his remark was being uttered, Charmian's thoughts were on other problems. There were plenty, professional and private, but after her outpouring to Kitty, and her long and peaceful night's rest, she felt better able to deal with them.

Talking to Kitty had cleared her mind. She still didn't know where Tom was – whether he was dead or alive – but she felt less guilt-ridden. She could wait. It was not really her problem; while the dead man and the robberies *were* her problems. They were her work.

The dead man could, also, in a way, wait. Other men – detectives, scientists, technicians – were working on him, studying his body, analysing his clothes, trying to check his movements when alive.

'But no one had seen him in Deerham Hills; no one remembers him,' Adam Lily had said sadly. 'The unseen Terry Jarvis. But he *was* here, even if he was brought here already dead, so we will find something somewhere in the end.'

And then there's the card, thought Charmian, as she listened to Adam's report. Something there for me, I swear.

For her, the man was an emotional problem, nagging away through that card, which was saying something personal and direct to *her*. If she could only get it clear *what*.

It wasn't because the name Ascham appeared on it, a water-dimmed ghost, although that was interesting.

'And then he was raped,' said Adam, with whom the fact rankled. 'Or as good as, so the doc says. Held down. Had it done to him.'

'I find that of relatively little significance,' said Charmian. 'Taken in the total context of his murder.'

No new facts about the dead man had emerged; only the old nasty ones were still there: that he had been abused, strangled, and dumped in the river.

'Oh, you can be such a bitch. It could have been you that did it to him,' said Adam Lily, stumping out, but he was careful to keep these words to himself, only saying aloud that he was off to do some more asking questions around the town and would report. 'You'll be here, will you?'

'Yes,' said Charmian thoughtfully. 'All day and into the night as well. I did have an appointment with a manicurist but I think I'll put it off.'

Accordingly, she rang up the shop, now operating full-time and full of the sound of hair-dryers, rushing water and pop music (Diana hated silence), and changed her appointment once again. She was aware that in so doing she was making it quite clear that her earlier visit to Diana's establishment had been a probe and she intended that Diana should know. She was sure that in some way Diana had to break. Only by cracking that assurance could she find out what this woman knew about the Deerham Hills robberies.

Diana herself answered the telephone, answering at once, as if she had been sitting by it. 'Hello?'

I can break her, thought Charmian. Only I've got to find the right way to do it. For one passing moment it occurred to her to use Gloria. Set the watching woman to watch Diana. Stroll across the shopping-plaza and say: 'I think you're a lunatic, but will you go and stare at a woman I want to disturb?'

Communications thus established, she and Gloria might have found much to say to each other, but Charmian did not know that. In a way – her way – Gloria knew, but she was unable to speak.

Over the noise of the salon, to which Baby's chirp was now added, Charmian announced her change of appointment once again.

Diana took it coolly, only remarking that it was usual

95

to make a slight charge for such late cancellations but that in this case she would waive it.

Charmian mentally saluted her nerve. 'A lot going on today for me. A clutch of crime, you might say. We've had some robberies here, you know. Small things, but tiresome. But I hope to have it all cleared up soon. It's pretty certain to be over soon.'

'Oh, really?'

'I think so. Tomorrow afternoon, could we say? Two-fifteen? I won't let you down.'

'Oh, I won't let you,' said Diana. 'If you're not here, I'll come down and get you in person.'

'A good threat.'

'Ah, who meant threats?' asked Diana with relish. Charmian caught the note in her voice and was surprised by it.

That woman will use me, involve me in some way, if she can, was Charmian's immediate reaction. What is there she knows about me that I don't know about her? What is there to know about her?

A sentiment echoed by Baby, and even more by Phil. As Baby manicured a client's hands, and watched Diana at the telephone, she remembered Phil talking last night over their late-night drinks.

Uneasily, Phil had said: 'Has it struck you that Di must have a criminal connection? Has it at her fingertips how and where to sell what we've picked. I delivered those goods and, though Bee did the talking, I did the listening. I could tell. It was all set up. By Di. She'd got it fixed to sell, and she knew what price to get. She didn't learn that by washing hair.'

'That's true,' said Baby.

'And something else: she must have been married once. She never says, but I can tell. I can always tell. Perhaps she is married still.'

'I never heard her mention a husband,' said Baby.

96

'Perhaps she learnt it all from him.' Phil leant forward, her hands on her knees, her expression earnest. 'She knows nearly everything about us, and we know nothing about her.'

She doesn't know everything about me, though, thought Baby, as she watched Diana put down the telephone, having finished talking to Charmian. She thought it a little unpleasant that Diana was smiling.

Charmian's follow-up to her talk with Diana was a telephone call to the Deerham Hills Chamber of Commerce to put a few questions to a friend there. She got the answers she had half expected.

Diana had come into the town with the money to set up her business. She had found the premises, established herself and hired staff, all within a few weeks. She seemed to have her plans ready-made. She explained that Deerham Hills was just big enough, just rich enough, and just far enough away from London to suit her.

'And that was the truth, anyway,' reflected Charmian's friend over the telephone. 'She sounded as though she meant it. But as for anything else – I don't know. Have you had a look at her salon? It's all been done on the cheap. Looks all right, but not much money's been laid out on it. If she walked out tomorrow, she wouldn't leave much behind.'

'Do you think she might do that?' asked Charmian curiously.

'No idea. She could do anything. One thing I am sure of: she knows the ropes. And she's learnt them the hard way somewhere.'

'I agree,' said Charmian.

'A hungry lady, I think. Isn't there a spider somewhere that eats you up for breakfast?'

'Husbands only,' said Charmian.

'Yes, she could do that, too, I should think,' said her friend. So, almost simultaneously, Charmian and Baby

97

and Phil arrived at the same conclusion: that Diana had a past that would bear investigating.

All the same, Charmian did not go for her rearranged manicure, and she made it plain that she did not intend to by sending a telephone message that same afternoon cancelling it. Her secretary did it for her.

'A bit of calculated cheek,' said Diana, staring down at the message scrawled on a pad by Baby, who had prudently cleared out.

Perhaps it was this that pushed Diana into action. The simple desire to show another, equally powerful woman what she could do.

But all she said was: 'Ask Phil if she'll have her car ready for me tonight, will you?'

And Baby did. Because Baby always did as she was asked, except when it did not suit her.

A great red finger pointed out from the wall at the group of women. Underneath was a question mark in yellow.

'Have you tested your urine today?' it demanded.

'Good Lord,' said Di. 'What's that all about?'

The three women, Diana, Phil and Baby, were standing in a corridor in the Hospital of St John and St James, Deerham Hills. At the end of the corridor stairs led up to the wards and down to a subterranean region of offices, cloakrooms and store-rooms. Although the corridor was short, signs and notices abounded on both walls. It was as well to be literate if you wanted to find your way about St John and St James.

'You can tell if you're pregnant from a urine test, I believe,' observed Baby.

'Well, that's not likely to worry *you*, is it?' returned Diana.

Baby gave her a hurt look and was silent.

'This is the diabetes clinic, I expect,' said Phil, with

irritation. 'Come on. Don't hang about here. We look so obvious.'

'But it's visiting-hours,' said Diana. 'No one will notice us. The place is swarming with strangers.'

'And none so strange as us,' said Baby with a giggle. She always bounced back, an enviable but not entirely lovable characteristic – at any rate, to Diana, who thought that Baby looked fragile but was probably indestructible.

The short corridor they were standing in was empty except for the three women, who were close together as if for protection. And they did indeed, in spite of Diana's brave words, feel vulnerable. But, at that moment, a young nurse wheeling a trolley laden with great kidney-shaped metal dishes passed by them without even looking towards them, and that gave them confidence.

'Whenever I come into a hospital I always feel as if someone is going to rush at me and order me to take all my clothes off and lie down and be examined,' whispered Baby.

'Trust you,' said Phil. She sniffed the air. 'Terrible smell in here. What is it?' The air was at once clean, rubbery, disinfected and drugged. 'I'd love a fag.'

'You can't smoke in a hospital,' Diana responded sharply. 'Not without drawing attention to yourself.'

Phil looked around her. 'You know, I'm beginning to think you could shout your head off here and no one would take any notice of you. They're so preoccupied.' Two young men in white coats, heads down as they talked together earnestly, brushed past them, oblivious and unheeding. 'See?' she said.

'Oh, come on.' Baby gave Phil a push. 'I know the way.' With eager little trotting steps she led the group towards the stairs.

At this point in the geography of the hospital many channels met, and many people were passing up and down the stairs. To the left was the bank of lifts. Diana looked at it carefully. In her book lifts represented an added danger to the unwary. People could appear on your scene so suddenly from lifts. It might be necessary to put a notice on that lift that said: 'Lower Ground Floor Only'.

'Downstairs,' said Baby. 'Just follow me. No one's noticing us. And, if they do, none of this lot will think it their business.' She took a quick appraising look around. 'Visitors. They're only thinking of themselves – just like the nurses.'

'Oh, don't be so chirpy,' growled Phil. She was always irritable when she was nervous.

'Well, it isn't as if we were going to *do* anything. Not tonight.'

Diana was silent, checking her watch. Timing was important. 'Shut up, you two,' she said casually. 'Keep your sex wrangles to yourselves. I'm in charge now.'

Baby opened her mouth, then shut it again. One day, she thought, I will claw that unsmiling face of yours from top to bottom, and it will be a pleasure. Her fingers, with their long red nails, curled in anticipation.

They had arrived at a floor where the lights were dim and silence and stillness reigned. A row of closed doors faced them on one side and a blank wall on the other. Baby went along, reading the names on the doors.

'All admin offices of some sort, I think. Just what I expected from what I was told.'

'And which is *the* door?'

Baby nodded. 'That one, Di. Just here where I'm standing.'

Diana tried the door. She gave the handle a hard turn, twisting so hard that the bones showed in her knuckles. 'Locked.'

'Sure,' said Baby. 'Of course. What do you expect? I'll get us the keys. Or a look at them, anyway.'

100

Diana looked down the corridor, which ended in a heavy glass-panelled door with the word *Exit* written on it in large red letters. 'And that's the way out?'

Baby looked at it. 'Yes. That door leads to an outdoor flight of steps and beyond it a side gate from the hospital. In fact, it leads to a car park.'

'Handy,' said Phil.

'I thought so.'

Diana marched over and tried the handle with the same force she had shown before. Baby watched her with a frown. Such force, she thought.

This time the handle turned, and the door swung open. Diana raised her eyebrows.

'It *should* be locked,' said Baby. 'But it's a short cut to the car park. Everyone uses it.'

Diana nodded. 'I wonder if that's good for us? It means anyone could suddenly pop through that door, and just at the wrong time for us.'

Baby shrugged. 'Well, you can't have everything.'

Diana didn't answer, instead she began to pace the corridor, looking about her, with Phil and Baby following like acolytes. When she had got to the end of the corridor, she turned round and walked back again.

For the first time, Phil showed signs of nerves. 'Do you think we ought to hang about down here?' she asked. 'I mean, we don't want to draw attention to ourselves, do we?'

Diana slowed her pace. 'I have to look. I'm very visual. I have to *see*.'

'Well, now you've seen, and let's hop it. In fact, we'll go out that door marked *"Exit"*. *"Exit"* is a word I like.' And Phil pushed past Diana, dragging Baby with her. She liked occasionally to assert her authority over Baby against Diana's: it showed both parties where they

101

'Someone's coming,' hissed Diana suddenly to their backs. 'Act normal.'

Phil lit a cigarette – her hands shook a bit – and Baby dropped her handbag.

When Baby had finished scrabbling for her possessions and got them safely back into her black lizardskin handbag, she stood up. 'Why, there's no one there.'

'Never was,' said Diana. 'I was testing you. Wanted to see how you'd react.'

'And how *did* we react?' asked Phil, her fury barely repressed.

'Not badly. Not badly at all. In character, anyway.'

'You are a sadistic bitch,' said Baby. 'You enjoyed it. You're enjoying it now.'

'I wanted to see how you would both behave in a crisis. Only a minor one, but still a crisis. Well, it wasn't bad. I said "Act normal" and you did. I think it would have passed muster.'

'Oh, good,' said Phil, still furious. 'I'm glad we performed well.'

'I had to test you.' Diana's voice was level and her face calm. 'I had to see you in action. I told you I was very visual.'

'And is that the end of the test, then? If so, let's push off.'

'Wait a minute. Supposing someone had come along and seen us here? Suppose we'd been questioned. What would you have said?' She swung round and looked at Baby.

'I'd have said I was looking for the ladies' cloakroom,' said Baby sulkily. 'And I soon shall want to, as well, after that shock.'

'Oh, come on,' said Phil, bundling them all off to her car. She had lost face before Diana, and she knew it. But Baby soon recovered her good humour and giggled as she got into the white Mercedes.

'Oh, your face, Di, when I said that about needing the lavatory. You're a bit of a prude, aren't you, Di?'

A round spot of pink colour appeared high up on each of Diana's cheeks. 'No, no, no,' she said.

But, obscurely, Phil felt that Baby had levelled things up for them.

When she got into her flimsily furnished apartment – if cardboard furniture had been available to her, then she would have bought it — Diana sat down at her kitchen table and drew one plan of the entrance-hall of the hospital and then another of the lower floor. An architect would have found the plans completely accurate even if crudely drawn. She had correctly described herself as 'very visual', because what she had once seen she did not forget. Or not while she wanted to remember it.

After completing her drawing, she started to make detailed notes of what she called her 'plan'. They were in her indecipherable writing, and covered several pages of a small notebook. After about an hour, she put the notebook in a drawer of her kitchen table and made herself some coffee.

Then she telephoned her sister. 'Hello, Bee.'

'Oh, hello,' said Bee, without enthusiasm.

'Can we talk?'

'Make it short. I'm busy.'

'Adding up figures?' asked Diana mockingly.

'Never mind what I'm doing.' She reached out and touched the man at her side and stroked his face. He murmured at her.

'You got anyone there?' said Diana in a rising voice.

'Of course not.'

'Good.' Diana relaxed. 'Because I want to talk. Things have started ticking.'

Tick-tock, tick-tock.

'Damn that clock,' said Charmian, sitting at her desk in

103

her office, where she was working late. 'Time goes fast enough, or sometimes slow enough, without having to hear it go as well.'

The clock was on Agnes's desk and was an old-fashioned carriage clock which had belonged to her grandmother. Charmian went over and turned it face down on the desk. Agnes had gone home long since, urging her boss to do the same. But Charmian had laboured on alone on the papers on her desk, which she had now reduced to order. She had answered those which required an answer; commented, in her neat writing, on those which required comment; and ignored those which could be safely passed over. Not so many of those.

The telephone rang and, after a pause for thought, she answered it.

'Ah, you're still there,' said Agnes. 'I guessed you would be. I said to myself: I bet she's still there; I'll try the office first and see if I can get her.'

'Well, you did, and here I am,' said Charmian patiently.

'It's that woman,' said Agnes. 'The one who stands and stares. For the first time I've had a good look at her. I was changing my library book. She's standing outside the library, on that sort of terrace alongside the Library Plaza, between the library and the post office.' Agnes sounded excited. 'She was outside the window and I was inside; I was close, really close, perhaps the closest anyone has been to her because she always moves away fast. I noticed something. I want you to come down and see for yourself.'

'Where are you speaking from?'

'A public call-box in the library. I'll wait for you.'

'Give me five minutes then.' Charmian looked out of the window, from which she could see the roof of the post office. She tidied away her papers, locked her desk, closed her office door firmly behind her and set off.

104

She wasn't in a bad mood; she just felt restless and full of a self-awareness that made her light-headed. Without being able to say why, she had the feeling that things might be about to happen. Agnes's phone-call fitted in with this notion.

The evening air was fresh and pleasant on her cheek. She walked briskly across the road, round the corner and into the Library Plaza, where she stood for a moment to look about her. The square, floored with black and white paving-stones and decorated with bay-trees in pots, was empty except for one figure standing outside the library building. As Charmian looked, the figure moved rapidly away and took a diagonal course across the Plaza, a path which brought her full into the lamplight at the point nearest to Charmian. Charmian watched her go.

Agnes came out of the library and walked towards Charmian.

'You're absolutely right,' said Charmian crisply. 'I suppose I knew it all the time. We all did. I saw it as soon as she walked away. You can alter a lot with clothes and make-up, but you can never fix the legs around the calves. They give it away every time. She's not a woman; she's a man.'

'I've got something, though,' whispered Agnes. 'She had one of those strange notices she wears; this time there was also one on her back, and it came loose. I picked it off without her noticing.' She held it out, and Charmian took it.

In large staggering letters in red was one word.

Charmian read it: 'Gloria,' she said. 'I suppose it's her name. Gloria.' She tucked the paper into her briefcase. 'Well, we've got something now. Two things: a name and a piece of paper. We can take it to that street-market in Midford where they put up notices written in a similar way and see what they have to offer.'

When she got home that night she didn't forget what she had seen. She kept thinking about Gloria; she had already discovered that no one who had seen Gloria forgot her readily. The image of that lost figure stayed in the mind. It was hard for Charmian to say what her reactions were; not angry or aggressive. She had sensed something innocent and strange about the woman; you still had to call her that – in itself, she supposed, a tribute to the force of Gloria. 'There but for the grace of God,' she said to herself; but when she talked about the matter next day to Adam Lily his face reddened and he became furious – an interestingly different reaction, she thought.

When she was prepared for bed that night, the memory of Gloria made her grateful for what she was. When she had undressed, she looked at herself in the mirror with detached interest.

Then she raised her hands above her head. 'I need a lover, that's what,' she said aloud.

Chapter Five

As soon as one fact was established about Gloria, such as the sex she wished to be, another appeared. The check on the street-market in Midford, the big town whose suburbs merged with the fields and woods around Deerham Hills, turned up the fact that all the notices that seemed to be in the same individual style as carried by Gloria were produced by one great family clan called Beadle. Successive generations of Beadles had sold fruit and vegetables in the market since the beginning of the century, or so they said.

Adam Lily came back with the news before lunch-time. 'The Beadles are a large family with many ramifications. A sort of spreading family tree, you might say, but they can't find anyone on it who would match up with our Gloria. Just as well, really, because I don't know what we'd do about it if we did identify her. He or she hasn't done anything criminal.'

Charmian was silent.

'Has she?' persisted Adam. 'Or do I hear you say a silent "Not yet"?'

'She is the cause of violence, I think.'

Adam looked incredulous.

'The innocent and unwitting cause. A kind of catalyst, perhaps.'

'I don't buy that,' said Adam. 'Our crime wave started before she/he came here.'

'Prove it,' said Charmian. She was remembering her interview with Jessie Buck, when Jessie had assured her that 'the Woman', as she called her, was the cause of the violence in town. Jessie or Adam, thought Charmian, which is right? They both know the town, but perhaps they see things from different points of view.

'I might just do that.' Adam's reply was delivered with belligerence. Then, perhaps feeling his aggression had gone too far, he went on: 'All the same, I have got something to offer you. The Beadles have mislaid one or two odd sprigs from their family tree, one of whom just might be Gloria. One was a boy called George, who used to work at one of the Beadle stalls, but left to take off on his own about three years ago. They heard he got a job as a hospital porter – preferred it to fruit, apparently. The other was a lad they called Pete, and they don't know where he went, except he said he was going on the road with a grip: he could sing, apparently.' Adam looked at Charmian. 'One of them could be Gloria. If it matters.'

'You seem to have found out quite a lot,' said Charmian grudgingly. 'Whether it matters or not, I wanted to know it. Thanks.'

'It turned out I was at school with one of the Beadles. He's got a stall in Midford market now. And a Jag and a Merc. Secondhand, of course, but in good nick.' He was wistful. 'He recognised me as soon as I turned up. I didn't know *him*: he'd got fat.'

'Comes of having two cars,' said Charmian. 'That ought to cheer you up.'

'Yes, it levels things up a bit.' And he departed whistling. 'Well, that's it, if it's any good to you. Don't believe it is, myself.'

Nevertheless, Charmian continued to think about Gloria, and the state of crime in Deerham Hills.

This included the dead man, Terry Jarvis, found in the river. No one seemed to know why he was there. No one claimed him; nobody wanted him, least of all Charmian, but while Walter Wing was still so ill she had no choice: he was all hers.

She wrote the words 'Dead End' experimentally on the

108

piece of paper in front of her, since that seemed to be where she had got with her case, to see if it gave her any idea.

Then she drew a circle and put Gloria's name in the middle of it and placed all the other events, from the finding of the dead man to the robbery at *Prettifurs*, at intervals around the circle. But it didn't look right. Gloria was surely too lightweight to be at the centre of so much.

So Charmian put a great cross through Gloria's name.

Then she drew another circle and put Diana's name in the middle of it. That looked much better. 'I like that,' said Charmian. 'Looks right to me.' She couldn't hide from herself that there was an element of aggression in her attitude to Diana, fully matched, though, by Diana.

Silently, she assembled in front of her the tuft of pale fur (returned by the laboratory with report attached) and the card found in the dead man's pocket. She knew now of what it reminded her. Previously she had been guessing; now she was sure.

But it was up to her to get proof.

'If I were casting someone's horoscope, and using these two objects as symbols, I would say they were an interesting conjunction of signs.'

Conjunction of signs. The words interested her. But the 'conjunction' of these two objects – if, indeed, they were, in any sense, joined – was in her mind only and fell far short of being proved.

'It's up to me to prove it,' she said aloud. 'But what a puzzle. I don't understand the implications of what I'm thinking, even now.'

Underneath the circle with Diana's name in the centre she wrote:

A blonde woman who works in Diana King's salon had caught in her bracelet a piece of pale blue fur similar to

109

the blue mink stolen from *Prettifurs*.

A card found in a dead man's pocket is the same shape and size as those in use in *Charm and Chic,* and it *could* have been the same colour once.

On this card my surname was written; whether by the dead man or someone else, I do not know.

After a moment's thought, Charmian traced streamers of pencil from each of these sentences to Diana's name in the centre of the circle. Having thus anchored Diana, she felt satisfied.

There was still Gloria loose in the firmament, as it were, and she suspected there were other happenings, of which she knew nothing but which must be fitted in. Yet Charmian began to see developing before her eyes a shape, a pattern, one which seemed to her of enormous significance.

Fascinating, she thought. I wonder if it *could* be so.

A fair burden of routine work then fell upon her in the day's usual fashion, but after she had dealt with it she walked across to the Library Plaza and went into the main public library of Deerham Hills.

Inside was an open area with plants in pots and a machine which offered weak tea and pale coffee when fed with the right coins. Perhaps the architect had planned it as a spot where friends could meet and readers pause to discuss their books with each other, but no one ever did pause here; they hurried through the swing doors into the lending library, or went upstairs to the reference library and the newspapers. Charmian went upstairs.

There she found a square bay, lined with books and classified *'Psychology'*.

With the air of someone who had been there before, Charmian took down a copy of William James's masterly survey of psychology in his day and took it to the table, where she sat quietly reading it, as if understanding it gave her inner strength.

As she went out, she met one of the librarians whom she knew. 'An interesting collection of books on psychology you have here,' she commented.

'Ah, yes. They belonged to old Professor Budgen. He left them to us when he died. We are unusually strong in that field.' She looked at Charmian. 'You've used it before, haven't you? I've seen you in there.'

'Yes. I suppose I use it to bolster up my own thoughts when they seem to need it.'

'I hope it's done so this time.'

'Yes, I think it did. Of course, to a certain extent you find what you are looking for.'

'But you found it?' The librarian smiled with pleasure.

Just before midnight on the same day, people queueing for the last bus in the High Street, Deerham Hills, were horrified to see two women leap from a car and attack two girls with their fists. The whole episode was over in a flash, and the women were back in their car and off down the street before anyone could reach them.

When the onlookers picked up the beaten girls, one had a broken nose and the other a split lip. They were crying and angry. Very angry, reported one woman who had offered a handkerchief to stem the blood and been deeply shocked at the flow of language issuing from the torn mouth. On the other hand, the girls refused to identify their attackers and would not talk to the police.

The men in the police car which had hurried to the High Street reported the incident, and later on this report was read by Charmian.

It was the other side of a much bigger incident, which she had to understand with all the means in her power, intuition included.

111

Perhaps the first way to view the episode was from the outside, as seen by one onlooker, a man of about thirty, the dog handler in charge of the dog patrols which guarded the lower reaches of the Deerham Hills hospital grounds at night.

He said his name was John Netherdowell, and he glowered as he gave it, having doubtless been the butt of many jokes because of it.

'I was late on my rounds last night. I have a lot of ground to cover and not much help to cover it with. That's because of economy cuts. There's only me and one other handler, whereas we ought to have several. I am the senior and I'm in charge. Only, of course, we operate pretty freely; it's that sort of job; you've got to be your own man; not much use to keep calling back for orders. We did have a lad helping us with the dogs, but we discovered he was doing a fiddle on the side, so he had to go. About a thousand pounds he must have turned over, and he looked like an angel. You can't trust anyone these days. I suppose I was about an hour behind, which made it about nine-thirty. It had been a bit of a shambles that evening, anyway. Some fool in a ward on the first floor set fire to his blanket by sneaking a smoke and, although the nurse put it out at once, they had to summon the cleaning-trolley to clear up the mess. Sister didn't half have 'em running. On top of that, the dratted lift was on the blink again. Chaos, as usual, it was. I'd just got to the bottom of the stairs when I saw a light was on in Mrs Sims's office when no light should be on. I started to hurry, and then the office door opened and three people came out like bats out of hell. No, I can't tell you which sex they were. They were wearing trousers and white overalls and turbans. They could have been anything. Sikhs, maybe. I shouted "Stop". One of them turned and shot at me with a pistol. The bullet just grazed my leg and hit the dog. No, the dog wasn't killed, but I reckon he'll always be a bit lame, and what future there is for a lame guard dog, I don't know. No, I couldn't say it was a lucky accident or good shooting that got my leg and my dog's. But it certainly prevented either of us running after them, because the dog bit me. Me! So they got clean away. Seven thousand pounds it was they took.'

'It was an accident,' said Baby. 'I didn't mean to hit the dog. I didn't even mean to fire.' She was still speaking thickly through the blood on her nose. She dabbed at a few tears on her cheek. 'It's the pain in my nose,' she said.

'I think you did mean to,' said Diana. 'That pistol had been burning your hand ever since I let you have it. My mistake.'

'Seven thousand pounds, two hundred and thirteen.' Bee raised her head from the notes she was counting.

Baby's tears miraculously disappeared. 'That's not bad. What price my little gun now?'

'Less than a thousand each,' said Bee. 'Allowing for the money for the emergency fund which we *must* build up.' Bee always had little emergency funds stowed away, squirrel-hoards against hypothetical crises. It seemed to Baby that too much of their seven thousand had gone that way.

'I'm your accountant,' said Bee. 'I never pretended to be anything else. I take my own risks.'

'I don't think there were so many risks,' Baby's eyes were pale and bright. 'It was easy.'

'Easy because I planned it, because I worked out all the angles. You were the biggest risk with that gun,' said Diana.

'I think the best moment was when we put the key in the lock and it turned,' said Baby, her eyes far away. 'No, I tell a lie. The best moment was when Mrs Sims came in unexpectedly this morning (nearly yesterday now) and I

113

got the key, and you got it cut, and we decided to do the
job straight away, that very night. I could do it all
again.'

'I believe you mean it,' said Phil.

Diana said: 'I don't think you're remembering it quite
accurately. I remember it differently.'

After their snap decision to do the hospital *now*, it had
been, as Baby said, 'all go'. Diana seemed to have it all
worked out in her head, and knew exactly what she
wanted everyone to do, and indicated it with her shiny
dark-red-tipped fingers, drumming out the orders with
taps of her nails that went through Phil's ears like a steel
band.

White overalls, as used by her staff, were produced
from the salon cupboard; they had never been worn
before. Each of them was to wear dark trousers and
rubber gloves: the trousers were their own and the gloves
were supplied from the cupboard, from those used for
doing tints and perms. Buckets, mops and brooms were
also provided by *Charm and Chic*. It was as if Diana had
been stocking up for just such an occasion. Phil,
summoned early from her job in the office of the local
architect, was at first angry, then resentful and finally
charmed into submission. There was no doubt about it:
Diana had a way with her when she wanted.

As they went out to Phil's car, which was discreetly
parked behind the back door of *Charm and Chic*, Diana
said: 'We had to seize the moment. Know the moment
when it comes, is what I believe, and that moment came
when the Sims woman walked in this morning.'

'I'd say it was when I got the keys out of her bag and
told her it would take her nails twenty minutes to set, all
in one breath,' said Baby with relish. 'Or perhaps it was
when I told her she'd need a false nail fixed.'

'Clever you,' said Phil, tugging at her turban; she had

rather large ears (but very well shaped, as she pointed out) and they were uncomfortable under her turban. Besides, she never wore a hat, although Baby had given her a soft felt kind of trilby, which was nice, but hats just weren't her thing.

'Clever me,' agreed Baby with pleasure.

Sitting in the back of the car, with Phil in the front driving, and among the mops and buckets which were part of their disguise, Diana silently produced a gun and put it on Baby's knee.

'For you. Don't use it. But produce it if someone surprises us while I get the money.'

'I heard you,' said Phil in a loud voice. 'I'm listening.'

'You keep quiet and concentrate on your driving,' responded Baby, shaking her gun. 'It's a phallic symbol, a gun. That's what a gun is. Did you know?'

'For God's sake!' said Phil, and the car swerved.

'It's a weapon,' said Diana. 'Remember that first.'

In the darkness of the car Baby smiled with genuine good humour. 'Of course. I know that. I know a gun's a weapon; I'd never forget that.'

There was a mutter from the driving-seat. 'She means it explodes when you pull the trigger. To someone else's detriment.'

'I know all about it,' retorted Baby. 'You keep quiet and concentrate on your driving. You nearly had that cyclist then.'

'Cow,' said Phil, but she didn't speak again, and she drove more carefully.

In the car-park, she chose a spot near the exit and left the car where it could be driven off quickly. As they got out of the car Baby and Phil collided.

'That's my foot. Get off my foot. My God, I think you've broken a bone. It's those bloody stiletto heels that I told you not to wear.'

115

'They suit my feet,' said Baby.

'Suit your feet! You look like Minnie Mouse.'

'Oh, indeed!' Baby swung round, ready to do battle on that one.

'Shut up, shut up, shut up.' Diana pushed herself between them. 'This is business, remember? Not some private party. Now, do it as I said: go in separately, attracting no attention, and we meet down below. If anyone questions you, just melt away. It only goes ahead if we all three get there unquestioned. Now move.'

One by one, they went into the hospital, first Baby, then Phil, then Diana.

Diana got there first; the corridor was empty, but in a minute Phil appeared, mop in hand.

'Had to take my time,' she said hoarsely. 'Some damned nurse kept on at me to go and mop up in her ward.'

'You didn't go?'

'No, of course not. I didn't answer. Just went on walking. She'd know me again, though.'

'Damn.'

'Don't worry. She'd only know me as what I look like now, which I don't normally. Thank God.' She looked around. 'Where's Baby?'

'I wish I knew,' said Diana. She looked at her watch. 'We can't wait long. Another three minutes and, if she doesn't come, this is off.'

'Are you nervous?'

'Of course I'm nervous. It would be stupid not to be.'

At that moment Baby came sauntering down the stairs and along the corridor, her bucket clattering.

'What the hell have you been doing?' snapped Phil. 'Putting some more lipstick on?'

'As a matter of fact, I haven't.' Baby put her bucket down. 'I just didn't rush, that's all. It would have looked silly. And I had further to come than you two. I used that

116

back door, remember. Nearly got lost as well.' She was insouciant.

'You took your time deliberately,' said Phil. 'You kept us waiting on purpose.'

'Oh, be quiet, you two.' Diana had the key in the lock. 'Now, just act calm and normal. Nerves can sometimes draw other people to a spot like it was magnetism.' She slid the key round and the door opened. 'In.'

Diana put the centre light on boldly, but drew down the blind in the glass-panelled door. The curtains were already drawn over the window. There was a certain amount of disorder in the room and she noted this with satisfaction.

'Obviously the room hasn't been done yet, anyway, so we could reasonably say we were cleaning up if we are challenged.'

Baby said: 'The safe is behind that wall poster.'

'How d'you know?' challenged Phil.

'I just do know.'

Diana said abruptly: 'She's right. That's the only place where it can be.' She pulled the poster aside. 'There it is, lock and all.' Once more she put a key in the lock. There was a moment's pause, while they all waited. 'It's turning,' she said softly.

'Oh, our luck, our luck.' Baby clapped her hands together.

Suddenly from the floor above they heard running footsteps. A moment of silence, then more feet came thudding across the floor.

'They're on to us,' said Baby, her eyes wide.

'Don't shout.' Diana went to the door and listened. 'Someone's coming down the stairs.' She snapped out the light and leant against the door. 'Keep quiet. And don't move, either.'

Someone – it sounded like Baby from the squeal that

117

followed – stumbled against a chair and it fell over. Phil swore.

Feet ran down the corridor and then ran back, wheeling something. The rattle of wheels and metal could be clearly heard. Feet and wheels passed. Then there was the sound of metal clanking as the vehicle was dragged up the stairs. Diana raised her eyebrows assessingly. She had put an *'Out of Order'* notice on the lift. There was silence.

Diana took a deep breath. 'Gone. It was only some medical emergency. Nothing to do with us at all.'

'Just someone dying,' said Baby.

Diana put the light on again. Phil and Baby were standing close together by the overturned chair. 'You were trembling,' said Baby to Phil. 'I could hear you shaking.'

'Never,' said Phil. She bent down to straighten the chair. As she did so, her foot came down heavily on the mop she had been carrying. The handle swung up and whacked down on Baby's nose.

Baby gave a shrill scream and her hand went up to her nose, from which blood was already running.

But Diana had pulled the safe-door open and was filling a big polythene carrier-bag brought out from her pocket with bundles of notes from the safe. 'Help me,' she ordered, barely looking round.

'My nose is bleeding.'

'Use a handkerchief, then. Oh, thanks, Phil. That's right. You hold open the bag and I'll shovel the stuff in.'

'Stuff,' said Phil. 'That's lovely money.' Having drawn blood, she was in a good mood.

'Now, out!' Diana looked round the room. 'Don't leave anything behind.'

'Except my blood,' said Baby.

Diana opened the door. She went first, then Phil, and Baby was last.

As they ran out along the corridor they heard a man's voice shouting to them to stop. Only Baby looked round and she felt as though what she saw – the man and the dog coming towards them – were imprinted for ever on her eyeballs. Whenever she closed her eyes she would see them coming.

She fired at once. Then Diana pulled her away, out through the door and to the car.

For a few minutes they were all quiet, as Phil got the car out of its parking-bay and on to the road, and then, when it became clear no one was following them, they all started to speak at once.

While they talked, relief and success making them light-headed, they stripped off turbans and overalls. Baby helped Phil to take off her overalls as she drove. The road was quiet but they were overtaken by an ambulance with lights flashing and bells ringing, which drove on past them to the town centre.

'Back to the shop,' ordered Diana. 'Bee will be waiting for us.'

As they turned the corner into the road where *Charm and Chic* stood, Diana gave an exclamation. 'There's something wrong. Don't drive round the back, Phil. Go right up to the front of the shop and let me look.'

'Is it the police?' Phil got ready to accelerate away.

'I don't think so.'

As they reached the front door, they could see that it was swinging open. A glass pane in it had been broken and knocked out, and someone must be inside the shop.

As they drew to a stop, two girls, probably about fifteen, rushed out and down the street.

'Little beasts,' cried Diana. 'They've been at the wigs, and that was a big bottle of scent one of them had. I recognised that fair one: I did her hair this morning. You can't trust anyone these days. After them, Phil.'

119

Phil grunted as she swung the car round. 'Haven't you got a burglar alarm or something?'

'No,' said Diana. 'Go on. There they go – round into the High Street. Catch up with them, Phil.'

When the car drew level, Diana and Baby leapt out, while Phil stayed at the wheel. Baby snatched the stolen tresses of blonde and titian from the girls' hands while Diana gave each young face several hard and wounding blows.

Then they leapt back into the car and Phil drove them away.

When they got back to the shop, Bee was there, already tidying up the mess the two teenaged girls had left behind them.

'Why weren't you here earlier?' demanded Diana. 'What took you so long? You could have stopped this happening.' She looked around at the litter on the floor from rifled drawers, and the broken glass from the door. 'Vandals.'

'There was an accident at the traffic lights near the shopping-centre,' said Bee. 'All the traffic was blocked and I got stuck.' She looked at Diana, who nodded.

'We did it. Big success, I'm glad to report. Our best effort so far. Yes, I think we can congratulate ourselves. Don't bother with all that now. I'll get the door fixed later. Come along round the back and start counting.'

'And everything went all right?'

'Everything. Except that Baby had to start shooting.' And Diana stared accusingly at Baby.

'It was an accident,' said Baby.

'There's bloou on the floor in here,' said Charmian as she inspected the rifled office in the hospital. 'As well as outside.'

'Not from the dog,' said Adam Lily. 'Must be from one of them.'

'Oh? But no one fired a shot at them. So that's odd.'

'Yes, it is. Perhaps they were fighting amongst themselves.'

'Yes, perhaps they were,' said Charmian thoughtfully. 'No prints, I suppose?'

Adam shook his head. 'They were careful. You see, if it weren't for the fact they were seen by the guard, no one would have known they'd been here until the safe was opened again. They had a key.'

'And except for the blood,' amended Charmian.

'The cleaner might have washed it away. I suppose they're used to blood in hospitals.'

'Well, we have the blood. I wonder if it will have anything to offer? Rare blood-group or something?'

'We shall have to find the donor,' said Adam with a grin.

Charmian had her thoughts about this, but all she said was: 'You took your time getting here. Why were you so slow?'

'There was an accident in the town centre,' said Adam briefly. 'It slowed us down.'

'A bad one, then?' said Charmian absently, her own thoughts engaging her. 'I suppose we'd better get after the lad that was dismissed from the hospital for fiddling. Might be something there. Because whoever did this had a key.'

While Bee and Phil were packing up the money into their allotted portions, Diana and Baby cleared up the shop and tidied themselves. Euphoria had departed and everyone was quieter.

Bee said thoughtfully: 'I know why Diana's in this, or I think I do. And I know why I am, but why are you? Why are you in it?'

'For the excitement, I think,' said Phil. 'And to please Baby.'

'And why is Baby in it?'

'She likes pretty things,' said Phil, almost apologetically. 'It seems a way to get them, I suppose. What about you and Diana?'

'Oh, Di thinks it's a job she can do,' said Bee shortly. 'As for me, it's simple: I want to get married. I've got to be the money-raiser; my fellow never will be. It's all right. I don't mind supporting him. Best way, really. I'm up to it, and he isn't.'

'It's as well to know where you are.'

'Oh, I always know where I am. Hope you do, too. Here's your money. Catch.'

A look of comradeship, unconscious but genuine, passed between the two women.

'Funny,' said Phil. 'When I first met you, I thought you were slow.'

'And now you don't?'

'No, I don't,' Phil announced. 'But I'm sorry for you having a chap who can't support you.'

Bee shrugged. 'Oh, I don't mind that. I'm no beauty. Lucky to get anyone, I reckon. And he suits me.'

Bee and Phil looked at each other again: the look that fallen archangels exchange in hell.

Suddenly Bee said: 'You know what they tell you about what to do if a wild dog attacks you? Grip its jaws inside and force them sideways. Breaks their hold or something. Sometimes I feel I'll have to do something like that with Diana. Not literally, of course. But something similar.'

'What a terrible thing to say.'

'Yes, isn't it?' said Bee. 'Well, let's get on, and get home with the money.'

When they had at last cleared up at Diana's and got home with their money, both Phil and Baby were dead tired.

'You look rather sweet with that pale blue bruise on

your face,' said Phil tenderly. 'And your poor little nose all puffy. Like a kid that's been crying. It suits you.'

'Wonder who was in that ambulance we passed,' said Baby dreamily.

'Doesn't matter, does it? Not important.' Phil stroked Baby's bruised cheek. 'Battered Baby, eh?' She put her arm round Baby and cuddled her up.

'Dunno,' mumbled Baby from Phil's shoulder. 'Just think it might be, somehow. You know I suffer from precognition.'

'Oh, come to bed,' said Phil.

'It was a man, I think.'

'What on earth does it matter to us?' demanded Phil. 'Not important.'

'Supposing it was?' said Baby. 'Supposing it did?'

Chapter Six

The name of Gloria had spread rapidly among the police force in Deerham Hills and was used familiarly by everyone. 'Seen Gloria today?' was the morning greeting. Everyone knew Gloria's name, and everyone used it. Gloria was halfway between a joke and a menace; Gloria, the Terror of Deerham Hills. No one was more terrified than Gloria, but few were in a position to know that, although her landlady's husband strongly suspected it. 'Poor girl, poor girl,' he muttered to himself, hearing, as he sometimes did, her uneasy but heavy tread on the floor above him. All his wife did was complain that Gloria was shaking the paintwork.

The young detective constable called James Wise, who was an assistant to Adam Lily, knew all about Gloria and had studied her once or twice from a discreet distance. The discretion was Gloria's. She retreated rapidly the moment she became aware of his scrutiny.

James had his own opinions about Gloria, which he passed on to Adam, and more distantly to Charmian, who could hear him through an open door. 'She's a tease. She wants attention and then she wants to run away. A natural victim, I'd say.'

'Gloria is not your subject today,' was all Adam said. 'Today you are looking for a lad who may or may not have had something to do with the hospital break-in. He was dismissed for dishonesty. He had a contact; he had a chance to have a key.'

'His contact was the woman in that office who had charge of the keys? Mrs Sims.'

'Yes. She befriended him when he first came. Ap-

124

parently he was one of those lost souls with blue eyes that women always like.'

'Taken in, was she, then?'

'Ah, they got entangled – sort of mother-son relationship. Or that's what she thought. I don't know what *he* thought. He worked in the hospital. Had problems, and she took him in as her problem. She may have been a bit in love with him. But he'd been flogging hospital equipment, and when he was found out he melted. The hospital never took action. Mrs Sims again. So he got far, far away. At least, no one's copped him yet. Now, it's your job to get hold of him.'

'He's not likely to have been part of this robbery, is he? I mean, there's no evidence.'

'You just go looking, lad, and leave the thinking to me. Georgey Burdomesky is what he called himself here.'

Wise was surprised. 'Was he a Russian, then?'

'As English as you or I, but that was the name he fancied.'

'A play-actor, then?'

Adam was silent. 'But he liked to be called Georgey by his friends. Georgey with a soft *G.*'

Wise was baffled. 'Is that significant?'

'No, I don't suppose so, but you might bear it in mind as you go around looking for him. Georgey with a soft *G*, remember, not a hard one.'

Wise remained baffled. 'People like that make me want to spew,' he said unhelpfully: he had strong reactions to anything that departed from the norm.

'Don't be more stupid than you have to be, Wise. Just find him. Be sick later in your own time.'

'I'll start with Mrs Sims,' said Wise.

But Mrs Sims, tearful, was convinced that Georgey had never taken her keys, although he had had the opportunity. Nor did she know where he was. She fanned out her beautifully manicured nails and stared at them, before turning to James Wise. 'I don't know if I ought to tell you – it seems disloyal – but he has been a wicked boy and he'll have to pay for it. This I do know: before he moved into the room in the hostel I got for him, he had lived at an address in Allerton Road, Midford. The number I don't know.'

The address led Wise to another in Midford, farther back in his quarry's history, and then this one led on to another, a much more recent address, a post-hospital address. By this time Georgey Burdomesky, Georgey with a soft *G,* had another name. He had been born George Beadle.

'One of the fruit market Beadles?' Jim asked. Jim Wise, an old hand at enquiries in the market, knew the name well. 'Related?'

'They're all related,' said his informant. 'I was at school with him, so I ought to know. That's why I let him have a doss here when he was out of his luck. Didn't stay, though. Moved on. Didn't leave a forwarding address. Can't say I blame him.' A grin.

'Why's that?'

'Oh, you'll find out when you meet him. I don't know the actual address, but I think he's moved to a house in Allerton Road, in South Midford. He always goes back to somewhere in Allerton Road if he can. One of his haunts. Everyone has got their favourite places and that's his. Wouldn't be mine. I followed him there one night. Took a bit of doing, too.' Again a grin. 'There was what you might call a hiatus in the middle. Anyway, that's the road. You'll find him easy enough.'

'Oh, yes. Sure.' Jim Wise pocketed the piece of paper on which the address was scribbled. 'Thanks.'

He felt the grin following him to the door and burning a hole in his back. It made him cough.

As he plodded down the road where his quarry now lived, he felt a little shiver of excitement – or was it even

126

apprehension? – start up inside him. 'I wonder what the boss will make of all this,' he pondered as he walked.

But there was no telepathic communication with Charmian, who was not thinking about *him* at all at that moment. She was sitting in her office, staring over a mound of paperwork, and listening to Adam Lily. 'Go on,' she said. 'So the man found dead on our patch was on bad terms with his wife. Well, I'd expect that. And so she's disappeared?'

'Well, gone anyway. Not living where they did live. But it was never a happy house. He used to beat her. Or did she beat him? They didn't seem too clear on that in the manor where he used to live, and where we wish he'd died. But the relationship between the two of them was bad. Wicked, by all accounts. And there were other women in droves, too.'

'Go on,' said Charmian. 'I like the word "wicked".'

'Not my word, I borrowed it from the chap that was telling me what he knew of them. He said they were vicious to each other, and I believed him. Real hate there, he said, on both sides.'

'H'm,' said Charmian. 'And so.'

'Still, they stayed together, till he went inside last time. And then she took off. Rumour has it she went off with what cash he had stashed away. He left it with her for safe keeping, or some such. So he must have had some trust in her. Misplaced, though, as it turned out. Or maybe he thought she didn't know where he kept his money, but she did, and took her chance when it came to clear off with it. Opinions are about equally divided as to what happened.'

'So what did he do?'

'What could he do? He was inside until recently. I bet he was thinking about her, though. There's no doubt

127

where he would have gone when he got out: to look for her.'

'And he ends up dead here,' said Charmian.

'He had plenty of enemies,' said Adam. 'I can give you a list.'

'Anyone we know here?'

'No. Not a name. But that doesn't mean much. He could have been killed elsewhere and just dumped here.'

'Except for the phone number of my husband, written on a card he had in his pocket,' said Charmian.

'Except for that,' agreed Adam. He put his head on one side. 'I think a nutter did him in.'

'Why?'

'He was sexually attacked.'

'A lot of people may have felt like doing that to him,' observed Charmian.

'It's not common,' said Adam drily. 'That way round. Still, we're farther forward.'

'Probably not,' said Charmian thoughtfully.

'There's one other thing: the pathologist thought to do a bit more investigation of the body, and it turns out the chap had what looked like a black ball in his heart; he had a malignant melanoma. He was going to die, anyway. Of a black heart. Totally irrelevant, of course.'

'I wonder,' said Charmian, and she drew a little pattern on a scrap of paper.

There it was: that circle again with Diana in the middle. And there was the dead, strangled, raped man with a black heart and the hospital now on the periphery of the circle, but perhaps ready to be moved farther in.

A lump got into her throat and she gave a cough.

'Starting a cold?' enquired Adam.

At that moment Detective Constable Wise had arrived at Allerton Road, Midford. In the next minute he had spoken

128

to the lady of number 12, and asked if he could interview
her lodger, and by the minute after that he was marching
up the stairs leaving a bemused landlady protesting behind
him.

Behind this door should be Georgey Burdomesky,
Georgey with a soft *G*, otherwise known as George
Beadle.

He tapped on the door, and a voice called: 'Come in.'

He opened the door and then stopped short on the
threshold.

'By God,' he said. 'We've got Gloria here.'

Charmian assembled her life before her, and put the
jagged bits together. Her dead husband and his son
certainly formed one such edge and, however hard she
tried to rub it smooth, it still stayed ragged. But now, in
her working life, she had some more pieces to fit into the
jigsaw.

First, she knew a few more facts about the strangled
man.

His doctor in London had been traced, and reported
that Terry Jarvis had known of his condition, and had
been angry. He talked to Charmian on the telephone.

'No other way to describe it: he wasn't frightened or
despairing or regretful, any of the things you might have
been. Just plain angry, as if a treat that had been promised
him had been whisked away. Although what treat his life
had ever been to him I do not know.'

'Was he in an angry state when he came to see you, or
only when he heard what his illness was?'

'Oh, afterwards, I'm sure of it.'

'That's interesting,' said Charmian thoughtfully. 'It's
such an abnormal reaction, isn't it?'

'Not usual, anyway,' agreed the doctor. 'But who
knows?'

'I think he *did* have something to look forward to,

which the shortness of his life would prevent him enjoying,' said Charmian.

'And what was it?' The doctor, a young man, was interested.

'I don't know. But I think it lay in Deerham Hills, and I shall find out,' said Charmian.

'I suggested that he attend the clinic at the hospital in Deerham Hills. Indeed, I arranged it. To be honest, I did not think he could be helped much, but I knew one of the doctors there was interested in cases such as his.'

'And what did he say about going to Deerham Hills?'

'He said he had known someone who had lived there once. "That dump," he said. "It'll be the death of me yet."'

'So it was,' said Charmian.

In addition to this new information, she now had direct contact with Gloria, and she knew Gloria's real name, which was George Beadle, and she was learning a little of Gloria herself.

Gloria had refused to leave her room, and so Charmian had driven herself to Midford to talk to Gloria there.

Gloria sat huddled on her bed in one corner of her room staring at Charmian with great piteous eyes. She wouldn't talk; she sat silent with her lips held tight together. Charmian thought that, if they once opened, a whole life would pour out of them.

'I've been looking forward to meeting you properly. Getting to know you,' she said gently.

Gloria did not respond, just shifted her gaze away from Charmian and looked out of the window. She was wearing full make-up, with her eyebrows crayonned in by heavy black lines, and her lips a deep red, the upper lip coloured into a false and profound bow far beyond the natural lines of her mouth, so that it seemed to reach up to her nose. It was ludicrous and infinitely touching. Or, anyway, to

130

Charmian. How could such artifice make her look womanly?

'It's been quite hard to meet you,' went on Charmian. 'Every time someone approaches you, you run away.'

Silence. No word from Gloria on the subject of her evasiveness. She didn't even look at Charmian.

Charmian tried again. 'We've all been looking for you, really. In a way we thought you *wished* to be looked at.' Gloria turned her head round sharply so that she could see Charmian. 'I'm sure there is something you wanted us to know. But you always ran away.'

'Everyone does,' said Gloria hoarsely. 'Or wants to.'

'Not quite everyone. I don't, for instance. I don't want to run.'

'Yes, you do.' Gloria gave her a brief glance. 'Fast and far. I can see.'

Charmian was silent. She's got me there, she thought. 'All the same, I haven't run very far,' she observed mildly. 'I seem to have a built-in brake.'

Gloria did not answer; she was not even looking at Charmian any longer, but down at her own feet. She had large feet, adequately but not smartly encased in patent-leather strapped shoes. Charmian could see them as a solution to what must have been a problem. They were safe if not fancy, and fitted Gloria's muscular feet.

Gloria hadn't given her a reply, but Charmian fancied that she had seen her mouth 'Keep trying' under her breath.

'When I say we've been looking for you, Gloria, it wasn't just to get a look at you,' went on Charmian gently. 'Although you are quite a sight, aren't you, Gloria, with your make-up and your notices hanging round your neck?'

Gloria's hand went up to her face, and she touched her lips as if she was now doubtful of their validity.

'Those notices of yours are a sort of hint as to where

you come from. I suppose you learnt how to do them in the market?'

Gloria didn't answer.

'But why do you wear them? Why do you stand and stare? Why do you behave like this?'

There was a dead silence, which endured for a minute and then for another minute, a long time for two such people to sit silent.

'I'm miserable, that's what,' said Gloria suddenly.

'Oh, yes, I understand that,' admitted Charmian. 'I am miserable myself, too, as a matter of fact. But why else? Because there *is* another reason.'

Gloria switched her eyes away from Charmian again and stared out of the window. Search me, she seemed to be saying. If there is another reason, then you find it.

'Why did you come into Deerham Hills? Tell me that.' Charmian was genuinely curious. One more fact she wanted to know about this strange creature.

'I didn't want to come. Not really. I was drawn. Drawn.'

'And what drew you?'

'The women.' Gloria's face lightened and became almost expressive. 'I heard that Deerham Hills was the place for women.'

And what the hell does she mean by that? thought Charmian, sitting back and wishing she had not given up cigarettes.

'So that's what drew you to Deerham Hills?'

'Oh, yes. It's like a star, like a fire.'

'And what do the women do in Deerham Hills?'

Gloria blinked. 'Why, they're altering the whole town. It's going to be theirs. I feel it. It's a conflagration,' she said dreamily. 'And I am warming my hands at its radiance. Don't you feel it?'

'Yes, I do,' admitted Charmian. 'I feel the heat, anyway. No one more.'

132

And all because a small group of women are behaving criminally, she thought. And does *she* know of it?

'But apart from the glorious feeling of being drawn towards Deerham Hills as to a bonfire,' she enquired cautiously, because she did not totally believe in Gloria's intuition, 'how do you know what is happening in the town?'

Diffidently, in a mumble, Gloria allowed her to find out that it was the gossip of the market area in Midford, as well as being common talk among those in Deerham Hills whose circle collided with the law.

'I see,' said Charmian. 'So it's common knowledge, more or less?'

Gloria nodded.

'Well, it certainly explains a lot,' said Charmian, thinking of the tensions in Deerham Hills, the violence under the surface, the abnormal outbreaks of crime. The accepted balance of life was being upset, and the result was disquieting. When the surface of any organism, whether it's as big as a world or as little as a cell, is broken, the forces inside spring apart and energies are set in motion that cannot be controlled.

There were tensions in plenty inside Gloria, the restless flick of her eyes made this manifest, and, like the thoroughly disorganised world she so much resembled, her volcano was about to blow.

'You know,' said Charmian. 'It's quite hard to know what to call you now. I suppose I should call you Mr Beadle.'

Gloria said: 'Everyone has a right to choose their own name. I've chosen several in my time. Now I choose Gloria. I *am* Gloria inside myself. You call me that.'

'All right,' agreed Charmian peaceably. 'If that suits you. It won't always do in public, though, but I dare say we can reach an accommodation.'

'You can call me Beadle, then; that's neutral.'

133

They settled for Beadle.

'Why did you milk the hospital, which was treating you well, of so much? You don't look like a greedy person to me.' Nor a well-provided one, thought Charmian, looking around the room.

Gloria, or Beadle, looked surprised. 'It was to launch me on my new life. As me, as what I know I really am.'

'A woman, you mean?'

Gloria nodded vigorously. Charmian was still finding it hard to think of her as Beadle.

'And have you spent all the money?'

'No, I bought some clothes. I've put the rest away. Saved it.'

'What for?'

'For my operation, of course. You can get it on the National Health, but I don't think I shall. I'm not popular with doctors.' Gloria was matter-of-fact, seemingly reconciled to her unpopularity with the medical profession. 'It's my right, but I should never get it. So I just took what I wanted another way.'

'You were lucky the hospital didn't prosecute. You owe that to Mrs Sims. She seems to have a sympathetic feeling towards you.'

Gloria's quick glance showed Charmian that she had not only known of Mrs Sims's sensibility, but had also counted on it. Charmian could see that without the garish make-up Gloria or Beadle must have been a pretty boy. Suddenly she was Beadle to Charmian.

I could have liked him myself, she thought, and was surprised at herself.

It was a tribute to the hypnotic quality that Beadle undoubtedly possessed that Charmian had forgotten one of the main purposes of the interview.

'Where were you yesterday evening, between eight o'clock and midnight?' she asked.

'I was at Deerham Hills near the library until after

134

eight.' Beadle cast his eyes down. No need to ask what he had been doing. 'Then I got one of my migraines. I could feel it coming on, like a great hammer banging on one eye. So I came back here and went to bed.'

'Did anyone see you come in?'

Beadle looked blank. 'I dunno. The pair of them downstairs watch me, but what they see I don't know.' And she smiled her secretive smile.

For some reason this irritated Charmian. 'I don't think you're in a position to make jokes.'

'A joke? Was that a joke? A sick joke, maybe, like me. So what happened last night?'

Charmian ignored the question. 'Do you have migraine often?' She could see a tumbler of water by the tumbled bed and a bottle containing tablets of some sort. She picked up the bottle: *Medigaine*, it said. 'Yes, I see you do.' The room looked like the room of someone who had been sick, but it didn't prove anything, of course. She guessed that Beadle was capable of creating such a scene if she wished.

'Pity no one saw you in bed.'

'Nobody sees me in bed,' said Beadle in a savage voice.

Charmian felt the truth of this. 'No, I suppose not.'

Reluctantly, as if by doing so she had raised a curtain on her privacy, Beadle said: 'But I expect *she*, Mrs Wills downstairs, knows I was here. I was sick, and she heard me being sick.'

'Well, I'll ask her.' Charmian began to move towards the door, slowly, because she was thinking.

'So what was it I didn't do, then? You might tell me.'

'Rob the hospital,' said Charmian, with a smile. 'Or not in person. Did you have access to the keys of Mrs Sims's office?'

'No, never,' said Beadle promptly. 'Never even saw them.'

Charmian didn't quite believe that, but she did believe Beadle had not been present at the burglary. She gave a grimace.

'What's the matter with you?' asked Beadle.

'Just a pain,' said Charmian.

'Ah. Well, that's where I score, anyway. If it *is* a score. And watch out – you could have an accident. Always more accident-prone then, I believe. And worse-tempered,' she said, observing the expression on Charmian's face.

'I don't know what we're going to do with you,' Charmian replied. 'But something.'

'Send round a psychiatric social worker, I suppose,' said Beadle sharply. 'Don't bother. I've had those. Just leave me alone. I'll make my way.'

But where to? thought Charmian. 'Well, lay off Deerham Hills,' she said. 'I think we've seen enough of you there. And what *was* on those cards and notices of yours?'

Beadle stared at her blankly. 'It's all there for you to see. You have only to read the message.' And she held up her last pronouncement.

And it was true that when you looked carefully among the scraps of newspaper and cut-out capital letters you could see that certain letters conveyed in black ink, with here and there a red variation, the message: *Women protect women.* Yes, the message was there; but, like all communications which came through the disorganised being of Beadle who was Gloria, it was confused and hard to read.

'I've read the message,' said Charmian, 'and I don't make much of it.' Beadle looked at her, bright-eyed and tense.

'It's women like you that are the enemies of a woman like me.'

'Woman?' said Charmian, before she could stop herself.

'I know what I am.' Gloria was fierce. 'I know better than anyone else. Let me have this operation. It's all I need.' Long fingers tried to grip Charmian's hand. 'I know what it is to be a woman.'

This time it was Charmian who dropped her eyes because she did not want Gloria or Beadle, whichever was chiefly present, to read the denial written in them.

No, you can never know what it is to be a woman, for that awareness starts from the conception when the ovum splits, setting up that subtle glandular rhythm which you have never known. Nothing can change the XY pattern of the chromosomes and the body chemistry which goes with them, and without which you are just someone in whom the surgeons have excavated a hole.

Aloud, she said merely: 'It's not as simple as you think.'

For answer Beadle burst into a loud ungrateful laugh, and he (or she, if that was how she felt) went on laughing and laughing till the laughter was weeping and weeping turned into groans. The volcano had erupted. Charmian summoned medical help and saw the still moaning Gloria carried off in an ambulance. But with the first laugh the balance of power in the conversation shifted decisively to her; unfairly so, Charmian felt; but she emerged from the interview with an important impression: that Gloria was innocent of any involvement in the robbery at the hospital, and that she, Charmian, knew who was guilty.

It was mid-morning when Charmian had finished her interview with Beadle; she rushed home, feeling the need to re-establish her identity by refreshing her make-up and changing her tights, before going back to work.

Charmian changed her tights and shoes, and put on some new lipstick and a spray of scent. She was

137

menstruating and she was glad of it, because it established another fact that Gloria could not match. She was even glad that she had not put herself on the Pill, because the bleeding then was simply withdrawal bleeding and not menstruation. It flushed out the uterus and provided a reinforcement of their feminity for those who wanted it, but it was not genuine. Today Charmian was glad to be genuinely bleeding. The tears of the disappointed uterus, a gynaecologist once called it. Trust a man to think of that description, thought Charmian, as she tidied herself.

She hurried out of the house to start her car. Kitty, staring out of her window, as so often in her housebound baby-obsessed life, said: 'That girl needs a visit to the hairdresser's. Thought she was taking herself in hand. She's slipping again.'

Charmian swung her car round and down the hill with only a percentage of her concentration on her driving and the rest absorbed in her problems, of which she thought she (and Deerham Hills) had far too many: the murdered man, the robberies, and Gloria.

Nevertheless, with inbuilt caution, she was not going fast, so that when the car in front of her skidded on the greasy road and slewed round until it faced in the opposite direction from which it had been travelling Charmian had sufficient time and control to swing aside. She escaped with a long scrape of the paint on her car door and a severe dent in her temper.

She got out and looked at the damage to her Volvo. 'Damn.'

The other driver, a plump elderly man, had also got out of his car. 'That was a near thing,' he said, puffing with relief. 'I don't seem to have collected any damage. A miracle, really. You've got a scrape, though.'

'I've noticed.'

'You were travelling a bit close, you know. I remember noticing as I came down the hill. That woman's driving too

138

close, I thought.' He was fumbling in his pocket. 'Here's my card. A knock for a knock, eh?' He sounded quite cheerful. 'I suppose, by rights, we ought to report it.'

'No need,' said Charmian, as she watched a police car from the traffic division of the Deerham Hills police approach them. 'It's going to be done for us.' She recognised the driver and noted the broad grin on his face as he came level with them.

Charmian had the uneasy feeling that events were getting out of her hands and she was in no sort of control, even of herself. Perhaps that was how Gloria felt all the time.

Work piled up remorselessly. There was a fire in a factory, and arson was suspected; a schoolgirl went missing – both events requiring action from Charmian. All work for Charmian.

On top of this, all the officers concerned in the hospital raid were required to attend a conference. 'Progress negative,' said Charmian sardonically to herself, keeping a straight face and reporting on Gloria.

There was no conference on the murdered man, where stalemate seemed to have been reached.

Only Charmian knew that the man was not entirely dead, that he still had a little life in him, enough to maim one or two people. He was still limping around, on one leg possibly, but making movement.

Charmian *felt* the movement, but she wasn't sure who else did, although she thought there must be one other at least. But it wasn't the only thing she had on her mind, and at the moment not the dominant one, either.

'I think I'll visit my hairdresser,' she said thoughtfully, as they left the conference room.

Adam Lily thought she was talking to him. 'I don't go much on hairdressers myself,' he said, passing his hand fondly over his shorn locks. 'Prefer a plain barber's shop.'

139

'Oh, they do men, too, in my hairdressers,' said Charmian. 'They'd do you. Probably eat you up.'

Adam looked at her sideways. 'You mean something by that, but I don't know what.'

'Not important. Let me do my own thinking.'

'I always do,' was the feeling response. 'We all do. Ever seen yourself when you're interrupted?'

'Wonder where that schoolgirl is?' asked Charmian. 'Hope she turns up soon.'

By that evening they knew that she had done nothing more alarming than get on a train to go to visit her grandmother, having quarrelled that morning with her younger sister. 'Mum's pet,' was her bitter comment.

With all this, the Deerham Hills force was badly stretched, with all the officers overworked and tired.

'Work, work, and more work,' grumbled Adam.

'Oh, Lord, I'm tired,' said Charmian. 'And my head aches. In fact, I ache all over, now I come to think of it. I'll give *Charm and Chic* a miss tonight. They'll still be there tomorrow.'

'They your hairdresser, then?' enquired Adam.

'That's what I call them,' said Charmian, after a pause. 'A team of bandits really.'

That night a bank in the shopping precinct in Deerham Hills was robbed. The branch was one that specialised in dealing with women. It was a major robbery, involving many thousands of pounds, and with one or two strange factors, such as the disappearance of the manager, a woman.

The news was given to Charmian on the telephone the next day as she made her early-morning cup of tea.

And with it came the message that there was a patient in Deerham Hills Hospital who wanted to see her.

Chapter Seven

On her way to the bank, Charmian took the trouble to drive past *Charm and Chic* to see what she could see. Although it was so early, there were signs that it was business as usual in the establishment. It was no more than she had expected. Professionals all, she thought.

Inside the shop, Diana saw her car pass, but no one else did. She did not spread the word around, although Baby was in the shop-window with her, and Phil and Bee were preparing to set out to their own places of employment.

In any case, Baby had something else on her mind. All four had been up all night and, in Baby's case, looked it.

'My face is frightful,' she said, smoothing on some eye-shadow. 'I can't do without sleep. I'm not strong that way. I depend on my full eight hours. Shows at once if I lose it.'

Diana's strong-featured face looked much the same as usual. Nor did she answer.

'I'm in that state where I look worse with lipstick on, not better,' lamented Baby.

'Don't do it, then,' said Diana. 'Just don't put any on.' Her own lips were shiny but bare.

'Of course, I know it was in a good cause last night.' Baby pursued her own line of thought. 'And well worth it, too. But it's taken it out of me.'

'I thought you enjoyed it.'

'So I did, as a matter of fact. I suppose I'm just cut out for a life of crime really. It's as well to know it,' said Baby.

'I mean, I might have gone to my grave without realising my full potential.' She tried a paler pink lipstick.

'Not you,' said Diana.

'I think this colour *is* better. But I still look very frag. Look at my poor little hand – all shaky.' She blotted her lips, erased the smudge her unsteady hand had caused, and drew in a perfect pink curve. Then she smiled at her face in the mirror. Apparently the curve was all right, because she left it at that. She turned round and looked at Diana.

'Di, where is she? Where did you leave her?'

Diana just shook her head with a little smile.

'She's not *dead,* is she?' asked Baby.

'You saw me drive off with her, alive and kicking. Literally kicking; I have a bruise on my shin to prove it,' was all Diana said, and she continued to smile. Bee would not have been reassured by her sister's smile.

'Just off,' said Phil, appearing in the doorway. 'See you this evening, Baby. Carry on as normal today, that's the show.'

'Right.'

'Where's my sister?' asked Diana.

'Coming up behind me,' said Phil, as indeed Bee was, wearing dark glasses and carrying a bag.

'What's worrying Baby?' asked Bee.

'The missing bank manager,' said Diana.

'Ah.'

'She was a manager and I managed her,' said Diana.

'I hate it when you joke,' said Bee.

'I have her safe. Leave her to me.'

'Good.' Behind her dark spectacles, Bee looked anxious. She raised her hand to touch the spectacles. 'They hide the bruise.'

'I wasn't exactly worried,' put in Baby. 'But one likes to know where one is. After all, we're in your hands, Diana.' Then she added: 'As you are in our hands.'

Diana laughed and turned away. 'You are a scream, Baby, the films and bad telly you must have watched. 'Bye, Bee. 'Bye, Phil. Keep in touch.'

Phil nodded. She gave Bee a reassuring pat on the shoulder as she went out to her car, and got a half-smile in return. The role of friendship between them, once struck, was growing stronger. They understood each other's position: they were both in love. Undesirable and almost unwearable as their love might be, it was a garment they had to keep wearing.

Bee and Phil departed and Diana and Baby, twin predators, were left to get on with their day.

Charmian visited the bank premises only briefly, but she saw enough. The usual investigating team had already arrived and were moving around, measuring, taking photographs and testing for fingerprints.

The staff, including the two women who did the cleaning and a tall ex-soldier who was one of the security guards, were all sitting on chairs in an inner office.

Charmian let her eyes wander over them appraisingly while she talked to Adam Lily, who had arrived before her.

'Apparently there was no forced entry,' Adam told her. He sounded happy about it.

'That's interesting.' Unobtrusively, she studied the faces of the three girl cashiers, and those of the ageing cleaners and the guard. Any signs of guilt or fear? They all looked mildly anxious. 'So the thieves had a key?'

'Yes, or somehow got the manager to open the door.'

'Mmm.' Charmian pondered on this, and also on the honesty of the manager herself. 'What about her? Angela Brown, isn't she?'

Adam consulted his notes: 'Angela Brown, aged forty-one. This is her first appointment as manager. Her record is impeccable. Not a stain anywhere.'

'There wouldn't be,' agreed Charmian.

'And we don't think she let them in. (By the way, it was *them*: unmistakable signs of more than one person present.) Her quarters upstairs have a separate entrance near her garage. That door was bolted on the inside.'

'So?' asked Charmian.

'There is an inner connecting door between her flat and the bank premises. This was standing open. Her bed looked as though it had been slept in and as if she'd left it in a hurry. Say as if she had heard something and gone to look.' He added: 'And there's one slipper on the stairs.'

'Like Cinderella.'

'She must have cold feet, wherever she is,' said Adam.

'And that's a problem, too. Anything to go on?'

'Well, she was tied up. A chair with rope still attached in her own kitchen.'

'Whose rope?' asked Charmian sharply.

'Her own, alas. She seemed to go in for skipping. So nothing there. But she'd put up a fight.'

'Where?'

'In the kitchen where she'd been tied up.' Adam motioned towards the upper floor. 'Take a look.'

'I will.'

On her way up the narrow staircase which led from a door in the manager's office to the floor above, Charmian saw the solitary slipper lying on the stairs. It was a dark-brown leather creation with a substantial wooden heel. You could injure someone with that, she thought.

Inside the kitchen she surveyed the mute evidence of a struggle: a chair overturned, china broken and a potted geranium lying on the floor with its pot broken and earth scattered everywhere.

'A short sharp little fight, I'd say,' said Adam. 'Before they got her tied up.'

144

'How many of them, do you think?' asked Charmian, moving around the room, taking it all in.

'Two or three, at least,' said the practised Lily. 'And they had a car outside, I reckon. Parked outside, ready to go. The tyres left an imprint on the mud. It was a heavy car with old tyres. We'll be able to identify it if we ever catch up with it,' he said with satisfaction.

'And how did they get in? Which door?'

'They went out by a side-door, a service-door used for supplies, I guess,' said Adam Lily. 'Because that door was left unbolted and unchained. If they left that way, then it's a fair assumption they got in that way.'

'With keys, and to a door which must also have been left unbolted and unchained,' said Charmian. 'So someone left it unbolted for them to come in. Interesting.'

'Yes,' said Adam. 'It smells inside job all over it.'

'I agree,' said Charmian. 'They had help from inside.'

Six people sitting downstairs, thought Charmian. Which one of them is it? Taking Adam with her, she went downstairs to take a look.

Three young faces, those of the bank clerks; two middle-aged, the security guard and one of the women who cleaned the bank; and one elderly face, belonging to a small frail woman still dressed in her overall, with a duster in the pocket.

Adam Lily had all their names and addresses.

Hilary Eden, twenty-four, with an address in Deerham Hills. A cheerful-looking girl behind the present air of worry.

Cynthia Ferningham, twenty-six, living in the country outside Deerham Hills. Huge round spectacles framing sharp blue eyes. Just as worried as her two colleagues, but not showing it so much.

Petra Lycett, twenty, the youngest person in the room,

145

living in Deerham Hills near the bank itself. Red-haired, freckled, and fidgeting with her hands.

Adelaide Goole, forty-five, and Jerry Latham, forty-nine, both residents of Deerham Hills, sitting together because they had recently become engaged to be married. A second marriage for each of them: Adelaide was a widow and Jerry was divorced. Wasn't there some rule excluding married people working in the same bank? But of course Jerry wouldn't be there all the time. This place was only one calling-point on his route. The two of them, sitting side by side, two strong-boned healthy people with the same carefully expressionless, wooden look, might even be married already, a perfect match.

That left Alice Udell, sitting with her hands in her lap, tired, old and fragile. She was over sixty, she had reported ambiguously on her age, and she lived in Deerham Hills. She had been married, but her husband was long since dead; she had one child, a son.

'I had the faint impression, the very faint impression,' reported Adam with a smile, 'that there was some worry over the son.'

'Mothers do worry over sons, and sons over mothers,' said Charmian absently. 'But she wouldn't rob a bank on that account.'

'I dare say not. I thought I'd mention it, though.' Adam scrutinised the seated woman. 'Anyway, she didn't rob the bank. Not in person.'

'But she helped those who did?'

'Could be. But look at that bouncy little girl with red hair who's playing with her hands. She's nervous.'

Indulgently, Charmian said: 'She's a baby.'

'Babies can be dangerous. Very, very dangerous. In the right context.'

'True enough,' said Charmian, remembering her friend Kitty. 'So what's the news about the hospital job? I gather there is some.'

146

Adam looked blank. 'Nothing new that I know of.'

'But I've had a message that a patient wants to see me.'

Adam shook his head. 'Nothing to do with me. Nothing by means of me or through me. In fact, it's news to me. Tell me what it's about when you get back.'

His unbroken calm irritated Charmian.

'Does nothing in your life surprise you?' she demanded.

'Nothing in my professional life, boss, and absolutely everything in my private life,' he said calmly. 'In my private capacity they've got me running ragged. That girl Agnes. I will *never* understand her.'

For some reason, what he said annoyed Charmian. 'Let's get back to work,' she said shortly. 'Get on with the questioning and get away.'

They were busy for some time after that, both of them anxious to get away.

When Charmian got to the Deerham Hills Hospital, the girl at the reception desk gave her a broad smile and acted as if she was expecting her. 'Oh, yes, I *am* glad you came in. I've just been on the phone trying to get you, Mrs Ascham.'

Charmian blinked at the name but accepted it. So it was a personal matter. She thought of her family, who obstinately clung to calling her Mrs Ascham, and actively disapproved of the use of her maiden name for professional purposes.

'He's poorly, I'm afraid, and Sister thinks a word from you would help.'

He? The word registered. 'Is it my brother, then?'

'I don't think so, Mrs Ascham.' The girl was abstracted, listening to Charmian with half an ear, the rest of her attention concentrating on the phone-call she was making. 'Sister Allen? I've got Mrs Ascham here. Right, I'll tell her to come straight along.' She put the receiver down and turned to Charmian with a smile. 'Sister says to go straight into Simpson Ward: Men's Surgical. Just follow the blue arrow.' And before Charmian could get another word out of her she was taking another call on the telephone.

Dutifully, Charmian followed the blue arrows which directed her through swing doors into a covered way to another building, then through a second set of doors and up a flight of stairs, and so to Simpson Ward.

Outside, she took a deep breath, and prepared to interview Sister Allen to see what it was all about. Senior police officers should not be summoned to a hospital in this way, was the thought at the back of her mind.

She pushed open a swing door and her nostrils at once met a smell made up of disinfectant and (to her surprise) tobacco smoke. She was amazed to see several patients with pipes in their mouths and one or two smoking cigarettes. Somehow she had supposed that in a hospital ward smoking was forbidden. But apparently not. A large colour television set was on and appeared to be showing the afternoon's race programme. There was an air of happy organised confusion in the place which astonished Charmian, who had expected quiet regimentation.

'Oh, good, here you are.' She was being hailed by a tiny dark-haired young woman with a fly-away white cap pinned precariously to her hair (although it never moved an inch in spite of her constant swift movements up and down the ward). She was advancing rapidly up the aisle between the beds, hand held out to Charmian. 'Reception rang through to say you were on your way up. Didn't get lost, did you? Good. We're really very well signposted. Last bed on the right, and come and have a word with me before you go.' And she was off again, hurrying past Charmian towards a group of doctors appearing through the swing doors.

The bank job or something about the robbery here in the

148

hospital? Charmian was asking herself as she walked slowly down the ward. Is it about one of those episodes I am going to be given information? And what reliance can I place on it?

She walked over to the bed, last on the right, and looked at the man. For a second she saw no one she recognised, then the mind dragged out its memories and imposed its own patterns. Click: the whole picture was there to be seen. Out of what felt like a long drugged sleep, she heard herself say: 'My God, *you.*' Weakness started at the back of her eyes, closing the lids, and travelled downwards, compressing her diaphragm and loosening her knees. She forced herself to open her eyes and stand upright. The bright ward had receded into darkness; here there was only the man and her and the bed at the centre, caught in a bright light as if on an operating-table. She closed her eyes again momentarily, and then blinked them open.

'Charmian.' Tom Ascham held out his hand. 'I've given you a shock.'

'I've nearly blown a fuse. In fact, I'm not sure if I haven't.'

She put her hand on her heart; it was beating regularly and strongly. She advanced closer to the bed, pressed against it, and stared at him. Tom looked sun-tanned and weathered, as if he had spent a lot of time in the open air since she'd seen him last, but underneath was a pallor that crept around the mouth and the eyes and along the fingers. There were so many questions she wanted to ask that she didn't ask any of them, but gazed in silence.

'Charmian,' Tom said again, still holding out his hand.

'I'm assembling my thoughts. Let me get them ready.'

Tom allowed his hand to drop, seeing that she showed no sign of touching it. 'I saw what you put in the papers. Took a while to make me move, but it did in the end. You

149

got quite a bite in those little messages, Charmian, and I thought: That's her, that's the authentic voice – and at first I was angry. Then I just wanted you. I was on my way to see you when I had this stupid accident.' He looked at his legs, over which a cage rested. 'Car crash. Gave myself a crack down there. My own fault. I believe the other chap's admitted liability, but I brought it on myself really. My mind wasn't on it. Any other time I'd have got myself out of his way fast. Called myself a good driver. Evasive action was my strong point.'

'That I know,' said Charmian.

'I was thinking about you.' Soberly, he added: 'And Dad, too. I'd only just heard.'

'Did you know I thought you were dead? That your father had been searching for you? He wouldn't believe you were dead, but he minded that you went missing.'

'I ran away. Silly thing to do, isn't it? What kids do. But sometimes you do regress twenty years or so. I was frightened. Of myself. Of you. I was working on an under-cover job, where I had ceased to be myself. It was easy to melt. Simple. I went to South Africa.'

'Whatever for?'

'Seemed a good place to go. Anywhere would have done. The moon, if they would have taken me. I would have preferred the moon, but I took South Africa. I worked there for a bit. Then I hitched my way to India. I fetched up in Australia. I felt I'd worked everything out by then and it was safe to come home.' He looked directly at her.

'Safe?'

'And now I've seen you and it isn't safe at all.'

They stared at each other coolly, neither playing the game of not understanding. Charmian let him get hold of her hand.

'There's a lot of things that have to be said, but I don't think this is the time or place to say them.'

150

'Not sure. I run away physically. You run away in another way, Charmian,' said Tom. 'That's been one of the troubles.'

A pretty girl in a violet and white striped dress, with a stiff white cap pulled down hard over her temples, came up and planted a cup of tea on the bed-table. 'Like one?' she said to Charmian, with easy good cheer.

'Yes, please.'

'That's a first-year nurse,' said Tom. 'Just learning the job. You can tell them by the striped dress and that funny cap. And the fact that she's usually running.'

'And I suppose they all bully her.'

'No, no one bullies her.' Tom showed mild surprise. 'No one bullies anyone in this hospital, least of all the patients. They all seem very kind.'

'It's not what I thought a hospital ward would be like.' Charmian looked around her. 'More cosy and comfortable. Things have changed.'

'Have you ever been in a hospital as a patient? Ever been ill?'

'I had my tonsils out when I was five,' said Charmian, accepting her tea with a smile of thanks, which was all her angel of mercy had time to receive as she whizzed off on her other tasks. 'Otherwise I'm as healthy as a pig. How are you? Are you in pain?'

'Legs smashed up. No, no pain.'

'Oh, well, that's good,' said Charmian.

'Yes. I suppose so.' He didn't seem quite sure.

'Oh, it must be.'

'Doctors are funny people,' said Tom, stirring his tea. 'They never seem pleased over the things you'd think they would be pleased over.'

A party of visitors had arrived for the man in the next bed. They were laughing and talking to each other in loud voices. Their unaffected uninhibited behaviour seemed to loosen a check inside Charmian.

151

'I am very glad to see you again, Tom,' she said, and suddenly she felt enormously happy, full of joy. 'Let's not talk about anything now. No explanations, no stories, but just enjoy the minute. It'll go quickly enough.'

They sat talking quietly, about things on the periphery of their lives, things which didn't now seem to matter much to them, like the histories of friends they had in common, the work he'd done in Australia, and some of the cases Charmian had worked on, while the warmth grew between them and they let it flow unimpeded.

It was not all euphoria.

'What sort of relationship *can* you have between a woman and her dead husband's son?' asked Charmian, with a touch of near-despair.

'I don't know,' he responded soberly. 'But we can investigate.'

They held hands, until he said: 'You'll have to go now. I can see my special squad of nurses bearing down on me. They'll draw the curtains around the bed and start doing things to my legs.'

Charmian bent down and kissed him. He gripped her hands hard, and, with his voice suddenly urgent, said, 'Only one thing we can do. Get out, get right away. Go to another country. Just us. No past, only a future.'

'See you tomorrow,' said Charmian, getting her hands free.

Then she remembered something she wanted to ask. 'Tom, did you call on me at home, one day? Call and find me not at home? My next-door neighbour said there was such a call. I wondered if it was you.'

'No. Not me. I thought about it once or twice but I was cowardly. I've been living in London. Trying to pluck up courage to make contact.'

'I see,' said Charmian thoughtfully.

'I did ring once or twice from the Chinese restaurant

152

where I used to eat. Once I got the wrong number –
another woman answered.'

'That was Kitty, my neighbour. And once I answered.'

'Yes.' He met her eyes, half ashamed, half amused.
'And I put the receiver down. Sorry, love.'

'Oh, I forgive you. *Now*. I'd better push off home. Do
you still have the house-keys?'

He shook his head. 'I lost them long ago. Accidentally
on purpose.'

On her way out, Charmian recalled the request to speak
to Sister Allen.

Sister was sitting at her desk in an alcove at the end of
the ward. She received Charmian with the cheerful smile
that was part of her professional equipment, as easily and
as purposefully put on as her rubber gloves.

'I wanted to have a word with you about your stepson,'
she began.

Charmian accepted without wincing this description of
Tom, which encapsulated her problem.

'Yes?' She said it encouragingly because Sister was
fiddling with a little tray of pencils in front of her and
seemed to want to get every pencil straight before she
spoke.

'He had a very nice blow on his spinal cord,' said Sister
decisively. 'For the moment the nerve is numb.'

'Numb?'

'Well, not passing on messages effectively.' The smile
was as generous as ever, the eyes cautious.

'You mean he can't move his legs?'

'Well, not at the moment.'

You're being handled gently, Charmian warned herself.
'And in the future?' she asked. 'He's going to recover?
Completely?'

The smile stayed in place. 'We have to wait and see. It's

153

probably just a question of time to let the natural healing process take place.'

'Time? How long?'

'Ah, that I can't say. I could make an appointment for you to see the surgeon. I expect you'd like that, Mrs Ascham?' Sister put her head on one side.

'Yes. Yes, I'd like that,' said Charmian. 'Not today, though.... Does he, does Tom know all this?'

'I expect he does really,' said Sister, the smile dropping from her face. 'But he hasn't been told officially. You might bear that in mind.'

The funny thing is, thought Charmian as she went down the stairs, I don't feel miserable or worried. I can't help feeling happy. That *must* mean something.

She drove herself home and put the car away. She could see Kitty moving about in her kitchen; Kitty saw her and waved a hand and mouthed something. Charmian read it as 'battery hens,' and decided that Kitty was on a conservation kick again, with which she wanted nothing to do at the moment, so she gave a placatory wave of her own hand and passed on into her house.

What Kitty had said was not 'battery hens' but 'battered women', a subject dear to her heart just then. She had given up battery hens for the moment; eggs had got so expensive that in her own interests she had been obliged to think more about egg production and less about the hens.

That morning she had been present as one of the organisers of a coffee morning and jumble sale in aid of a home for battered women. It had been Kitty's own suggestion that the name be altered from 'wives' to 'women'. You didn't have to be a wife to be given a black eye, Kitty pointed out. Her close friend Teresa took some exception to this, pointing out that it was in the family situation that the battering took place, therefore the word 'wife' was appropriate in most cases, even if not accurate. But Kitty got her way.

'I wonder if it's true that the number of wives being beaten by their husbands has increased in Deerham Hills in the last few weeks, or if we are just hearing more about them?' Kitty pondered aloud.

'I don't know. But one thing's for sure: we need a bigger hostel for them,' said Teresa.

'I could ask my friend Charmian to check the figures.'

'What, ask the fuzz?' said Teresa.

'She's not fuzz. Or not in the way you mean. She's extremely nice. You don't know her.'

'I've seen her, though. She looked a pretty tough customer to me.'

Kitty decided to be tactful. She knew that nothing was more irritating to Teresa, who held that tact was a female reaction to male aggression. 'The sale's going well, isn't it?' she said.

'M'mm.' Teresa nodded. 'See that couple over there? The pretty little fair one with the rather butch character in jeans? Well, the little fair one just gave me fifty pounds. Fifty pounds! She said it's in a good cause. Butch looked as though she'd have liked to take the money back, but she couldn't get it away from Blondie's hands. I wonder who they are?'

Kitty looked across the room. 'I know the fair one. She belongs to a reading and discussion circle I belong to. She's a beautician of some sort, I think. Hands, I believe.'

'Yes, she looks like that,' said Teresa. 'She is pretty, though. I wouldn't mind looking like that.'

'*You*, Teresa?' Kitty was surprised.

'Yes, a really pretty face might change my nature. My political views, too. You'd be surprised. Honesty forces me to accept the fact.'

155

Kitty thought about this at intervals throughout the day, and she was doing so when she saw Charmian through the window at home, and waved to her.

She gave Charmian about half an hour before going across to visit her.

'Oh, come in,' said Charmian; she was wearing rubber gloves and an apron. 'I'm just doing some washing.'

She led the way into her kitchen and plunged her arms up to the elbow in a bowl of froth and bubbles. There was water on the floor and a mound of soapsuds subsiding into a puddle on the draining-board, as if Charmian had not really had her mind on the job.

'Can I help you?' Kitty thought Charmian looked both exalted and tired.

'What?' said Charmian absently.

'Can I help?'

'Oh, no, it's just a few underthings of my own.'

Kitty watched her labours, as far as she could through the mountain of suds her friend had created. 'You ought to get a washing machine.'

'Can't be bothered.'

'A machine is very useful with a baby,' said Kitty, whose mind never wandered very far from that beloved object.

'I believe you. Put the kettle on, will you, and make some coffee?' Charmian turned back to her washing. 'Oh, blow!'

'What?'

Charmian held up a greyish stringy-looking object. 'Blow! That's the dish-cloth I'm washing, not my pants.'

Kitty was shocked. 'Charmian, it says something for your view of your underwear that you could think it *could* be, even for a second. Heavens, I don't think a woman ought to be a sex object, but can't you do something better for yourself than that?'

'Oh, I'm going to,' said Charmian. To Kitty, she did not seem to be talking to her, but directing herself to someone else. 'I'm going to attend to the lot: clothes, hair, skin and hands.'

'Glad to hear it,' said Kitty, puzzled. Not before time, she thought. 'That'll cost.'

'Oh, the money doesn't matter. I'll manage somehow.'

Kitty felt even more surprised. 'It's lovely to hear you like that again. So cheerful and outward-looking.'

'Again? I don't think I've ever felt like it before. Not totally and absolutely.'

Kitty was even more surprised. She was also touched, and, strangely, felt older and more mature than her friend. It did make you wonder, she told herself, what Charmian's emotional life had been up to date. She hadn't much doubt what was up: there was a man in it somewhere.

'I'm so glad,' she said. She waited but Charmian was offering no confidences.

'What was it you were shouting at me about battery hens?' asked Charmian, hanging out her washing.

'No, it was battered women. I am on the committee which was running a coffee morning and a jumble sale to help raise funds to build a home for such women and their families near here.'

'Did you do well?'

'Surprisingly well.'

'Why surprising?'

'Because it's not really a popular cause. I'm not sure why.'

'I suppose happy women can't help thinking it's partly the unhappy ones' own fault,' said Charmian.

'And, of course, women *are* economically under-

157

privileged,' observed Kitty crisply. 'They simply haven't got the money. I wouldn't blame them for stealing it.'

'No,' said Charmian absently. 'Maybe one wouldn't. In certain circumstances.'

'That's certainly a surprising thing for you to say. But I'm glad to hear it. I've always regarded you as a lost cause; you're so legalistic.'

'In my way, I've tried to level things up for women,' said Charmian.

'There's still a lot of levelling up to do. And I don't just mean money. Of course, it is a difficult problem about the Pill,' observed Kitty in a judicial way. 'I mean, it's so clearly the best method, but yet it seems to be risky for a woman to go on taking it for years. I think couples ought to take it in turns. Let the woman use the Pill for the first half of their marriage, and then let the man take over for the second. That would be fair. One should be fair,' she said virtuously.

'Some men I know would just change wives when it came to their turn,' said Charmian.

'Oh, you are cynical.'

'No, just realistic.' She looked at Kitty's downcast face. 'Oh, not *your* husband.'

'No,' said Kitty with indignation. But that evening, when Kitty put the case about half-shares to her husband, he began cautiously, 'How do we know when it's half-time?' and then, seeing anger spread into her face, he said: 'Ah, Kit, don't be angry with me.'

'You're *bargaining*, that's what you're doing, trying to bargain.'

'Just asking.'

'It's *moral* bargaining.'

Perhaps she felt the cold advance touch of this conversation as Charmian went on: 'But why did you come tonight? Any special reason?'

'Why did I?' Kitty asked herself, her mind still involved

158

with her husband and her own life. 'Oh, I know. One woman at the sale this morning gave us fifty pounds. Just gave us, just like that. Opened her bag and took it out and handed it over. A good cause, she said. I know who she is; she belongs to a literary circle I belong to. Anyway, she works in that hairdresser's —'

'A blonde, is she?' asked Charmian.

'Yes, small and pretty. Wrists loaded with bracelets and lots of jewellery. I rather like her. It was a lot of money, though. I wonder where she got it.' Kitty looked at her friend with a troubled face.

'I wonder,' said Charmian. 'Did you look at the notes? Singles, I suppose?'

Kitty nodded.

'I'm going to the hairdresser's anyway,' said Charmian. 'Not a bad plan to have a look round.' And she smiled. 'And don't look so worried, Kitty. I'm full of bright ideas tonight.'

When Kitty had left, the thought of that fifty pounds so casually handed over by Baby remained at the back of Charmian's mind, a thought never quite dealt with, but never put aside, either.

After Kitty had finished her argument with her husband (they declared a draw), she told him of the money and of Charmian's reception of the news.

'I hope I was right to tell her.'

'Oh, I dare say. And, after all, if it's clean money, your generous friend's got nothing to worry about.'

'I wouldn't call her my friend exactly,' said Kitty, 'although I do like her. We've only really met through my reading and criticism circle. But it's the effect on Charmian that puzzles me: I felt as though I'd planted a seed.'

'It's her job,' said her husband easily.

'No, it was in her private life, somehow, I'm sure of it.'

159

'I don't see how you could possibly be sure of that,' declared her sceptical husband, secretly glad to be back on good terms with his doughty Kitty.

'With Charmian sometimes I can be,' said Kitty.

Charmian went to her office early next morning and studied all the reports available to her on three cases: those of Terry Jarvis, the robbery in the hospital, and finally the bank raid. She read them all with care.

She only wanted to refresh her thoughts; her conclusions were already formed.

Finally, she flipped through the notes she had made of her conversation with Jessie. She had not forgotten that Jessie thought she had trouble close to home, and she still wondered what Jessie meant by it.

Agnes was watching her over her typewriter, a scrutiny which Charmian was aware of and irritated by. Agnes always seemed to be watching her these days.

'Jessie really is an offensive old woman,' she said aloud. 'Sometimes I think she invents foul things just to stir me up.'

'Would she do that? Be stupid, wouldn't it?'

'Yes, it would be, and she's not stupid. No, I was just exploding because she hit a nerve.' Charmian put the papers aside.

'About what?'

'Oh, it doesn't matter,' said Charmian irritably. 'She was trying to tell me I had trouble close to me. Trouble I didn't know about. Perhaps she means Tom.'

'Yes, I've heard he's back,' said Agnes, still watching her closely.

'And you can shut up about that.' She stood up and tidied her desk, spending time on it.

'You're not leaving that for ever, you know,' said Agnes, irritated, in the end, by Charmian's absorption.

160

'I like to leave it tidy. I will be out for some time. And not strictly on business, either. Well, half and half.'

'Oh?'

'Yes. Like my desk. As you say.' She picked up her handbag. 'Make the right excuses to everyone for me.'

'Suppose Walter Wing comes back? He's said to be looking in today, now he's so much better.'

'That much better, is he? Well, he won't be up in things, so he won't know the right questions to ask. Show him all the papers, though, and give him my love.'

Agnes watched her go out. 'Damn, oh, damn,' she said to her typewriter.

Chapter Eight

'Don't come up to me too close,' said Baby, with that maddening faint giggle. 'I think I ate a bit of garlic by mistake in my salad last night.'

It was morning, and Diana and Baby were in *Charm and Chic*, preparing for the day. The same day that Charmian and Agnes had just begun.

'Oh, how disgusting,' said Diana. 'I don't know why you can't eat a proper meal instead of all that greenery. Keep your face turned away from the clients, that's all.'

'As if it mattered now. We're only keeping this up for a front, aren't we? We could clear out tomorrow if we chose.'

'Of course it matters,' said Diana fiercely. 'We have to do it properly. A front's only a front while it looks genuine. Don't be so bloody sloppy. Be professional or keep away from me. Keep away from me, anyway, or suck a peppermint.'

'They'll think I've been at the gin!' joked Baby.

'Oh, rubbish. Just keep cleaning your teeth, then.'

'You are in a mood. I should think you'd be on top of the world.'

'I will be when it's all over. It's not all over yet, can't you see that?'

Baby shrugged. 'Suppose so. But as good as. I'm not worrying.'

'I don't trust that woman detective.'

'Oh, neither do I,' said Baby cheerfully. 'Not one little bit. But so what? We're not in the mutual trust business, are we? I mean, I don't trust you, and you don't trust me. Or not much.'

'I do trust you.'

'No, you don't. You watch me all the time.'

'Oh, that's because you're so silly.'

'I can look after myself. I'm probably in better shape than you now. Talking of which, have you heard from that mass screening for cancer that we went to?'

'No,' said Diana irritably. 'You don't hear unless there is something wrong.'

'Oh, good. I hope I don't hear. It would be *distasteful* to be ill now, wouldn't it?'

'Trust you to think of a word like that. How does taste come into it?' And Diana went to the window and gazed out as if she was looking for something or someone. Apparently it wasn't there, because she came back and sat down at her desk and stared at Baby.

'What will you do? I mean, how will you wind things up? Just leave everything and do a bunk?'

'Certainly not,' said Diana. 'That would be asking for trouble. I shall simply put the sale of the business in the hands of my bank and quietly leave the country.'

'I take it all back,' said Baby with admiration. 'You've got your nerve. Bank, indeed. "Put the sale in the hands of my bank." I love that. Is it the one we did?'

Diana stared at Baby. 'And what are you going to do? You and Phil, with your not insignificant pile?'

'Oh, I've got it all worked out. We're going to somewhere like Spain to soak up the sun. Then we'll come back here and set up our own little business.' She looked at Diana. 'Whatever I may do to other people, I'm good luck to me.'

'I believe you,' said Diana with conviction. To listen to Baby you would think the whole bank robbery job had been nothing more than a pleasant episode, a profitable evening out. Perhaps it had been like that for Baby, but for Diana it had had its hair-raising side. Obviously I didn't show it, she thought. So far, so good. But, by God, I remember that night.

The three of them, Diana, Phil and Baby, had made more of a noise than they realised as they let themselves through the side door of the bank, and Angela Brown, the manager, heard them and came down to investigate.

Diana knew as soon as she saw her face that the manager was scared and they would have trouble with her. All three intruders wore overalls, dark trousers and masks. They stood in a group at the bottom of the stairs and looked up, faceless and yet menacing.

'Get her,' said Diana. The three of them swarmed up the stairs and dragged the manager back towards her sitting-room. Diana had one hand held tight over Angela Brown's mouth; she had it pressed down so hard that she could feel the lips being ground against the gums. She knew she was hurting and she wanted to go on hurting. She got the heel of her hand against the mouth to get extra leverage. A streak of blood appeared on Angela Brown's face; her eyes were wide and scared. Powered by her fear, she was struggling against them hard; she was a big strong woman who was using all her strength to free her arms and kick them with her feet. One kick landed on Baby, who gave a hiss of pain beneath her mask. A slipper fell off as they went up the stairs, but they all trampled over it regardless. The heel of the other slipper scratched against the wall, marking it, as the quartet, bound together, arms and legs contorted and entwined like a group by Rodin, moved up the stairs. Diana saw the scratch on the wall and was angered, because the more signs of struggle the more the police could learn of what happened. She had planned it as a silent, speedy, traceless episode.

As they got their prisoner into the sitting-room, where all the lights were on and a radio playing, she stopped struggling and relaxed against them. Diana saw her eyes flick towards the telephone, and next to the telephone a bell-push set in a wooden panel which must represent a secret alarm system of which they knew nothing.

'Swing her round,' Diana ordered. 'Get a chair. Face her this way. Bring the rope.' What she can't see, she can't plan to reach so well, she reasoned. From her pocket she produced a small towel and, helped by a silent Phil, she tied it tightly across her victim's mouth.

This done, she nodded to Baby, who produced the revolver, cocked it and pointed it.

'Now, go downstairs and open the safe,' ordered Diana in a rough voice. 'Do that and we won't hurt you.'

Angela Brown shook her head. Diana slapped her face hard. 'Do as I say.'

Again the woman shook her head; again Diana slapped her face. Their eyes met, and incredibly Diana saw a gleam of what could only be recognition in the other's gaze. My face is covered, and I disguised my voice, but somehow she knows me, Diana thought. I shall have to dc something about it. She grabbed the gun from Baby and pressed it hard against the woman's rib-cage on a line with the apcx of the heart. 'Move,' she said.

For answer, the bank manager threw herself backwards, tilting the chair and reaching desperately for the alarm. Her hand stretched out, her fingers clawed at the bell, but slid past. Her head banged against the wall, hard.

Furious, Diana seized her by the shoulders and banged her head against the wall twice.

Behind Diana, Baby drew in her breath with a sound that might have been disapproval or might even have been excitement.

Phil put a restraining hand on Diana's arm and shook her head. She kept her hand there till Diana drew back, breathing heavily.

During all this time only Diana had spoken.

165

Blood had spurted from the injured woman's nose and run down the front of her dress. Without a word, Diana wiped it up with a tissue taken from a pocket. There was a sort of vindictive haste in her movements. Then, with help from Phil and watched by Baby, they got their victim to her feet and, one on each side of her, moved her towards the door, and then progressed, banging and bumping, down the stairs.

Baby, as she followed, thought: If this were a strip cartoon, there would be large bubbles with 'Crash!' 'Wallop!' and 'Thud!' floating above us. Crikey, that's what we are really: a strip cartoon of violence.

Suddenly she could see 'Crikey' floating about her head in large electric letters, as if they'd been made out of lightning. It was that sort of strip cartoon she was acting in. It gave Baby a queer feeling, as if life and art had suddenly met.

As the quartet got closer and closer to the manager's office, beyond which lay the strong-room and safe, it seemed to Diana that the resistance of the woman they were half carrying, half dragging lessened. It was almost as if she were willing to move forward with them; willing, but yet not wishing them to notice. But Diana, her senses sharpened by tension, had noticed and was at once alerted.

Of course, she thought, there must be yet another alarm system in here that we know nothing about.

She moved forward, slowly and cautiously, her eyes searching walls, doors and floor for a clue. She turned round and gave a quick look at their prisoner's face, and at once knew she had made an accurate guess about the situation from the expression in the woman's eyes, at once watchful and veiled.

She knows. And she's waiting for me to put my feet in it. Deliberately, she let a slow smile cross her face. Let her make what she likes of that, she thought defiantly.

166

All the same, it was with some desperation she went on with her silent secret scrutiny of the interior. Behind her she could hear Baby humming quietly, a tuneless sound which rubbed her nerves. 'Shut up,' she signalled fiercely, and at once Baby went quiet.

Walls, window and doors were all studied and offered up no easy answer. It wouldn't be easy, of course, because what she was looking for wasn't meant to be seen.

'What's up?' whispered Baby. 'What's holding us up?'

'Be quiet, I'm looking for something,' said Diana, almost soundlessly.

'Who isn't?' she heard Baby mutter.

I'll kill that girl one day, thought Diana, letting her eyes run again over the scene before her. She does it to me on purpose; she knows what effect she's having.

But anger must have sharpened her eyesight because her eyes fell on a small door, about a foot square, set in the wall at eye level. It was flush with the wall and painted the same dull grey.

Diana marched over and opened it. Inside was a panel from which two red and two green lights stared back at her. The lights were flanked by two switches. Of course, she thought. There's some sort of photo-cell unit working here. If anyone crosses the wrong area in this room, or touches the wrong piece of furniture, or perhaps even just crosses the room, an alarm will go off in the police station. Probably set off an all-car alert. *She* wanted us to walk into the trap.

Diana looked from the switches to the manager's face, or what she could see of it through the gag and bruises.

'Turn it off,' she whispered harshly. Baby held the gun steady. 'Now. This minute. One, two — Thank you.'

Ten minutes later – and it had felt like ten hours – Diana,

167

Baby and Phil gazed at the open safe. The unconscious body of the bank manager was slumped against the wall. Having done what was required of her, she was not obliged to be a witness further. Diana, having checked her breathing, had her own plans for her future.

What they felt was hard for each woman to sort out into separate strands of emotion, but Baby, of course, found words for it.

'Gorgeous,' she said. 'Gorgeous. There's no other word for it. I've never seen so much money in my life. And how neat they keep it. It never struck me before how tidy money is (I suppose I've never seen enough of it). I quite long to untidy it with my little hands.'

And before they could stop her she had plunged her hands in as if the paper money were soapsuds and Baby was the one to disperse the bubbles.

Diana remembered all that now and wondered just how far she ought to trust Baby.

Charmian called the hospital later that morning and learnt that she could visit Tom any time she liked that day – his condition was 'stable', and he was both 'comfortable' and 'progressing satisfactorily' – and then she went shopping.

She was surprised to find how much underclothes had changed since she had done any serious shopping for them, as opposed to grabbing something without really looking. More satin, more lace, more sensuous and about four times as expensive was her impression. And stockings and suspenders were coming back. Who'd have thought there could be sexual appeal in that little bump a suspender makes where it joins the stocking? But apparently there could be.

On the whole she enjoyed herself, and spent a fair amount of money. Her savings weren't going to last long at this rate. But it didn't matter: she had the house, and if she decided to sell it she knew it would fetch a good price.

It would leave her homeless, but she wasn't sure she wanted a home any more, and she was quite sure she didn't want that home.

Then she bought some paperbacks, making a wide selection, ranging from spy thrillers to biography. Carrying them, she went to the hospital.

'Here, these are for you.' She dumped the books on the bed. 'To further your education. You never did read enough.' She kissed him on the cheek. 'They told me I could visit you any time I liked. Within reason. I was surprised at that.'

'Oh, I'm an interesting case. Interesting cases get special treatment.'

'I suppose so.'

He looked at her parcels with interest. 'You've been shopping? Haven't you been working?'

'Just a few hours off. A few hours for me.' And *you*, she thought, but did not say so. 'I've got plenty of work on, don't worry.' She smiled. 'I thought you'd given up police work?'

'Can't help being interested.'

'Deerham Hills seems to be in the middle of a crime wave.'

'I know.' He pointed to a newspaper lying by his side. 'I've read about it in the local paper.'

Charmian picked it up. 'Oh, they've got on to it, have they? I thought they might. I see it's a whole article devoted to it. A friend of mine worked on it for a while, and still freelances for them.' She read it through quickly. 'I wouldn't be surprised if she wrote this for them.' It had speed of presentation, more than a touch of Kitty.

'Sounds interesting. What lies behind it? If you know.'

Charmian studied his face unobtrusively while she

169

refolded the paper. Now that yesterday's flush of excitement had faded, he looked much less well. There was a taut line to his mouth.

'I'll tell you.' Probably anything was better than letting him brood.

He listened carefully as Charmian recounted the history of the last weeks in Deerham Hills. 'My main problems are the sequence of robberies, *all* related, I'm sure.' She broke off and gave him a short summary of the robberies at the fur-shops, the jeweller's, the hospital and the bank. It was useful to talk to him and cleared her mind. 'And then there's the murder of Terry Jarvis. We seem at a dead end there, but what happened to him and the way it happened – the sex side – is crucial, I'm sure of it. Which brings me to Gloria.' Charmian took a deep breath. 'She's a symptom and an answer all in one. She seems to sum it all up.'

'I wish I could meet her.'

'You might yet. She's looking for a hospital to take her in,' said Charmian. 'And she's drawn to this town. We attract her here. And that's important, too. I'll fit it in with my robberies in the end. A psychic fit, maybe, but it'll be there.'

'You seem to have your own ideas about the robberies.'

'Oh, I have. But proving anything! There's that bit of coloured fur, of course. I told you about that and the hairdresser's? But it isn't enough. And the whole thing may be pure fantasy on my part – a kind of bubble.'

'But you don't think so.'

Charmian shook her head. 'No. But so many things are floating around in my head. Facts that seem to me important or, at least, indicative of something. I've been reading through all the reports this morning, and – I don't know – perhaps I was in an especially receptive mood –

I think I was – because certain things seemed to stand out.'

'Such as?'

'Well, there was that card in Terry Jarvis's pocket. It had our surname on it. Ascham. That was strange. Was that anything to do with you?'

'Nothing,' said Tom promptly. 'Never had any connection with Terry Jarvis in my life.'

'Sorry, but I had to ask,' mumbled Charmian.

'Suspect me of anything you like,' he said cheerfully. 'But I'm not guilty. Must have been either you or Dad that was meant.'

'Yes, but which of us? Perhaps I'll find out one day. But that's not all.'

'So? Go on talking.'

Charmian rapidly went over in her mind the things she wanted to dwell upon: the voice that the woman shut in the lavatory of the jeweller's had heard, saying, 'A proper inimitable horror, you are'; Jessie's heavy hint that Charmian had someone close to her who was not to be trusted; her own strong reaction to Diana; and the fact that the bank manager remained missing, with no trace of her to be found. Finally, she came out with what seemed to her the most important point of all.

'Inside information has been involved twice. At the jeweller's raid it was known when and how the burglar alarm operated. At the bank there was no break-in. Somehow, they walked in. So, they had keys. Right, but a bolt was left unpulled, and a chain undone, so they could open a crucial door. Who left that door unbolted, and why? Two differing kinds of inside help there, if you think about it.'

'I *am* thinking.'

'And Jessie more or less said that I had someone working with me who was bent.'

'I should go and see Jessie again,' said Tom.

171

'No. I believe she's told me all she can or will. I think I know who I'll go to.' Charmian remembered an anxious drawn old face seen at the bank on the morning after the robbery. 'I think I'll go and see a woman called Alice Udell.'

'Right. Go now. I'll read my books.' He picked one up. 'What's this, for heaven's sake?'

Charmian had a look. 'Oh, it's about a haunted house. I thought it might amuse you. Goodbye. See you again soon.' And she kissed his cheek.

'Wait a minute – what was that name again, the name of the dead man?'

'Terry Jarvis. Why?'

He looked at her thoughtfully. 'I seem to remember something. Stay around for a few minutes longer and let me scratch my memory.'

'Only a few minutes, then. Sister is giving me pointed looks.'

'Oh, ignore her.' He took her hand and sat there holding it. 'Terry Jarvis. It *does* ring a bell and it's something to do with Dad.'

'Oh? That fits in with what I've been thinking.'

'Telepathy,' said Tom lightly. 'You and I thinking alike. We always did, remember? It's what started us off together.'

'Go on about Terry Jarvis,' said Charmian uneasily. 'Don't talk about us.'

'I seem to remember Dad telling me about a man he knew. He said he was one of the prime examples of a self-made wicked man. I remember he said he married a woman he didn't like only because she was the woman his brother wanted to marry. He didn't like his brother. Dad said from then on he went downhill in every way. I think it was Terry Jarvis. I can just about drag that name from my memory, and I don't think I'm kidding myself. No, I'm sure, every minute it seems to get stronger.'

172

He was gripping her fingers harder and harder. Gently she pulled them away. 'Nothing wrong with your hands, anyway,' she said, flexing her own. 'I think I'm going to have bruises.'

'Have I helped you?'

'You've told me something about Terry Jarvis, and that illuminates a dark corner. So he was someone who got wickeder and wickeder?'

'Yes. Dad said it was a progressive disease. With him, anyway, and perhaps with everyone.'

'I wonder if it works the other way, and good people keep getting better? Doesn't seem to, somehow. Of course, no one talks about goodness now. It's out of fashion. I'm going now. Thanks for what you've told me. It helps. Get back to your books. Goodbye.'

'I'll probably sleep for a bit. I feel tired.' And he leant back on his pillows as if he were glad they were there. 'I'd like to get you to see Terry Jarvis right, because my instinct tells me it's important.'

'And you're a policeman, too,' said Charmian with affectionate mocking.

'And I'm a policeman, too. Or I was. Maybe will be again. Now, you hop it. I'm tired.' And he closed his eyes.

Charmian was aware as she left how quickly he tired, and as she said goodbye to Sister Allen, although today nothing was said to her, she received the distinct impression that Sister thought it even more unlikely that Tom would ever walk again.

Her reaction surprised her: it only heightened her resolve to push on with what she thought of as her destiny. Calvinism, after all, was her inheritance.

Without bothering to drive home to leave her shopping, Charmian drove straight to the district where Alice Udell lived. She anticipated no difficulty in finding her way to

173

Alice's door. She had lived in the area for a time in her earliest days in Deerham Hills, and remembered the geography of the streets.

The district hadn't changed much, if at all, in the years since she had left it, she thought, as she parked her car around the corner from where Alice Udell lived, still the same mixture of quiet semi-detached houses of the sort built between the wars and older poorer property.

Not to her surprise she discovered that Mrs Udell lived in one of these little older terraced houses, dating from the days when Deerham Hills had been so much smaller. She halted outside Alice's house to have a good look at it. Not much money to spare for new curtains and decorating there, she thought. Nevertheless, the little front garden was neat and well tended. Somebody here loved flowers.

She rang the door-bell and, after a pause, she rang again. The bell echoed emptily through the house. She took a few backward paces and stared up at the façade. Neat empty windows with no sign of life.

A flick of a curtain at a window of the next-door house caught her eye, a tiny movement but an interesting one. She turned to look: behind the lace curtains she could see a face observing her. Deliberately, Charmian looked back.

The face disappeared. Charmian went back down the road, and took a sharp left turn down an alley between two houses. She knew that at the back of this terrace of houses ran a narrow path which gave on to the back gardens. This was all that remained of what had once been a pretty lane skirting a cornfield. She passed down the track, along which a few stunted willow-trees still sprouted and where patches of may and wild briar hinted at ancient hedges, and as she went she counted the houses until she got to Alice Udell's.

But she would have known it, even without counting

174

the houses, because the flowers were so pretty. There was a back gate which opened easily and she walked up to the door, flanked by a metal coal-bunker and a dustbin. Tentatively, Charmian tried the door-handle; the door opened at once.

Inside was a small, neat and empty kitchen. A tap was dripping, but the dish-mop was ash-dry. A geranium in the middle of the table looked healthy enough.

'Anyone home?' she called, but no answer came, nor had she expected any.

Slowly she walked through the kitchen into the hall. A door was open on the right hand, and she could see into the sitting-room, which was sparsely furnished, as far as she could see, with a table and upright chairs and polished linoleum on the floor, odd and old-fashioned in the world of fitted carpets.

She took a step into the room. Hidden behind the door was a small sofa; on the sofa lay a quiet figure, head bent against a cushion, hands still.

On the table by the sofa were a glass and an empty medicine-bottle. Propped up against a framed photograph was a note. The note was addressed to someone called Amy, but Charmian read it, anyway. Amy was probably the only close friend Alice Udell had had.

Dear Amy, said the letter,
Brian passed away last week. I've just come back from the funeral. I did not tell you because I knew you could not leave Bert since his stroke. They never should have taken Brian away to that hospital, Amy. I knew I never should have let them, although they said it was for the best. I should have kept him here. He couldn't walk or talk but we understood each other. He was lost without me, and the fare cost so much I couldn't get there as much as I should. Now he's gone, I'm finished, too. Also, I've got something on my conscience that worries

175

me. I took money, Amy, to unbolt a door in the bank. I betrayed a trust; I wanted the money so I could get to see Brian, but it worries me now, so I'd best be off. Goodbye, Amy, my dear. You're the only one who will care I'm gone. And, after all, Amy, what have I been ever to you but a next-door neighbour?

ALICE

Charmian put down the letter and looked at the photograph on the table: it showed a much younger Alice Udell with a small boy balanced on her lap, behind her a man in sailor's uniform. The boy's round face and round eyes looked vacant but happy; the whole family looked happy. Charmian turned away from the photograph with pain. Well, they were all gone now. An hour later, after the ambulance bearing Alice Udell's body had departed, and after the necessary police enquiries had been set on foot, and Amy Giddons, the next-door neighbour, informed, Charmian left the house, closing the door quietly behind her. She looked calm, but inside her she was fiercely angry.

A wind had got up that seemed to blow from all directions at once, stalking Charmian as she went off on her next piece of work.

The wind and anger pursued Charmian into the town again and followed her as she parked her car near *Charm and Chic* and walked to the shop, pulling at her hair and making it look wild.

Diana saw her before anyone else did, although Baby was busily arranging her manicure-tray beside the window.

'Look who's here. Oh, how she does make me angry.'

Baby looked up. 'Ooh, what a wild lady . . . . Do you think you have the same effect on her?'

176

'Very possibly,' said Diana. 'I have reason to believe so.'

'I love that tension between you two.' Baby buffed her nails. 'I find it so exciting. Well, I'm off to my customer. *You* deal with our private personal fuzz. We're pretty busy just at the moment, but I expect you'll fit her in. Meet her eyeball to eyeball. You usually do.'

Diana got to the appointments desk just as the girl who worked at it was telling Charmian that they were fully booked. 'Oh, I think we can manage this customer,' she said smoothly.

'I want everything done,' announced Charmian. 'Hair, nails, and a total make-up.'

'Come right in,' said Diana, taking in the glitter of excitement in her client's face and making her own calculations. A little of the cold fine anger rubbed off on her. I was right, she said inside herself. I knew it. My intuition never lets me down. She's going to yield. To Charmian, she said: 'I'll look after you myself.'

Charmian was installed in a small curtained-off alcove in one corner of *Charm and Chic.* Here Diana cut and washed and set her thick hair.

'Pretty hair you've got,' she said, running her fingers through the thick shining mass. 'Lovely colour. Natural, too.'

'Hard to do anything with it,' said Charmian briefly. She was staring at herself in the mirror above the wash-basin.

'It's all in the cut.' Diana took a step backwards and then leant forward so that her face appeared in the mirror over Charmian's shoulder. 'If you were more regular in your attendance here, I could help you get yourself in order.'

'I'd like that.' Charmian turned round in her chair so that she could get a straight look at Diana. 'I feel I need it.'

177

'You do. I could do a lot with your looks if you'd let me,' said Diana with conviction. 'Put yourself in my hands.'

Charmian smiled. 'I've never done that with anyone.'

'No, no, you're too independent. I'd say it's your great fault. Or one of them. But you have to trust the professional, you know.'

Diana produced her skin-treatment tray, loaded with cleansing cream, astringent lotion, and a jar of face-pack. She put a pink towel round Charmian's shoulders and wound a padded neck-rest up to support Charmian's head. 'Put your head back and I'll attack your face.' She took up a ball of cotton-wool, soaked in lotion, and began to clean Charmian's face with firm determined motions. 'I can tell you're tense. I can feel the muscles all tight under the skin.' Her fingers prodded the angle of the jaw and then again round the mouth. 'Here, and here. Tense and taut, that's you.'

'I'm relaxing now.' Charmian closed her eyelids, which felt heavy and warm.

'I'll give you the special treatment.'

Charmian opened her eyes alertly. 'What's that?'

'*Deep* massage therapy.' Diana creamed her fingers and started a slow rhythmic pummelling with her finger-tips up and down Charmian's left cheek, at a bruising pace. 'I'm quite good, aren't I? I expect that surprises you.'

'I never said so.'

'Oh, you didn't have to. I can tell. There's something else I can tell: you want to be beautiful.'

'What?'

'Yes, you really want to be beautiful now. It's a bit late, but you do.' Charmian jerked her face away, and stared up at Diana. 'You didn't before. Now you do. So something's changed you. What is it?' The two women stared at each other. 'Well, it's a man, isn't it?'

178

'Does it have to be that?'

Diana laughed. 'You can't see yourself. You don't know how you've changed.'

'But you do?'

'Yes, I do. I'm good at that sort of thing. Besides....'

'Besides what?'

'You came in here for a purpose today. Not just your looks. There's half a dozen places in Deerham Hills could do a job on you, better perhaps than me. But you came here. To me. You wanted to come . . . . Here, let me get the cream off your face.'

Charmian submitted to have her face cleaned of the massage cream; she felt naked. 'I've been a client for a few weeks now,' she said.

'Yes. You've been in. And gone out. You've been watching us. Well, let's face it: we've been watching you.'

'I had a feeling the watching was mutual,' said Charmian drily.

'Of course, I don't know *why* you were watching us,' said Diana.

Charmian smiled, and let her gaze flick towards Baby.

'But I can guess,' said Diana. 'Can you guess why I was watching you?'

'Because I was watching you,' observed Charmian.

'Oh, no. Well, yes, perhaps the first look. But after that it was because I liked you.'

'Liked?'

'Yes, I thought. There is someone who watches me. We have a lot in common. Sisters under the skin, and that sort of thing. We both know what it is to have trouble and how to handle it. I've handled plenty and I guess you have, too. And I could tell you weren't content. I'm not always content myself, so I know where it shows in other people.'

179

'I suppose I had a sort of twitch where it ached,' said Charmian sarcastically.

'Yes. You did. A mental twitch. Perfectly apparent to those who know where to look. I've got one myself. Gives me hell sometimes. Doesn't yours?' Diana did not wait for Charmian to answer. 'Now, let me finish your hair and face, and then you can get your nails done. Then come and have coffee in my room at the back. I'd like to talk to you. We've got plenty to say to each other, I think.'

Thoughtfully, Charmian said: 'Right.'

Baby was preoccupied and quiet as she worked on Charmian's hands. Charmian had already noticed that, in fact, she did not talk much, contenting herself with occasionally throwing off a bright remark, like a cat preening itself. That was Baby at work. Perhaps she was different at home.

When her manicure was finished, Baby sat back and admired her handiwork. 'That looks good. You should always wear that pinky-tan varnish.'

'I can't always. My job, you know.'

'Oh, yes. Fancy me forgetting.'

'Well, I don't think I ever mentioned it.'

'But I know, of course. You're our local gorilla. Can't keep a thing like that quiet in Deerham Hills.'

'No.' Charmian gathered her things up. 'It all binds together, doesn't it? One fact interlocking with another like a piece of knitting.'

'Watch your nails,' said Baby.

'Or a steel vest.' Charmian reached out for her handbag. 'A piece of chain mail.'

'There! You've smudged it.' Baby sounded vexed. 'Let me do it again for you.'

'No, don't bother. I'd probably only smudge it again.'

'Well, if you *won't*. Let me carry your bag for you. What was that you were saying about a steel vest? I never wear one myself Be chilly, I should think. I've often

180

thought a chastity belt would be a good idea. In case of rape, you know.' Charmian glanced quickly at Baby, but she did not appear to be joking.

'I'd like to talk to you about your boss some time,' said Charmian. 'A few questions I want to ask.'

'Oh, you talk to *her*,' said Baby, picking up her velvet cushion and bowl and bottles. 'She'll do her own talking.'

'Some questions I'd like to ask you, too, for that matter.'

'Oh, she'll talk for me as well.'

'Thank you for telling me,' said Charmian. 'I suppose it *is* better if you all talk with one voice.'

'And exactly what do you mean by that?'

'It makes me think, this place,' observed Charmian.

'What of?' said Diana, appearing from her eyrie behind a dividing wall made of boxes of tints and shampoos.

'Oh, just what a good front this shop provides. People naturally coming and going all the time. Men as well as women, and no need to ask questions.'

'I've given up unisex work,' said Diana. 'It didn't pay.'

'Still, you did a bit at one time, and I suppose you still get the odd man wandering in to ask for a cut.'

'Sometimes. Not often,' said Diana.

'It would not surprise anyone, though, to see a man coming in. Or any number of women. Yes, a very useful front.' She looked around her appraisingly. 'Be a waste if you didn't use it. I don't think you waste much.'

Diana stepped aside. 'Come back here and have some coffee.'

Coffee-cups were laid out on a small table, together with a plate of biscuits. Diana took one and nibbled it, her strong white teeth crunching it into little bits. 'Of course, I know we excite your imagination. Take a biscuit.' She pushed the plate and a cup of coffee towards her visitor.

Charmian took a biscuit. 'Not without reason.'

'Oh, no, you've got your reasons. Those you know, and those you don't know.'

Charmian raised her eyebrows at this, but did not answer directly. Instead she took a good look round this inner sanctum.

'Seeing what we're made of?' asked Diana, watching her.

Charmian continued her inspection. 'Do you get many obscene telephone-calls?' she asked, picking up her cup of coffee.

'No. Why?'

'You look the sort that would.'

'I suppose that's a compliment.'

'It's a comment, anyway.'

'You get a bit near the bone sometimes,' said Diana. 'It's true I am aggressive and that most men don't like me and that some men would like to attack me. All of which is true of you also.'

Charmian continued with her leisurely absorption of the room. Diana's coat was hung up next to a pale cream tweed with a ginger fox collar that must belong to Baby. Naturally neither of them wore a hat, although a row of various-coloured wigs on stands suggested that both of them wore different hair-pieces as desired. A patent-leather handbag rested on a pile of books.

'Someone's a reader.'

'Oh, those are Beryl's. Baby's.'

'A wide range of reading: Hemingway, Virginia Woolf, Kenneth Clark.'

'She belongs to a kind of club – they read the books and then talk about them to each other.'

'I see she's got one called *The Amityville Horror*,' said

Charmian, picking it up. 'I've just bought a copy for a friend.'

'She introduced that to them. Gave them all the creeps.'

Charmian smiled and put the book down.

'All friends now, are we?' said Diana. 'All sitting comfortably and waiting for Mother?'

'Don't talk like that to me.'

'You think I'm being flip. Really, I'm holding out a hand to you. And you're ready and willing to have me do it, although you don't like to admit it. I can tell.'

Deliberately, Charmian said: 'I have reason to believe that you and the woman you call Baby, and probably at least two other women, have been involved in a series of robberies. Specifically: the robberies at the Sable Shop, at *Prettifurs*, at Benton's the jeweller's, at the hospital, and now at Grimbly & Hughes Bank.'

'Reason to believe,' said Diana mockingly. 'The way you talk.'

'Three people were seen by the security guard when the hospital was robbed, and I think at least two other people have always been involved with you.' continued Charmian.

'None of this really matters. It's not the way life is going to go. I'm telling you that now,' interrupted Diana.

'Of course, I'm not yet talking about proof,' went on Charmian, 'although once pointed in the right direction proof will certainly be forthcoming. What I'm talking about are straws in the wind that gave me ideas. A strand of coloured fur – mink, as it happens – that seemed to have come from your manicurist. It was caught in her brace-let.'

'Go on. You talk. *I'll* talk later,' said Diana.

'I think I can tie you into the jewellery raid,' said Charmian, 'because one of your band said something and I think I'll get her voice recognised when I ask her to

183

repeat the phrase she *really* uttered. The person who overheard it got it a bit wrong but, then, she was shut up in a lavatory at the time. All the same, I think she'll come through. A voice identity parade will be heard, instead of the usual line-up.'

'I suppose that's a joke. Hear me laugh.'

'No joke. But your colleague or co-criminal was making one. The woman shut up in the lavatory thought she heard a voice call someone, *you*, I think, "an inimitable horror". She didn't know what that meant. But it wasn't what was said. "An Amityville Horror" was the phrase used. By your manicurist. She was making a joke about a book she was reading.' And Charmian dragged the book out from among Baby's property and tossed in on to the table for both of them to see.

'Funny thing to call me,' said Diana.

'Not at all. She'd read the book, and I've looked at it, and it's about a case of possession, the demonic possession of a house and a family. I think *you* possess and manipulate people.'

Diana blinked.

'Or perhaps she just meant that *you* are possessed by a devil. I don't know for sure.'

'Why don't you ask her?' suggested Diana.

'From what I've seen of her, I don't believe she'll remember what she meant, even if she remembers saying it.'

'You underestimate Baby.'

'On the whole, I think she meant you were the possessor,' said Charmian, her voice level. 'In at least two of the robberies you had inside help. At the jeweller's you knew that the manager was to have been out at lunch-time (although as it turned out she was not) and you also knew that the usual alarm systems were not operating at lunch-time. To know that, you had to have inside information. I think you bribed a police officer to tell you.

184

As far as the bank goes, I believe you bribed a cleaner called Alice Udell to leave a vital door unbolted. (She's dead, by the way, killed herself. Are you sorry?) I say "leave a door unbolted", not unlocked, because we both know that in every case you had keys. Very useful keys, which let you through vital doors. And you got those keys because in each case a woman in a position of authority in each establishment had the keys in her bag when she came as a client to this place, to have either her hair or her hands done. I think your manicurist stole them, you got them copied quickly, or took an impression, and Baby put them back. I expect you've had my keys.'

There was a long silence. Then Diana said softly. 'I came in through your front door and I looked at you once. I had called earlier – you were out. Later that night I came back. You never knew. I looked down at you as you slept. I knew you were wide open to me then.' Charmian opened her mouth as if to speak, and Diana motioned with her hand to stop her. 'Oh, not sexually. Don't think I meant that. Don't equate me with that mixed-up creature I see parading round the town.'

'My God, you're so arrogant,' said Charmian.

'And so are you. And riding for a fall.' The two women confronted each other, but it was Diana who swept on: 'We're two of a kind. I keep telling you that. Why don't you take it in? Don't fight us, join us.'

It was out: the incredible statement uttered, the unspeakable spoken, falling between them like a sword.

In spite of herself, even although she didn't want to do it, Charmian found her lips parting in a stiff smile like a rictus. The silence seemed to stretch out into minutes; and through it Charmian became aware of the hum of the hair-dryers and the soft murmur of conversation from the salon beyond. All the same, it was she who broke the silence.

'I have joined you,' she said. 'I joined you the minute I walked through that door this afternoon.'

Diana took a deep breath. 'That's great; you've come over. Look, we can't talk here. Come round to my place tonight. Meet me here and I'll drive you. Meanwhile, fudge up the records, will you, so that none of your colleagues jumps to the same conclusions that you did?'

'I don't know that I can quite do that, although I can certainly make things difficult for them. I expect they'll get there in the end, although I suppose I had special opportunities denied to them.'

'It's luck,' said Diana. 'It's all luck.'

'That's it,' said Charmian.

'And my special sensitivity. I had you marked down. Anyway, now you know the first thing you can do for us. The other thing is to help us with the money from the bank job. It's got to be cleaned. I'll admit to you that we got more out of it, a lot more, than we expected. But it has to be handled.'

'I should have thought you knew how to do that.'

'Oh, I do, I do. I know a route to the cleaner's. But it costs. It would take over half of what we've got. I won't have that. Now, don't tell me that in all your years on your side of crime you haven't learnt some names and methods.'

'One or two,' admitted Charmian. 'Not cost-free, either.'

'But I shall look to you to make a better bargain than I can. I expect you've got the material with which to twist a few arms if you want.'

'So I will protect you, I will organise your profits into respectable money, but what will I get?'

Diana looked surprised. 'You'll get your share. Money, good hard cash. Isn't that what you want?' She looked assessingly at Charmian. 'It's your price. I'm willing to

186

pay it. Although hard, I am fair.' She called to Baby beyond the barrier of shampoos and tints. 'Baby, aren't I fair?'

'Oh, very,' called back Baby.

'And you have something you want to spend the money on.'

'I have,' said Charmian. 'And I want as much as I can get.'

'Stay with us,' said Diana with a shrug.

Thoughtfully, Charmian said: 'I may not want to. I may want to take what I've earned and get out.'

'With the boyfriend?' asked Diana.

'What boyfriend?'

'Oh, there is one. With women like you, whatever you may think, underneath and beyond anything, sex is the driving force.'

Charmian stared at Diana. 'I shan't answer that.'

'Don't.' Her hand fell heavily on Charmian's forearm; her touch was cold and yet with an inner warmth coming through the skin that was disconcerting. 'So you're one of us?'

'I said so.'

'Then prove it.'

'What?'

'Prove it. I believe you. But this is business. I have to be dead sure. I owe it to the others. So do something to show me it's real.'

Charmian stared at Diana's face looming so close to her own that she could see the tiny fair hairs above the lips. She licked her own dry lips. 'How?'

'You say.' Diana's eyes were bright.

'I could come on a job with you,' offered Charmian.

Diana drew back, dropping her hand. 'Not likely. What, and have you turn up with a couple of your professional friends and have us arrested on the spot? Besides, we haven't got anything planned.'

'You suggest something, then.'

'I know. Take me into your office and show me your files. Things I would never see unless you took me there. I'd like that.'

'I couldn't do that,' said Charmian decisively. 'Practically speaking, it would be impossible. Dangerous, too.'

'Yes.' Diana considered. 'Bring them out, then. Bring out all you've got on us, our activities. And hasn't there been a dead body? Bring what you've got on that, too. I'll photograph bits and we'll both date and sign them.'

For Diana that seemed to be it. She stood up, and slowly Charmian did the same, her thoughts fully occupied. 'See you later,' said Diana. 'Come round here about ten tonight. Bring everything with you.'

'I will.' Charmian started to move towards the door, gathering up her possessions as she did so.

Before she reached the door, Diana called out, 'Wait a minute. Come back here. I've had an idea.'

Charmian turned round to look at her. 'Well, what is it?' She didn't like the look in Diana's eyes.

'Take me to meet your man. I know there is one.'

'I don't think that's a good idea.'

'It'll be a mark of confidence,' said Diana. 'Just a look. I don't ask more. Do it for me. To show trust.'

'I'll see what I can arrange,' said Charmian, turning away. To herself she said, Damn, damn – but inside herself an excitement was rising. It's not such a bad idea, she thought. I'd *like* Tom to see her.

When she got home, Charmian first telephoned Kitty to tell her that she expected to be away for a few days and not to worry if the house was empty. No point in arousing speculations in her Argus-eyed neighbour if they could be restrained at source. Then she sorted through the papers in her desk and destroyed a number, burning them carefully and stirring the ashes. Afterwards she arranged

188

on her shelves all her pretty new clothes, sparing them a wistful valedictory look before she closed the door on them.

'Were you coming to see me tonight?' It was Tom. 'I've been lying here, reading and wondering.'

'I was thinking of it.'

'Well, don't, then.'

'Why not?'

'I'm tired and ready to sleep. Spent the day having a variety of tests.' His voice was cheeky, but a sort of empty fatigue echoed behind it.

At once alert, Charmian said: 'Is anything wrong?'

'Not as far as I know. They seemed quite pleased, in fact. But I am tired.'

'I'll see you in the morning, then,' said Charmian. 'I've been making plans. For us both.' No need to mention Diana just yet.

Then she left the house, checking the door was closed behind her, and drove down to the town for her meeting with Diana and the others.

On her way down the hill she heard the sound of a fire-engine, and before she had travelled many more yards two machines had passed her, travelling fast towards the town centre. Charmian was interested, but too preoccupied with her own life to give her mind to the sight.

She went into her office, selected various documents with some care and then put them into her briefcase. Then she sat down at her desk and wrote a report, signed it and placed it in an envelope, addressed to Walter. Appearances must be kept up.

What had happened was that a man called William Edwards, who had been employed as a cleaner in Benton's jewellery shop when it was raided had lost his job because Benton's suspected, falsely, that he had been

189

implicated. William Edwards was bitterly upset. He bought himself a bottle of whisky and got drunk. Drunk, but not showing it, he went into the public library to read the papers. There he lit a forbidden cigarette, dropped a lighted match into a waste-basket and then fell asleep in a corner with a lighted cigarette and a newspaper. No one was in there at the time, and all was nicely smouldering before the fire was noticed. Smoking at all was, of course, strictly prohibited in the library.

Then an illegally opened fire-door and a strong draught spread the fire beyond the reading-room.

Within the hour, the store next door was alight and a rising wind was making the flames leap from area to area. In spite of everything the firemen could do, most of the library premises and rows of shops on either side were burnt out. Their façades remained curiously intact, although scorched, but they were hollow shells. In fact, the whole plaza was declared unsafe.

Diana might not yet have succeeded in her declared ambition of taking Deerham Hills apart, but she had certainly begun to burn the heart out of it.

Chapter Nine

Next day Charmian was on her way to her office good and early. After all, she had documents to replace and files to tidy. She felt surprisingly self-confident. Last night she had let Diana see the documents she had requested and had noted Diana's avid interest as she read. Not to her surprise, Diana had produced an efficient camera and had taken instant photographs of certain pages, and also a posed photograph of Charmian holding all the documents. There really had been no need for a parade of signing and dating the photographs after that, but Diana had insisted. It gave her pleasure, she said, to do things properly. Now Charmian parked her car and walked briskly towards the main entrance of the police building, where she met Adam Lily coming out. She turned her head away from the burnt-out town centre, which she preferred not to see. It represented a failure.

'How are things with you?' she said to Adam.

'Fine.' He looked cheerful and happy, not a care in the world. 'No, I feel great. Just a naturally lucky fellow, I suppose. Mind you, workwise, I don't seem to be making progress on any of the cases we're confronted with just now, but I'm plodding on. I'll get somewhere in the end.'

'Yes, I expect you will.' Charmian nodded; she knew Adam's power of steady relentless application and, indeed, believed that he would turn something in at last. But I might not be around to see it, she thought. 'Just off, are you?'

'Mmm.' He nodded, raising the collar of his jaunty short overcoat against the damp rain-promising wind.

'Got to see a man about another man. Also, Walter Wing's on the way back to work. Had you heard?'

'Word had reached me.' Charmian gave him a wave and walked on; her feet felt preternaturally heavy, as if she had lead in each shoe, but she forced herself forward. Lucky Adam, she thought. Men really do have it easier. Or most men. There was always Tom, who was having nothing easy.

Perhaps I should tell Agnes everything, she thought. Perhaps one owed it to one's friends to tell them of the bad things in one's life so that they could have a chance to feel sorry for you. But she knew she was not about to do it. Anyway, Agnes was better not involved.

'How are things with you?' she said to Agnes. The girl was seated at her desk, looking through the day's letters, reports and requests.

Agnes stared at her. 'I see you really mean that,' she said finally.

'I do.' Charmian waited. For a little while it looked as though she wasn't going to get an answer.

'Then my reply is that my state is hopeless but not serious.' Agnes's eyes met Charmian's perceptive gaze. 'Joke,' she said uncertainly.

'A bad old joke,' replied Charmian in a level voice.

Agnes banged her hands down on her desk. 'Oh, come on, what's behind this? What are we talking about? What are you asking? You don't really care how I feel this morning.'

'As it happens, I do.'

'You're serious. *Serious.*' Agnes sat there for a moment looking at her hands; she saw a slight bruise forming where she had banged the knuckles. 'What is it?'

'A little while ago I had it strongly hinted to me by an old woman who probably knew what she was talking about that someone close to me in my working life was corrupt. Receiving payment for information. I think that someone from this office passed on details about the safety precautions taken by business firms and shops in the neighbourhood. Perhaps information about a lot of them, certainly about one, the jeweller's, Benton's. I had a list made, remember? I think it was either you or Adam. I've seen Adam this morning, and to my mind he's cleared that hurdle. That leaves you.'

Agnes stared at Charmian, wide-eyed. Charmian saw fear in her eyes.

'I think it was you. Why did you take money, Agnes?' Agnes made a noise at the back of her throat, as if a giant hand had taken her and squeezed her. 'I won't ask how she got on to you, or knew you might be up for sale, because I think she's the sort of woman who has an instinct about that sort of thing. A sort of moral buzzard. But why, Agnes? Why?'

Agnes said: 'Don't look at me. Look out of the window and I'll tell you why.'

Charmian got up and walked to the window, looking out, and presenting her back to Agnes. From the window she could see the traffic passing quickly down the main street. The shopping-precinct and the burnt-out library, once the haunts of Gloria, were just visible, gleaming with damp and depressing. This was said to be the heart of Deerham Hills, but at this moment Charmian doubted if towns had hearts. She saw no reason to believe so – or, at any rate, not feeling, loving hearts. These were hard enough to come by with human beings.

Behind her she heard Agnes's voice.

'You knew about my early abortion —'

'Yes, I did.'

'What you didn't know was who the man was. It was Adam. And what you also didn't know was that I couldn't pay for it. It wasn't so early, you see, not nearly early enough, and it isn't so easy to get that sort of abortion on

the NHS, even if it were easy to get one at all round here
– which, as a matter of fact, it isn't. So I went private. And
it cost. Try having an abortion on the instalment system
and see how it makes you feel.' Agnes took a deep breath.
'It makes you feel dirty.'

'Didn't Adam . . . ?' Charmian did not turn round.

'I wanted to marry him,' said Agnes. 'That's why I left
it so late. Silly of me. He's quite ruthless in his way. He
did what he could financially. But it wasn't much. He had
obligations,' said Agnes wryly. 'His car, for instance.'

'I am so sorry,' said Charmian, turning slowly round.
'I wish I'd known at the time.'

'I told it you the easy way then – you had troubles of
your own. I've only told you now because of what it made
me do. Take the money, I mean. It wasn't so much, but
I needed it desperately. And now I've told you what are
you going to do?'

Charmian walked over to her own desk and stared down
at the neat piles of folders and correspondence on it. 'I
don't know yet. I shall have to put in a report about it, of
course, but I'll make it as good for you as I can. But
there's something else I have to tell you: I'm applying for
leave of absence. Starting at once. I'll hand over and be
off.'

Agnes sat down abruptly. 'You mean you got all that
out of me and now you're clearing off?'

'Yes, I do mean that.'

'But that's — ' Agnes's voice rose.

'Yes, it's a rotten thing to do. But I had to do it. Sorry,
Agnes.'

'I don't think I'll ever forgive you,' said Agnes, her lips
white. 'I only told you all this because I trusted you and
thought you would be around here to help me through
whatever was coming to me. But you got it out of me and
now you mean to go away. For how long? How long will
you be gone?'

194

For answer, Charmian started to pack together her possessions, but her simple actions raised the level of Agnes's anger. 'Well, I've got news for you. Walter Wing is back. Sooner than expected. He walked in ten minutes ago. You won't get away without facing *him*.'

Half an hour later, Charmian closed Walter Wing's door behind her and went down the stairs and into the cloakroom. It had been a difficult interview; Walter was a hard man to lie to. What a pity he couldn't have stayed away a bit longer.

Meanwhile, all this time, the bank manager remained missing. It was now beginning to be said that she was in the robbery, too, as an accomplice. Charmian was thinking of all this as she combed her hair and applied some lip-gloss. For a moment she hesitated, then she went back to her room, where she picked up her telephone and called Diana.

'I'm coming down to get you so that you can take a look at that man you wanted to see. Remember? And then we'll go to that place where I am going to stay. Remember that, too?'

'I remember.' Diana sounded pleased. 'I'll be waiting at the door.'

Charmian collected Diana from the salon where she was standing with a slightly sardonic smile on her lips.

'Ready and waiting,' she announced. 'As arranged. Where are we going?'

'You'll see.' Charmian drove them straight to the hospital. Diana's eyebrows went up as they arrived, and Charmian thought she looked alert and suspicious.

'It's all right,' she said as she drove into the car-park. 'Nothing sinister here. No plot against you. I'm keeping my word.'

'That's good,' said Diana, relaxing a little, but by no means letting down her guard. 'I've got those pictures, remember.'

'Oh, I do remember.'

Charmian led the way in, a route she knew well by now.

'Are you allowed to go in and about here just as you like?' questioned Diana.

'Just follow me.'

'I suppose he's a doctor or something.'

'No.'

'Coincidence him being here. Not sure I like coincidences.'

Charmian led her to the entrance of the ward where Tom was. Nurses were bustling around at the end of the ward well away from where the two women stood.

Tom was lying in bed, more pillows than before supporting him, reading one of the books she had brought him.

'There you are,' said Charmian. 'The last bed on the right. Just look. I'm not taking you any further.'

'How do I know?' began Diana suspiciously.

'You know,' said Charmian. Tom looked up from his reading at this point, and as he saw Charmian, he smiled. She waved back. 'You know now.'

Diana smiled. 'Well, I never. Explains a lot. Thanks.'

'Satisfied?'

Diana was still studying Tom, and now he was looking at her. For a moment their gaze held.

'That's enough,' said Charmian, breaking the moment as if she were jealous. 'You go now. I'll see you afterwards. I'm going to speak to him.' And without a backward look at Diana she went towards Tom.

'How are you this morning?'

'Pleased to see you.' He looked white and tired, but plainly wanted no questions on his condition. 'And reading, as you see.'

'Enjoying them?'

196

'Well enough. You chose some good books. I can see your tastes and mine match up.'

'Good,' said Charmian absently. Books were not really what she wanted to talk about.

'Who was that woman with you?'

'Gone now, has she?' Charmian looked towards the door.

'Went as soon as you came over to me. Who is she?'

'Someone who wanted to see you. And, to tell the truth, I wanted you to see her. What did you make of her?'

'Difficult to tell from one glance.' He was frowning. 'Good looking, well dressed. Hard.'

'Yes, she's all that.'

'What is she to you – friend or foe?' He was half laughing.

'It's business, really.'

'A difficult woman to beat, I should think.'

'I think so, too,' said Charmian. Then she added: 'I've come to say goodbye for a few days. I might not be able to visit for a while. I'll keep in touch by telephone. I can do that, can't I?'

'Yes, they bring round a phone on a trolley and plug it in,' he said, 'but don't rely on getting through just as you wish; that phone serves two wards and gets plenty of use. I'm sorry you're going, though. I suppose it's work?'

'It's a job,' said Charmian evasively. 'Perhaps my last job. And it's for us both. Or partly so. Yes, perhaps I do have more than one motive. Perhaps revenge comes into it.'

'No, I don't like that sort of talk; you're not talking like yourself.'

'Yes, I am. I've only just realised what that self is. But it includes you.'

Tom frowned. 'I expect that I'm made stupid and addled by drugs, or I'd understand you more. But I'm

197

worried. Alarmed for you. As if you were going into danger.'

Telepathy, Charmian thought. Illness and weakness have made him reach out beyond the flesh to catch the thought in my head. I *am* in danger. As if it mattered.

Aloud, she said: 'Not if I do it right. No danger if I do it right.'

'Got the Deerham Hills crime wave all tied up, have you, then?'

'Oh, yes,' said Charmian. 'All tied up with ribbon and ready to post.'

'Will you ring me as often as you can? I wish you'd tell me where you will be.'

'Better not,' said Charmian.

The night before Charmian had confronted Diana with a demand.

'You'll have to find me a room to live in. I'm not going back to my own place. Not till all this is over. Perhaps not ever.'

'Well, that poses me a problem,' began Diana doubtfully.

'Can't I move in with you?'

'That place I've got's only a *pied à terre*, as they say. A hole in the wall.'

'Yes, I noticed.' When Diana had taken her to her one-room apartment, Charmian had noticed that it was strictly a fly-by-night accommodation. It was in no sense a home; Diana could have been and probably was intending to be out of it in half an hour.

'Just suits me for now,' said Diana. 'I don't know where to put you.'

'Try,' said Charmian.

'There's my old family place,' Diana had said after a while. 'Bee's there on and off.'

'Don't either of you really live anywhere?'

Diana more or less ignored this question. 'She's most

198

often with her man at his place. She thinks he can't exist without her looking after him and telling him he's alive. Soft fool, he is.'

'Is he safe?' asked Charmian.

'If you mean, will he talk, he doesn't know anything. I didn't have to tell Bee not to talk – she wants him kept innocent. She says it's nicer to come home to.' Diana gave a short laugh. 'Doesn't want him to know what sort of money he's spending. Protect the men and babies, that's always been her idea. Anyway, I never tell Bee more than I have to tell her.'

'You don't trust her, then?'

Diana shrugged. 'She's my half-sister. She'd never let me down.'

'But you trust me.' It was a statement, not a question.

Diana half smiled, a cold half-smile, without answering.

Charmian had felt a shiver run up her back. She felt as if she had put her head in the mouth of the tiger and the tiger's rough tongue had licked her hair. 'What did you do about the bank manager?' she asked. 'Corrupt her, like you have me?'

Diana was pleased with herself, and showed it. 'That's right. I made her an offer she couldn't refuse. All right, then. You can have a stay at my dear old family home.'

Charmian was thinking of this as she went to find her car in the hospital car-park. Diana was sitting in it. Charmian got in and then she turned to Diana. 'I've done my part. Now you do yours. Take me to where I'm going to hide.'

'What are you going to do about this car?'

'A good question. I'm going to take it to a friendly garage I know and sell it for cash. And then we're going to get in your car and you're going to drive me away.'

'Got it all set up, have you?'

199

'Yes. I telephoned the garage this morning. It's not far from *Charm and Chic*. Convenient, really. They're expecting me. I won't get much of a price, but that doesn't worry me.'

'In the circumstances it shouldn't,' said Diana. 'But you've got a nerve. I'm not going to appear.'

'Wait outside, then.'

Without waiting for an answer, she drove off straight to the garage. Diana was out of the car almost before it had stopped.

'I'll walk to my own car. It's parked outside the salon. Just get in and we'll be off.'

'Give me fifteen minutes,' said Charmian, and she was punctual to her time. Diana relaxed a little when she saw her.

'Get in.'

Charmian got in, stowing her overnight bag on the seat behind her. They were off.

'Leave an address behind you?' enquired Diana as she drove away.

'I had none to leave,' Charmian reminded her. 'You could say I've left home.'

'True.' Satisfied, Diana returned to her driving. 'It's a bit isolated, you'll find, but none the worse for that.'

'Telephone?'

'No telephone. There's a call-box at the end of the lane. You can use that if you have to. You'll be able to make yourself comfortable there, though, I think. There's not much in the way of food but, in any case, tonight we are going to Phil and Baby's to eat. They've invited us for a meal.' She looked at her watch. 'So you just dump your things, and we'll be off.'

Hardly looking where she was going, but driving as if her muscles knew the way, Diana took the car five miles out of town, and swung it leftwards down an unmade road. Charmian was surprised that such a road existed

200

within five miles of Deerham Hills, surprised at herself for not knowing of its existence. On either side of the road were small sour-looking fields given over to the production of thistles.

Three hundred yards down the narrow rutted lane, a building appeared, a low, double-fronted, turn-of-the-century house, now badly in need of paint and repair. Behind it stretched outbuildings which looked like small barns. And beyond that was a bend of the river which eventually ran through Deerham Hills. Someone – Bee presumably – had repainted the front door and had had a shot at laying some paving-stones to the doorway – a poor job, they looked like irregular blobs set in cement. No wonder Bee, if it had been Bee, had given up.

Charmian looked around her with curiosity. 'I suppose this was a small holding once?'

'Yes,' said Diana. 'Belonged to my grandparents. Then my father had it. He was a butcher. He used the fields for grazing. Belongs to me and Bee now. We ought to do something about it.' Her tone was indifferent.

What an enigma you are, thought Charmian. Here you have this piece of property from which you might legally and justifiably have made a profit. Even these few neglected acres are valuable in this part of the country, so you could have sold them for a good price, or even made use of them in some way, but, no, you turned to crime. Why?

'Of course it's mortgaged to the hilt,' said Diana, partly answering Charmian's question. 'Anyway, I hate it. Grew up here. What a grind. I couldn't get out fast enough.'

'To London?'

Diana didn't answer directly. 'Anywhere did.' It *was* London, thought Charmian.

'But you've come back to Deerham Hills.'

'I suppose you always come back.'

'Home means something?'

201

'"Something" is right,' said Diana with a laugh. She stopped the car and turned off the engine. 'Here we are. We get out here.' She was already scrambling out of the driving-seat and leading the way into the house. Charmian, clutching her overnight bag, followed more slowly.

On the very threshold, the smell of damp and disuse swept over Charmian. She saw a narrow hall with rooms opening on either side and a steep staircase rising at the end to block her further view. Dark paint, dim and dusty carpets underfoot and the sad smell of a dead dwelling-place.

'I think that smell's dry rot,' she said prosaically. 'You ought to get it looked at.'

Diana shrugged. 'Who cares? One day it'll fall down.' She opened a door and showed Charmian an old-fashioned kitchen. 'Bedroom's upstairs. Can you make yourself comfortable?'

'Yes,' said Charmian, looking around at the room where a wooden dresser lined with blue and white china faced an antique sink and gas cooker. 'It'll do.'

'Won't be for long.'

'I feel like a prisoner,' said Charmian, with a shiver.

Diana gave her a sceptical look with raised eyebrows. 'Ever been a prisoner? You'd know then.'

'Have *you*?' asked Charmian pointedly.

'Not in an HM prison, no,' said Diana. 'But there are other sorts of prisons. Especially for women. For women, prisons come in all shapes and sizes.' She added, in a brisk voice, 'Anyway, you won't be alone here much. I shall be in and out.'

Like a prison officer, thought Charmian, but naturally did not say so. 'It doesn't look as though anyone comes here much,' she observed.

'I do now,' said Diana briefly. 'And Bee always did pop in. Old times' sake, you know; I believe she keeps her kid

202

toys here and old schoolgirl annuals. So, shall we get off now? Go to this supper at Baby's? We'll make it an early night because of London tomorrow. That's the idea, isn't it?'

'Yes, early tomorrow. I've set up the meeting with my contact, and he will start the ball rolling about the money.'

'It had better roll fast,' said Diana. 'But come on now.'

The apartment shared by Baby and Phil was the essence of the cosy. This quality Baby had endowed it with, for there was none of that softness about Phil, who cultivated awkwardness, sometimes deliberately ruffling up the little prettinesses arranged by her mate. 'Move those bloody silly little cushions out of the way,' she said, kicking aside a scatter of confetti-coloured cushions, some satin, some velvet and some patchwork. 'So that Di and Co. can sit down.' She picked one cushion up as an exhibit. 'And look at this object: quilted blue satin with an eye painted on it.'

'I painted that on it myself,' said Baby, snatching it away. 'So it would always keep an eye on you.'

'You're mad,' said Phil. 'Come in, girls, let's eat. Whatever else, this little creature here is a good cook.'

'You married me for my cooking,' said Baby, straight-faced.

'Sure.'

'And then I turned out to be a good crook as well.'

'Oh, you're sparkling today,' said Phil. 'Come on, you lot. Supper's spread. Sit ye down.'

'She's having one of her North Country girl kicks,' Baby told them. 'But do sit down. I've got everything ready. I *do* like pretty food, don't you?' She waved a hand at the dishes of mixed salads, cold meats, and the sliced cucumber in lime jelly.

203

'Colour-matched,' growled Phil.

'Oh, you bear.' Baby herself was gay. 'Now, do sit down, Charmian. Sit on Phil's right.'

'Thank you.' Charmian slid into her appointed seat.

'And don't be shy. You're acting a little shy.'

'Shut up, Baby,' said Phil. 'It's a strange position for her to be in, eating here like this with us. I should think even you could see that.'

'I'm fine.' Charmian spoke up hastily before battle was joined. 'Just fine. Quite at home.'

'Now, that's more like it.' Baby looked in triumph round her table. 'Here we all are. And I'm so glad. We're a gang. Bound together by affection and loyalty.'

Phil's jaw dropped. 'What?'

'To money,' concluded Baby smoothly. 'That's where our loyalty lies.' She surveyed them. 'Don't laugh, anyone.'

Diana said: 'I hate you when you're jokey. I truly do.'

'Salad, Di? A little sweet pickle? No? Try the garlic bread.' Baby broke off a good chunk for herself and put it on her plate. 'So, what's the plan for tomorrow?'

Diana looked at Charmian, who said: 'Tomorrow we go to London, Diana and I, and I set up the arrangements with my contact there.'

'He knows you, does he?' said Phil.

'He's never seen me, but he knows me, yes,' said Charmian.

'And that's good? That'll do the trick?'

'It's what I know about him that counts,' said Charmian, her expression unconsciously grim.

'If you knew it, you people – the police, I mean – why wasn't it used before?'

'We were saving it up. It would have been used in due course.'

'And now you're blowing it. Alerting Mr X,' said Baby thoughtfully. 'Your old lot *will* be pleased with you.'

'She'll be clearing out, won't she?' said Diana with barely suppressed irritation.

'I wonder how far she'll have to run.'

'Far enough,' said Charmian.

Baby studied her face. 'I don't think I really understand you. Or why you're doing this.'

'I do,' said Diana.

'Oh, yes, you do. We all know about *you* and your famous intuitions.'

In spite of the fact that Baby obviously chose her food for its looks, the meal was tasty and good, and to her surprise Charmian found herself enjoying the evening. In their way what Baby called 'the gang' were good company; Baby and Phil were likeable people, and even Diana's steady astringency had an amusing quality. Bee didn't say much; perhaps, Charmian thought, she was, of all of them, herself included, the cleverest and so saw most clearly their predicament.

Or perhaps she's just the sanest of us, thought Charmian, looking at that sad long face of Bee's with the shrouded bespectacled eyes, and knows that life's no bargain packet ever, whereas the others in their different ways still believe in happy endings.

'I'd better get off,' she said, looking at her watch. 'Got an early start to make tomorrow.'

'Oh, you can't go off to that dreary dump of Di's,' protested Baby, who appeared to know the details of all the arrangements. 'Stay here with us. We've got a spare room.'

'Well . . . ,' began Charmian doubtfully. 'If you could let me have a toothbrush and a nightgown.'

'Plenty of everything here,' said Baby.

'You might as well,' conceded Diana. 'I don't know if I fancy that drive out there tonight myself.'

205

'That's settled, then,' said Baby. 'Phil – you go off to bed. You look all in. I'll clear away.'

'You take that trip often enough lately,' observed Bee to her sister, coming in quietly with a slow remark.

'We'd better be off now,' said Diana, ignoring her sister. 'I think we're all tired. It's been a wearing time. Nice it's coming to an end.'

There were kisses and hugs all round as goodbyes were said, and Charmian promised to be ready when Diana drove up in the morning. When Diana and Bee had departed and Phil had gone to bed, she and Baby washed up the dishes together.

'Friends?' enquired Baby. 'I'll wash, you dry?'

'Of course. To both questions.'

'I'm glad. But it's hardly likely to be a long friendship,' said Baby thoughtfully. 'I suppose we'll be ships that pass in the night, as they say. I think that's romantic, don't you?'

'Yes,' agreed Charmian. She wondered exactly what sort of relationship was in Baby's mind.

'Of course, nothing could ever come between me and Phil,' went on Baby, partly enlightening her. 'I'm totally loyal to Phil. I'm a very loyal sort of person.'

'I know,' said Charmian. 'I can see you must be.'

'That's why I came into all this. I won't ask you what your reasons are, but I bet they aren't far removed from mine. I wanted the cash. Free, flowing money in the hand, to do with what I like. Not for selfish reasons, no. Someone's got to look after *her*.' And she nodded in the direction of Phil's bedroom door. 'Thinks she's tough. Not so strong as she thinks she is. Got a bit of a heart. In both senses, cardiac and loving. She has to be looked after. She's *too* generous, a real giver. All bark and no bite.'

'You can tell,' agreed Charmian.

'Of course, if I'm honest (and fundamentally I am an

honest woman), I have to admit I did fancy a few luxuries like furs and jewels. No one was ever going to *give* them to me, so I had to get them for myself in the only way I could. Wrong, of course. I know it's criminal, but I can't seem to make it mean anything to me . . . . All those old rules.' She lowered her voice and spoke earnestly to Charmian. 'Why, they grew up in the old days when they mattered in primitive societies. They meant something then, but they don't mean anything to me. Once, if someone stole a man's crops or his beasts, he probably starved. No one's going to starve if I take a few fur coats or some banknotes.'

'There is an answer to that,' said Charmian, 'but it's long and complicated and it would take the recounting of the whole of human history to explain it.'

'I don't understand you.' Baby cocked her head on one side.

'Never mind.'

'I'm glad you're with us, though. We can do with a bit of help. Between you and me, we were properly done over those furs, I suspect. We've got to hang on to the money, of which there was much more than we'd expected, much more. I helped Di and Bee pack it up.'

'How much was there?'

'Bee keeps the accounts,' said Baby evasively. 'But plenty. Provided we can keep it, and not be fleeced the way we were over the furs and jewellery. Criminal, that was. Not that all was entirely lost.' And Baby gave Charmian a seraphic smile. She put down her mop and went over to a cupboard. On a shelf, almost hidden behind stacks of crockery, was a box. Baby withdrew the box and opened it for Charmian to see. Inside was a pretty little tabard of blue and pink fur. 'I kept this for me. I always believe in looking after myself.' She smoothed the shining fur and put back the lid. 'No one knows I've got this; I

207

didn't mind showing you, because I think you admire me.'

'I admire all of you.'

Baby turned startled wide eyes towards her. 'You sound as if you mean that. You said it in such a natural voice, as if it wasn't remarkable at all.'

'Unremarkably, I do,' said Charmian.

Charmian and Diana set off early the next morning, with Charmian driving Diana's car. On the seat behind them was a neatly packed suitcase. Every so often, Diana cast a protective eye towards it; Charmian wondered why she didn't have it chained to her. By now, Charmian had spoken to Bee and knew how much was in it. She caught Diana's eye.

'I thought you'd wear a head-scarf and dark glasses.'

'Why?' Charmian braked as a car drew out in front of her.

'Disguise. I didn't think you'd want to be recognised.'

Charmian gave a short laugh. 'Too late for that.'

She drove on smoothly for a few minutes, then said: 'It's pouring with rain, you know. Don't you think dark glasses might be *more* noticeable? Cuts down the vision, too. And the last thing we want is an accident.'

'God, yes,' said Diana, startled. 'Aren't you driving a bit fast, though?' she asked nervously.

'No. We have an appointment and I want to keep it. The man we're meeting doesn't give second chances.'

'Oh.' Diana digested this information. 'You know him well, then?'

'We've never met. I thought I told you that.'

'Well, I didn't know how much to believe. Naturally, you'd keep some things to yourself. If you've never seen him, how will you know he's the right man, then?'

'If he says the right sort of thing, he's the right man,'

said Charmian, driving, if anything, faster. 'He can wear any face he likes.'

They drove on for another mile or two in silence. The outskirts of London began to appear. Charmian didn't get lost in the complex system of roads and freeways. Diana noticed that.

'I'll never admit to anything,' she said suddenly. 'They can put me on the rack, and I'll never admit to a thing.'

'There are no racks at the disposal of the police force,' observed Charmian, hardly sparing her a glance.

Again they drove on in silence, an unbroken silence this time. Charmian took her route without hesitation. Steadily they were driving farther into the heart of London.

Suddenly, Diana spoke again. 'You know your way here.'

'No.' Charmian answered without much expression.

'But you haven't got lost.'

'I have a good memory for routes.'

Diana looked out of the window. 'Where are we now?'

'Hammersmith, I think. And at these traffic lights we turn left. Yes, and now a right turn.' Charmian drew up outside a row of shops in a terrace of Edwardian houses of great respectability and solidity. 'And here we are.'

Diana looked around her with interest. 'I'd never find my way here on my own. So it's in a shop?'

'Well, over one. Over that betting-shop at the end.' Charmian pointed.

'Yes, I see.' Diana got out of the car, gripping the case firmly in her right hand. 'The place looks all right. About what I expected. When we get in there, do I talk or you?'

'Me,' said Charmian, following her. 'I've done all the preliminary work.' She led the way up a staircase which rose between a travel agency and the betting-shop. On the first floor was a solid-looking oak door, with a brass plate, well polished, which said *Leisure Days Ltd.*

'Promising name,' said Diana. 'Leisure, here I come.'

Behind the brass-plated door was a small outer office, with a pretty girl seated behind a large electric type-writer.

'We're expected,' said Charmian. 'For Mr Foster.'

'Oh, yes.' The girl smiled. 'I'll just tell him you are here.' She slipped through an inner door and presently emerged to say, still smiling. 'Please go in.'

Mr Foster was sitting behind his desk, sipping a cup of coffee. He had a genial middle-aged face, with hard little brown eyes hiding behind spectacles. 'Come in, dears,' he said. 'Oh, pet,' he called to his secretary, 'bring in some more coffee for these ladies. You'd like some, love, wouldn't you?' he said to Charmian.

Charmian took a deep breath. She had burnt all her bridges now. 'Love some,' she said. 'We both would.' She felt as though she would never breathe any more.

Half an hour later, they were both outside again.

'Well, that's over,' said Charmian. Somehow she had started to draw breath again.

'Yes. You did well, really well,' said Diana. She turned exultantly to Charmian: 'I always knew you were lucky for me.'

Charmian did not answer.

Chapter Ten

The evening of their return from London was a repetition of the night before, and once again they gathered around Baby's pastel-coloured food. It seemed to be agreed that she was the one to feed them.

'We have to hang on for about a week – more, possibly,' said Charmian. 'It will take that long for the deal to go through.' She was trying to hide her unease.

Baby fluttered her eyelashes experimentally. 'Just trying to see if I've still got them on,' she said. 'It's so silly not to have matching eyes! I used to tap my contact lenses with my fingernail to see if I'd still got *them* in, but Phil didn't like it. Oh well, a week's nothing. Nothing, really.'

They all agreed it was nothing, except for Phil who said honestly that she'd be glad if it was over tomorrow.

'Feeling nervous? There's nothing to worry over,' Diana assured her soothingly.

'I'm not nervous; I'd just like it over,' said Phil stoutly.

Diana turned to Charmian. 'I'll take you out to the old place tonight.'

Charmian agreed. 'Probably better not to stay here two nights running.'

All the same, she and Baby washed up the dishes in the kitchen together while the others slumped in the living-room, as if they two alone were able to cope with everyday living.

'What are you going to do when this time's over?' asked Baby.

'I've made plans.' Charmian polished a plate.

211

'I bet. Told anyone? Because you're planning for someone and something. I get waves of planned thought emanating from you.'

'You do?' Charmian was startled.

'Yes. You've got a way of staring into space; then I think: She's at it again – dreaming. Then you click back into the present.'

'There's someone, a man; I want to get away with him and into a new world,' said Charmian. 'Right out of things as they are now. To somewhere warm and quiet, where we can be alone.'

'Told him what you plan?'

'Not really.' Charmian fiddled with a spoon. 'I thought we'd just pack our cases and go.'

'Just walk out?'

'If he *can* walk.'

'What's that?' Baby was busy creaming her hands and checking the cuticles of her valuable nails.

'Oh, nothing.' She turned back to her task. 'That's the last of the spoons and forks. Anything else?'

Baby took off her frilly apron and hung it over a chair. 'No, all done.' She lit a cigarette. 'You wouldn't let us down, would you? Betray us, I mean? Because what is loyalty, after all, and why should you feel anything for us?'

'I do, all the same,' said Charmian reluctantly.

'Yes. Funny, that. Just grown up, hasn't it? Because we're all women, I suppose, and women must stick together.'

Yes, what is loyalty? thought Charmian, remembering what she had done to Agnes. It's a problem to know what to be loyal to – a person or an idea. It seems to be better thought of if you stick to the idea and jettison the person. 'You've got your thinking look on again,' said the alert Baby. 'There – it's gone now. Good. Baby prefers you without it.'

'I was worrying about someone, or perhaps something. It's hard to know which.'

'Don't worry about Baby: she can look after herself,' said Baby. She gave her confident high-pitched giggle. 'Friends?'

'Friends,' said Charmian.

Diana dropped her in her desolate hiding-place and drove rapidly away. Charmian tried all the doors and found that only the kitchen and bathroom and her so-called bedroom were unlocked. Cagey Diana had the keys. One room on the ground floor and several on the upper were barred from her. As she undressed and climbed into her cold bed, Charmian decided that tomorrow she would have a look round.

After a dark and restless night, with sleep punctuated by dreaming moments of sharp fear, she woke up and went downstairs to make a cup of tea. As Diana had promised, there was a modest array of provisions.

She tried the front door, to discover that it was locked and that Diana had taken away the key.

Well, she had always known that Diana did not trust her.

I'm a prisoner here, thought Charmian. I got myself into this fix and it's for me to get myself out. She wondered how Tom was feeling about her, how much of the story she had told him about her movements he had believed, and what he really thought she was doing.

For a moment she contemplated knocking Diana down and taking the key when she arrived to let her out, but it would hardly further the plans of either of them.

'It's for your own protection,' explained Diana. 'It's a funny neighbourhood round here.'

'You don't look as though you slept, and yet you were so confident yesterday.'

Diana shrugged. 'Sometimes I feel confident, some-

213

times I don't; that's human nature.' She put the kettle on to make some more tea. 'How will we get the message to tell us our transaction has gone through?' she asked uneasily.

'Well, I'm a novice, too, remember; I've never been through the procedure before, but I imagine you will get a bank statement from the banks you named, saying the money has been credited to you.'

'I'll be watching the post,' said Diana grimly. Presently she urged Charmian to get herself together and come down to *Charm and Chic* where she could spend the day more or less hidden at the back of the establishment.

Waiting was a time of trial for them all, and nerves were liable to become frayed. The five of them were much thrown together, the relationship between them uneasy and taut. Sometimes their meetings were full of laughter and excitement, but equally sometimes a sullen silence prevailed. They didn't want each other's company, but they felt compelled to keep seeing each other. Charmian waited for an explosion.

She didn't sleep much at nights, but during the day she never felt tired. It was as if she were living on a bag of energy hidden inside her. She was conscious of losing weight. Diana seemed to be putting it on, although Charmian had not noticed that she was eating excessively. She attributed it to an unconscious vampirism. Manifestations of strain were showing themselves amongst the others in different ways. Baby, for instance, was becoming more angel-child by the minute, excessively, almost obsessively so. Her curls were curlier, her eye-shadow bluer, and her clothes frillier and silkier. A bit more and she'd be fit for the top of a Christmas-tree. Phil was smoking non-stop now, lighting one cigarette from the butt of another; as a consequence her cough was, as Baby put it, 'shocking'. Bee hid herself behind her spectacles

214

and her silences, as Charmian suspected she had always done. The others were taking care of their appearance: Phil took significantly less. There are different ways of hiding, and too much make-up can tell the same tale as too little. Charmian thought this every time she looked round at her associates. It made her remember Gloria.

In her uncomfortable bed one night, unsleeping, Charmian decided that she needed a weapon to protect herself with. She had one to hand.

She got out of bed and from her handbag took one of the cards used by *Charm and Chic* to record the dates of appointments for their clients. You wrote down when you were to come, slipped it in your purse, and then forgot about it. On one side was the space to write down the date, and on the other a prettily set-out display of the name and telephone number of the salon. Without doubt Baby had had a hand in the design: it had her dainty paw-marks all over it.

The card found in Terry Jarvis's pocket, on one side of which he had written her husband's name and telephone number, was identical in shape and size. It was probable that even the coloured ink used in the printing had been similar.

The coincidence was interesting. To Charmian's mind the card had come from *Charm and Chic*. And that placed his death fairly and squarely in the middle of the picture.

Someone at *Charm and Chic*, or closely connected with it, had known Terry Jarvis. It could be a customer, but Charmian's money was on Diana, Baby, Phil or Bee. And if either one of them made a move that threatened Charmian's safety (and she did not hide from herself that behind the good cheer probably lay suspicion), then she could use her knowledge as a counter-threat.

'The whole house will come down on top of me if I have to do that,' she said thoughtfully.

215

The knowledge was oddly calming and she crawled back into bed and went to sleep, although a dream of a sort of Bacchic hunt of women pursuing her disturbed her sleep. Even when she woke she remembered it, which was unusual with her dreams. Hadn't the female followers of Dionysus (who was the same as Bacchus) torn him apart? Difficult to equate Dionysus with Terry Jarvis, though.

She shook her head, trying to clear it. Really, it wasn't very comfortable, this camping-out life she was leading, but it certainly produced interesting reactions in the psyche.

The five women were even more noticeably on edge with each other the following day. Charmian spent it sitting at the back of the salon, endlessly reading and thinking. Before the shop closed, both Bee and Phil drifted in as if they could not keep away.

Tense, very tense, she thought, looking from face to face. I suppose I look the same. She turned and saw her face in a wall mirror. Yes, there it was, that tight hollow look around the eyes. It was impossible to have any illusions about your appearance in Diana's looking-glass world. 'Charmian through the looking-glass,' she murmured to herself. 'Charmian down the well.'

Waiting was boring as well as nerve-racking. 'Let's *do* something, go somewhere,' said Baby fretfully. 'All this hanging about is like having a disease. I'm wasting away from it.'

'We're better all together,' said Diana.

'We could all go out for a drink.' This was Phil's suggestion.

Baby rejected the idea. 'All of us together? What a spectacle we should look!'

'I know somewhere we could go,' said Charmian. 'I don't think we'd be noticed. It's a quiet sort of place.'

216

'If it's a cinema, I tell you here and now no film is going to take my mind off the drama I'm living through.'

'No, nothing like that. I've been thinking of suggesting it for some time, as a matter of fact. Very soothing, very relaxing.'

As a policewoman Charmian had always needed a place where she could go and feel anonymous. She had such a place where because she was naked no one noticed her. In the sauna she felt completely unknown. Because it is by her clothes, by her make-up, by her hair-style, that many a woman announces her individuality. Steaming and naked, hair limp, eye-shadow gone, all faces looked much the same. In the sauna, as in the labour ward, a woman is faceless.

'The sauna: there's a good one about three miles away. I often go there. They know me, but they don't know who I am. We needn't all go at once. Sort of filter in. They have quite a few hot rooms and showers. Pools as well. It's an anonymous sort of place.'

'Not a bad idea,' conceded Diana. 'Do us all good. Relax us. I could do with a rest myself. Might get a nap.'

'I think you would.' Charmian studied Diana's face. She did seem tired. It looked as though neither of them was getting much rest. 'Well, let's go. You pay as you go in, and the attendant there is remarkably uncurious and invisible. She keeps out of the hot rooms, anyway – can't stand the heat. See you there.'

'I'll come with you,' said Diana speedily. 'The others can follow.'

'Yes, do,' agreed Charmian. 'But I'm not going to run away.'

'Where could you run to?'

'Where could any of us?' asked Charmian.

'When we've got our money we can go,' said Baby. 'Can't we just? I can't wait.'

Everyone except Baby felt guilty, Charmian decided, and what *that* meant, knowing Baby and knowing the others, was anyone's guess. When they all met in the sauna, she was still guessing.

The Floris Sauna had a small entrance foyer, then beyond that a cloakroom with lockers, where customers could undress and leave their possessions. Beyond an inner door was a series of hot and hotter rooms with slatted shelves on which to rest. Pools and showers were sited to one side beyond swing doors. Lights were low, the atmosphere was hot and placid.

One by one they assembled on the threshold of the hot rooms.

'We the only customers, then?' said Diana, peering through the gloom.

'I expect there are a few other women here. There never seem to be many. It's a quiet place, as I said. And all the hot rooms are built into recesses and alcoves so you can have a private corner. We all can. You can drop the towel then.' Charmian glanced briefly at Diana who was wound up in a white bath-sheet with another towel wound, turban-like, round her head. 'I usually lie on mine.'

'I couldn't lock my things up. There was no key on my locker,' grumbled Diana.

'I've never lost anything.'

Baby and Phil shuffled in together. Phil wore a brown towel-robe. It was only loosely belted, but she wasn't worrying.

Baby had on an elaborate bath-cap with flowers of blue and green. Her eyes were hidden behind huge tinted glasses. Twisted chiffon scarves covered her top, and another scarf was tied round her waist. She clutched two

218

huge towels, a couple of cushions, a beach-bag decorated to match her hat, and a book.

'Good Lord, look at you,' said Diana. 'What do you think you look like?'

Baby minced forward in her flip-flops. 'I'm shy. Don't want everyone looking at my little knobs and bumps.'

'Be uncomfortable in the hot rooms,' suggested Charmian. 'You'll be better naked then.'

'I'll undo them,' said Baby, moving slowly into an alcove and suiting her actions to her words, allowing her bosom to appear slowly. 'I'll be on my front.' And she smiled, arranging her bosom on cushions in front of her for her greater comfort. There was a cold-blooded cheek about Baby.

She's as bold as brass, really, thought Charmian, and it was a comparison which suited Baby.

Silently, her charges distributed themselves in separate places in the hot rooms. Diana lay down, face on her hands, in a corner in the hottest of the rooms and announced her intention of sleeping.

'You could die in there, it's so hot,' said Bee. She wiped her spectacles free of steam and retreated to a cooler spot.

Charmian lay down on her back on a wooden bench, closed her eyes and waited for the heat to invade her body. For some minutes her body seemed to hold out against the attack, and then it yielded and little spots of sweat appeared. She sighed deeply and opened her eyes. The ceiling, made of the same pale wood as the slats on which she rested, seemed to have come closer. Here and there on it were darker spots as if the wood were sweating, too. The source of the heat was an electric stove pretending, but without much conviction, to be a stove burning wood. Since it was a phoney it was forbidden to throw cold water on it, as if it were the authentic article.

219

Charmian closed her eyes again. The heat was invading her windpipe and lungs and making breathing an effort. She wondered how Baby was getting on with her book. I love the smell of heat and hot wood, she thought.

Presently, she got up to take a cold shower. As she went out she noticed that all her charges seemed suitably disposed of and were quiet. Diana seemed to be asleep.

After she had had a cool shower, shivering and gasping, she wrapped herself in her towel and went quietly around to the lobby, where her friends had hung their clothes.

No one was about, and so, keeping an alert eye on the door, she searched their coat pockets. The opportunity for this search had been one of her motives in bringing the party here. The pockets were empty except for a handkerchief smelling of scent in Baby's coat. Then she turned to the handbags. Baby had hers with her, and she went through the other three quickly. Phil had very little in her bag, except money, cigarettes and a clean white handkerchief, man-sized. Diana's was crammed with her possessions. She seemed to carry a whole range of cosmetics. Charmian noticed a bottle of fairly strong painkilling pills. What pain was Diana suffering from, then? In the bottom of her bag was a large wad of banknotes.

She could get to the moon on that, thought Charmian, counting it quickly. Or, more important, to somewhere like Spain or Portugal. She was prepared to bet that in Baby's handbag, which, of course, she could not examine, was a similar roll.

Bee's handbag contained little money, and not much else except a spare pair of spectacles, but Charmian was surprised (or was she?) to see that she carried a packet of contraceptive pills.

There was one other thing: each woman seemed to have a supply of the trade-cards for *Charm and Chic,* even if they were only used, like Phil's, to write racing tips on.

220

Charmian left everything tidy and quietly returned to the hot rooms and lay down on a bench. No one was near her, but she had seen her friends' hot pink limbs and flushed faces as she passed through. Baby had given her a little wave before returning to her reading.

Over the next half-hour one or other of them would get up to take a shower or a dip in the pool. Only Diana did not move.

Perhaps she is dead after all, thought Charmian, and got up to take a look. But Diana was breathing quietly in her dark corner and, after a pause, Charmian left her to her sleep.

She went to lie down again; her pulse was beginning to race. Time to leave soon.

Slowly, one by one, rounded up by Charmian, the group reassembled to dress.

'I feel all swollen,' complained Baby. 'Puffed up like a balloon.'

'A shiny red balloon,' said Phil nastily.

Baby was hurt. 'Don't be beastly. You don't look so good yourself. Your face is all blotchy.'

'It's all that stuff you had tied round you. Did you move at all?'

'Yes, I did. I had a shower and a jump in the pool,' said Baby, with a toss of her head, so that all her flowers quivered. 'Don't be rotten.'

Bee was silently puffing scented talcum powder on her hot body when Diana appeared.

'I'll never be able to get my tights on,' she said.

'You should wear trousers like me,' said Phil, who was pushing her legs into pale-blue jeans.

'Oh, God, you look awful,' said Baby. 'I shall be ashamed to go home with you.'

'You look to yourself,' snapped Phil. 'Your heat trip hasn't done you much good. I thought we were all supposed to be the better for this?' she demanded of Charmian.

'You will later. Give it time. At the moment your blood pressure is probably right up.'

'Make you very sexy as you cool down,' said Baby, with a little giggle. 'Bound to. All that lovely cool smooth skin. I can feel mine's smoother already, can't you?' She appealed to Charmian.

They were interrupted by a scream from Diana. She was staring over her shoulder at her naked back in the mirror. 'Look at my back. Just look at it. How did that happen?'

Across her pink shoulders was scratched a great *X*. Sensitised by the heat, the scratch had come up in an angry weal.

They all crowded round to look. 'Someone came and kissed you as you slept. How romantic!' It was Baby's voice.

'I shall have a scar, I'm sure I shall. I've always had a sensitive skin.'

'No, it's only come up like that because of the heat. Honestly, it'll go down quite soon. You may have a red line for a bit, but even that will soon fade,' said Charmian soothingly.

But Diana refused to be soothed. 'Which of you did it? It was one of you, I know. One of you did it while I was asleep.'

No one of them confessed to the exploit, so Diana accused each of them in turn, her voice rising angrily.

'It was only a silly joke. I don't know who did it,' said Baby. 'I know it wasn't me. I was reading all the time. I wouldn't know. But calm down, Diana.'

Diana dressed and combed her hair, putting on her self-control with her make-up. But it was an effort, as Charmian saw. Diana was shaken and angry, and would probably get her own back if she could. She had probably

222

guessed as had Charmian that only Baby would have done it. The psychology of it was Baby's.

'She can't bear her body touched,' whispered Bee to Charmian. By way of apology, Charmian thought.

Thus, so far from soothing the mind and relaxing the body, the trip to the sauna appeared to have inflamed both. Charmian waited to see what would happen.

On the next day, a day on which all five had met as usual, drifted in and out, quarrelled and made up again, an envelope containing a photograph had been slipped into her pocket.

When she looked she saw she was staring at a picture of a young woman in the full skirts and bouffant hairstyle of the early 1960s, sitting on a bench with a young man. Contrary to what is sometimes thought, recognition of a face in a photograph is not always instantaneous. Charmian found she had no idea who the girl was, except that it was not herself. But, from the manner in which it had been deposited in her pocket, it must have come from one of the four women, Diana, Baby, Phil and Bee, and it must be a picture of one of them.

She studied it carefully: it was meant to tell her something, but what?

And also why? But the answer to that came quickly. Within the group, the knives were out, and someone else among them, other than Charmian, now thought she had a weapon.

And, if this unknown woman had sent Charmian the photograph, it must be because it was expected to say something to Charmian. As she studied the face of the woman and man Charmian thought sadly of all the police records and resources she could not make use of now. Still, she had to make some use of the photograph. Clearly, it was expected of her.

'And I won't let down her expectations,' she said aloud. 'Whoever she is.'

It was a quiet day at the salon. Charmian was getting to know the routine now: the way in which Diana arrived first and unlocked everything; the arrival of Baby, followed by the setting out of fresh towels and bottles of shampoo and hair conditioner. Considering that few customers now arrived, it was amazing how easily both Diana and Baby kept up an appearance of being busy. Both were old hands at the game of make-believe.

Diana had earned the right to see the photograph first.

'How's your back?'

'Fading. But I'll always have a scar.'

'Oh, come on. It was only a scratch – hardly that, even.'

'I'll always feel it there on my back,' said Diana fiercely. 'Whether you can see it there or not, I shall feel it there.'

Charmian was silent. More than one way of showing egomania, she thought, and Diana was manifesting several. She wondered whether egomania was a disease or a disturbance of the metabolism.

She produced the photograph. 'Did you ever see this before?' Diana picked it up. 'No,' she said with absolute indifference. 'Never did. Silly bitch.' She handed the photograph back to Charmian.

'Why do you say that?'

'She's holding his hand. What a mistake. Never hold a man's hand.'

'I can't see that she is,' said Charmian.

'Just look closer.'

'I suppose I can just see it,' said Charmian, studying the snapshot.

'You suppose you can just see it,' mimicked Diana. 'Honestly, the way you talk. Where did you get this pretty picture?'

'I – found it.'

224

'I don't believe that, dear, for a minute, but I shan't question it. I always knew you were tricky, and tricky you are being. Right?' She didn't wait for Charmian to answer. 'Anyway, it's nothing to do with me, nothing at all.'

'Have a cup of coffee. I've just made one.' Charmian pushed across a steaming cup, black of course – Diana was watching her weight.

Diana sat down and lit a cigarette. 'Yes, I think I will. Thanks.' She kicked her shoes off, as if ready to relax. This encouraged Charmian.

'Why did you start up all this business, Di? I mean, your life in crime?'

'You know why. The reason is on its way to a bank in Switzerland.'

'Money? Yes, that I understand. But apart from that, what else?'

Diana shrugged. 'Because I thought I could do it. As it proved.'

'Yes, I see. Like Everest. Because it was there.'

Diana gave her a blank stare. 'You're getting to be a bore, dear. Reverting to type. Asking too many questions and giving yourself the answers. I'll be glad when you go your way and I go mine. Take my advice: just leave it.' She finished her coffee and stood up. 'I've got an errand to do, so I'll be going out.'

'At the old house?'

Diana ignored that. 'So I'll leave you in Baby's care. She knows what to do.'

Baby made a charming gaoler. If that was what she was. 'Nice to be on our own for a bit. I've bought some delicious smoked salmon for lunch. A little treat.'

Pink, thought Charmian, Baby's favourite colour.

'Diana can be the teeniest little bit oppressive,' went on Baby, arranging salad on a plate. 'I'm very interested in anthropology, and Diana's definitely a sort of priestess figure, don't you think so?'

225

'I've been thinking so for some time,' said Charmian.

'Have you? You are clever. I've always thought so. Yes, that's what Diana is. It's what makes her so uncomfortable to be with. Priestesses are always a bit baleful, and there's more than a touch of that with our Di.'

Charmian laughed. 'And what about *you*, Baby? What are you?'

'Oh, I'm strictly secular. I don't think I fit into any classical category. They'd have to make a new one for me.'

'I believe you,' said Charmian. She produced the photograph. 'Ever seen this before? Do you recognise either of the people in it?'

Baby picked it up. 'No, can't say I do. Years old – no one wears their hair like that now. And her skirt – no style, no true style. You can't see her hands very well, but I'd say she didn't give them the treatment they deserve.'

Always this obsession with hands, thought Charmian. 'What about the man?'

'Not interested,' said Baby. 'No idea. You can't see his face much, anyway. It's in shadow.'

'And you recognise neither of them?'

'Don't think so,' said Baby. 'I wouldn't call it a good photograph. Probably not a good likeness even then. Why? Why do you want to know?'

Charmian said: 'Just interested.'

'How'd you get the photograph?'

'I found it.'

'You ought not to ask so many questions about us girls,' said Baby seriously. 'Just leave us alone.'

'You think it's a photograph of one of you, then?' asked Charmian.

'It must be, mustn't it?' said Baby. 'If you're interested in it.'

'I'm just speculating.'

226

'Plenty of scope for that with us. Although I'm ordinary enough, and so is Bee. Arcane, Diana is.'

'A mystery? You may be right.'

'Now, that's what I like about you,' declared Baby. 'You accept me using a word like "arcane". If I said that to Phil, she'd just say: "You've been reading too many good books, Baby." She's not my intellectual equal. I love her, but she can't reach up to me. Increasingly, I'm afraid that there may be a gap between us. She won't develop, and I still am developing.'

'What about you, Baby? Why did you get into crime? After all, women don't usually.'

'Increasingly, I'd say.'

'Perhaps. But why did you?'

'I grew up beside a toy-shop. Always used to have my little face pressed against the window, looking in. Made me greedy, I think.' Charmian was never sure when Baby was being serious. 'I never got anything. My father didn't believe in children having what they wanted. Rather the reverse. Thought they ought to have what they didn't want. In the end, I decided as he obviously wasn't going to give me any treats I'd better go out and get them myself.'

'But it wouldn't have happened if you hadn't met Diana?'

'We were looking for each other, I reckon,' said Baby, with a smile. 'And she says she was looking for someone like you. She has got a flair, you know, old Di.' The sound of the door opening made her turn her head. 'Oh, hello, Phil. Come and have a salad with us.'

'No, I've had a pint and a pork pie down the road,' said Phil, slouching in and sitting down beside them. The force of her sitting down dislodged a tower of shampoo-bottles which fell to the ground with a crash.

'You ought not to eat in a pub,' reproved Baby, getting on her hands and knees to retrieve the bottles. 'It may

227

make you fat. I don't like fat people. Damn, one of these bottles is broken. I'll have to mop the floor and put these bottles in the cupboard.'

'Pooh, what a stink,' said Phil, screwing up her nose. 'What has that stuff got in it?'

'Flower bouquet.' Baby was taking an armful of bottles through to a walk-in cupboard. 'Or so it says on the label. It is a bit strong.' She turned her head to Charmian. 'This is going to take me some time. Look after Phil, will you?'

'Wouldn't mind a cup of coffee,' said Phil. 'And I'll have a fag.'

'And you do too much of that, too,' said Baby sharply from the depths of the cupboard.

'Oh, you shut up.' And Phil pushed the cupboard door shut behind Baby.

'Won't she suffocate in there?'

'Not she. If they cut off her oxygen, she'd learn to breathe in neat carbon dioxide. Got more lives than a cat, that one. What about that coffee?'

While Phil drank her coffee and Baby clattered away behind the closed door, Charmian produced the photograph again.

'Did you ever see this? Do you recognise either of them?'

Phil picked it up. 'What is this, identity parade?' She did not wait for an answer. 'No, I don't know who they are. Friends of yours?'

'I don't know who they are.'

'No loss, I should say. Grim-looking pair.'

'They do look a bit serious.'

'Just had a quarrel, I should think.'

Charmian studied the picture. 'Perhaps you're right.'

'Think so. Got that look. I'm sensitive about that sort of thing. Baby thinks I'm not, but I am. I'd say they were against each other. I usually know.'

228

'But they're holding hands,' Charmian pointed out.

'You call that holding hands? Looks to me more as if they were hurting each other.'

'You've silenced me,' said Charmian.

'Yes, I often do. I've noticed that. It used to worry me. I knew I wasn't fitting in. Not getting things right somehow. But Baby taught me to live with it. "I like it, Phil," she said, first time we really talked. "You be yourself. You stay the way you are." We hit it off straight away. She calls me her father figure.'

'And what do you call her?'

Phil blushed deeply. 'My little fairy. But that's a secret. Don't say. I've never said it aloud to her. Just inside. Before I had Baby I only had an old dog, and he died. Rover, he was called.'

'It's a good name for a dog,' said Charmian.

The cupboard door opened and Baby bounced out.

'Not dead, then?' said Phil.

'Not a chance. Were you hoping? Well, I've tidied up in there. Waste of time, really, but it looks neat. You'd better clear off now, Phil. I can see Di's car, and she's getting wacky at you being here so much.'

Phil got up. 'Yes, I'd better get back to work. See you this evening, then.' And she trudged off.

Baby gave a deep sigh. 'She's not herself at all. I just long to get her right away into the sunshine. Roll on the day. Oh, hello, Di.'

Diana came in and hung up her coat before speaking. 'Have you seen Bee?'

'No.' Baby sounded surprised. 'Not today.'

'Not rung up, or anything?'

'No. Specially not anything.'

'Oh, don't be jokey. You know I hate it when you're jokey.'

'Sorry for breathing.'

'Oh, be quiet. You can be very tiresome when you like.'

'I know,' said Baby.

'Bee's not been in to work today. I can't find her.'

'Telephone where she lives.'

'I did. And she's not there. That man she lives with is, though. He's moved in. He's there permanently now.'

'They're probably married,' drawled Baby.

'No. No, Bee would never do that without telling me. She wouldn't dare. Besides, he has a wife.'

'As good as married, then,' said Baby. 'What does it matter?'

'Where is she? That's what I want to know.'

'She'll turn up. I don't suppose she's lost.'

Diana made herself some coffee and sat down to drink it, ignoring the gestures of a customer who had come through the door and was trying to attract some attention. 'Baby, go through and tell that woman that she can't have her hair done. Tell her we're closed.'

'She can see we're not,' grumbled Baby, but she went, and presently they heard her uttering fluent excuses.

'Bee's left her job. They told me when I rang up,' said Diana.

'Well, that's understandable,' said Baby, coming back in time to hear. 'I got rid of that woman. Told her the Health Inspector had closed us down.'

'You didn't!'

'No, of course not. So, Bee's retiring. So shall we all be.'

'But she never told me. She always tells me. Anyway, we agreed to carry on as normal till I gave the word.'

'Are we being normal?' said Baby.

The telephone rang and Diana grabbed it. 'Oh, it's you, Bee,' she said, relief in her voice. 'Yes, I have been after you. Where are you? What? Why a doctor? Are you ill?

230

Yes, I suppose you'll need immunisation if you're going abroad, but you could have waited.'

Briefly, Charmian remembered those contraceptive pills, and wondered.

'Look, Bee, I want to see you. Soon as possible.' No denying the crisp command in Diana's voice, but Bee was obviously giving trouble. 'Come. Just come, that's all. When, then? This evening, then.' And the receiver was slammed down. 'She's coming over around six tonight,' Diana announced to the other two. 'We'll have a good talk. Now we're coming to the end of things here, we must see things are done properly.'

Whatever that means, thought Charmian.

'Think Bee'll come?' asked Baby, under her breath, when Diana's back was turned.

Charmian shrugged. 'We'll have to see.'

'I don't like it,' said Baby. 'Funny thing, Bee turning evasive. She's always been so good. Servile to Di, almost. Di doesn't like it, you can tell, and I don't blame her. I think it's a bad sign. The sooner we get this thing wound up the better. Think it'll be long now?'

'I honestly don't,' said Charmian. 'Not long at all.'

'We all get letters to tell us about the money being in the Swiss bank, don't we?' Charmian nodded. 'But, if you get to hear first, slip me the word, will you?'

'If I can.' Charmian was non-committal.

'I wish I could have a word with Bee. On her own, I mean, without Di breathing over us.' Baby frowned. 'I'll have to see what I can fix.'

'Do you know her telephone-number? Or where she lives? I don't.'

'Di's never told me, but I know all the same.' Baby grinned. 'Not hard to find out what you really want to know. *You* ought to know that. Yes, I'll ring her and ask her to come to see me and Phil tonight. Say I've got to talk things over. Ask her not to tell Diana.'

'A good idea.' But I don't think you'll get away with it, thought Charmian.

In a little while, when Diana was occupied at her desk, where she appeared to be sorting out papers, Baby slipped out through the door.

'Where's she gone?' said Diana alertly, raising her head from her work.

'I don't know.'

Presently Baby came back and gave Charmian a triumphant little nod. Fixed it, she seemed to be saying.

Diana swung round at once. 'And what does that mean? I saw.'

'I just popped out for a newspaper.' Baby had a copy of an evening paper under her arm. 'Must read my horoscope, you know.'

'And I suppose it was a good one?' said Diana cynically.

'Marvellous.'

'And that's why you looked so pleased with yourself?'

'That's right.'

'Liar!'

Baby blinked.

'I know what it is. You're ganging up on me.'

'*No,*' said Baby. 'You know me better than that. I don't gang up. I'm for me, and me only.'

'Still, you went out for something,' said Diana, narrowing her eyes. 'What could you want in the newspaper shop? I know, there's a pay-phone there. You made a phone-call. One you didn't want me to hear.'

'Just a private call to Phil,' said Baby sulkily.

'Private? There's nothing private about you. You're the most public person I know. You'd go to bed with Phil on the table in here in front of me if it suited you,' cried Diana.

'That's not true,' said Baby in a prim voice.

'You were phoning Bee. That's it. You were phoning Bee!'

'Oh, blast you,' said Baby. 'I just wanted to talk to her, that's all.'

'You are a fool, Baby. Do you think she wouldn't have got in touch with me about it, told me, rung me back?'

The telephone on the desk rang. Diana let her hand hang over it for a minute while her eyes held Baby's, then she picked it up. 'Hello, Bee. Somehow I knew it would be you. Hang on a minute.' She smiled at Baby. 'No, don't go away. Just listen. Hello, Bee. What is it, dear? Supper with Phil and Baby? Why, of course, you go. I'd like you to. Yes, lovely. Have a good time. No, in the circumstances, don't bother to come round here tonight. Bye, Bee.'

She put the receiver down in triumph. 'See? See what I mean?'

'So you've got her tethered,' said Baby. 'Well, you haven't got me. So Bee's got your permission to visit me. Oh, thank you very much. Well, it's off, then. No little visit.'

'Oh, but there will be. Only we'll all come. One of our cosy evenings. All of us. Including you,' Diana said to Charmian. 'Can't leave you out.'

'Of course,' said Charmian, who had very nearly achieved the end she was aiming at.

At the door, as they were getting ready to leave, Charmian managed to whisper to Baby: 'Try to distract Di somehow this evening, and leave me to talk to Bee.'

When the three of them arrived at Baby's flat, they found Phil slumped in a chair with her feet on a low table, a comfortable if inelegant figure. 'Oh, it's all of you.' She struggled to her feet. Charmian thought she was none too pleased.

The room was as beautifully kept and as spotless as

ever but, all the same, there was a change in it. Some of the sweet fluffiness had worn off the mimosa, which was a day too old. Baby's heart was no longer in it.

'Bee's just walked in. Said you were expecting her. She's in the bathroom being sick.'

'What?' Baby and Charmian exchanged looks, but it was Diana who went into the bathroom and emerged with a white-faced Bee.

'Just something I ate,' said Bee. 'I don't think I'll have anything now, Baby. I didn't know it was a party.'

'A party's us?' demanded Diana.

'Oh, you must eat, love,' said Baby. 'I'll cook you a lovely little omelette. Cheese or tomato? I do a very good cheese omelette.'

'Nothing, thank you,' said Bee weakly. 'I'll just have a cup of tea.'

'Well, some toast, then,' began Baby. 'With scrambled eggs?'

'A cup of tea and some sandwiches,' ordered Phil. 'I think that's about all any of us can stand.'

'We need to have a talk,' said Baby. 'We've got to talk this over between us. We're all flying apart.' She turned to Bee. 'You all right, now? You sit down and I'll make a pot of tea. Phil, you cut some sandwiches.'

She switched on the television set to while away their waiting-time. 'With sound or without?' she asked brightly, as she tuned it in.

No one answered her, so she left the sound off. Diana leant forward and turned the sound up as soon as Baby had disappeared into the kitchen. 'Silly fool,' she said. 'She gets under my skin sometimes.'

Baby was back very soon with a steaming pot of tea. She handed a cup to Bee, and then one to Charmian. As she started to pour a cup for Diana her hand twisted and a boiling jet of liquid shot into Diana's lap. Diana screamed and leapt to her feet.

'Clumsy idiot.'

Baby darted forward, dabbing at her. 'Come into the bathroom and let me dry you.'

'I'll have to take my skirt off.'

'I'll help you.'

Phil appeared at the door of the kitchen with a plate of cheese sandwiches; when she saw what was happening she shook her head and went back again into the kitchen.

Charmian said to Bee quickly: 'Bee, are you pregnant?'

'No.' Bee looked startled. 'But I'd like to be.'

'I see.' Charmian thought she saw. 'And can't you?'

'Di wouldn't stand for it. She'd force me to have an abortion.' Bee shook her head. 'She's getting very angry with me. That's why I was sick. I'm so nervous. I feel sick nearly all the time.'

'I know the feeling.' Charmian produced the photograph. 'Have you ever seen this? Do you know who it is?'

Bee didn't touch the picture, and hardly looked at it. 'No. No idea,' she said, as Diana and Baby came back into the room.

The five women spent a quietly uneasy evening watching television. It was difficult for Charmian to get a private word with Baby, but as Diana went off to put on her now dry skirt Charmian said:

'Couldn't you have thought of something better than the tea? Diana suspects, I'm sure.'

'I had to do the best I could on the spur of the moment. I'm not an original girl. So what's up with Bee?'

'Nothing much. She's nervous. She wants to have a child.'

'She does? Good for her, then. That explains a lot. Don't see it happening, though.'

Charmian was saved from answering by the arrival of

Diana, who shepherded her back to her desolate bed. Charmian was beginning to dread her nights there.

But, as she lay sleepless that night, she knew who had put the photograph in her pocket, and because she knew who had put it there she also knew who were the two people in it. And because she knew who the people were she knew why it had been left with her.

So I have to go forward, she thought. There's no going back now.

The next day and the day after passed quietly; Diana showed a distinct tendency to keep a surveillance on Charmian, but that was entirely understandable. And, after all, *she* was watching Diana.

She had written to Tom, and by careful pre-arrangement was able to receive a call from him in a public call-box.

'How are you?' he said at once.

'I ought to be asking *you* that question.'

'I'm sitting up in bed with the telephone beside me on a little trolley. They wheel it up to you. Handy, really . . . . I wish I knew what you were up to.'

'I've told you. More or less.'

'Mostly less – but I can fill in the gaps.'

Fervently Charmian hoped that he could not. 'What progress on your side?' she asked, to change the subject, although she wanted to know, desperately.

'I think I can waggle my toes,' he said, half doubtfully. 'It felt as though they were moving, but perhaps it was my imagination. I told the doctor, but I'm not sure if he believed me; he humours me a bit. My legs ache, as if they weren't there; it's a funny feeling. Or perhaps the pain is in my head and I'm only imagining it's in my legs. Sometimes I think that's what it is really: sort of phantom legs, you know.'

'Can't they give you something for the pain?'

236

'I think I'd rather keep my pain,' he said deprecatingly. 'I feel that if I lost my pain I might lose my legs.'

There could be something in that, Charmian thought; the pain must relate to the nerves of the leg, and the sensation must indicate that the nerves were alive. She wished she knew more about the workings of the human body. Wasn't there something called 'referred' pain?

'I think it's a good sign,' she said decisively. 'A very good sign. Must be. Look, I'll write you another letter.'

'Can I phone you again?'

'I'll tell you when.' And she rang off. On the ninth day she said to Diana: 'You don't have to watch me like a hawk. I'm not going to run away.'

'No, I suppose not.' Inevitably, Diana's strict surveillance of her largely unwanted guest was weakening. That day, Charmian had satisfied herself as much as she could, by looking through the keyholes, that the locked rooms of the house contained nothing but old furniture and old clothes. She had investigated the bathroom carefully, examining some bottles in the cabinet with interest. Early that morning she had climbed out of the kitchen window and inspected the outhouses and sheds situated farther along the narrow path which led to the river. They looked desolate and empty, but were as well locked up as anywhere else in Diana's domain. Even the narrow stretch of river which ran a few yards from the buildings looked grey and sour. Charmian had seen a dead rat floating in it, belly up.

'We'll both soon be free.' Charmian looked round the cubby-hole that Diana had created for her at *Charm and Chic*. 'I've read all the magazines here. You ought to get a few new ones.' Across the wall of cartons of hair-dye she could see Baby at work. Only Baby and Diana remained on the staff of *Charm and Chic*. Diana had given a holiday (it was going to be a permanent one, only they didn't know it) to the apprentice and junior assistant. She

237

herself did the hair of such few clients as she booked in, but they were very few. From the outside *Charm and Chic* looked normal; inside it was a hollow shell. 'What did you do to that bank manager?' she enquired thoughtfully. 'I notice she's never surfaced. Did you corrupt her the same as me?'

'You? No, not like you. You were halfway to corruption before I ever set eyes on you.' Diana gave a hoot of laughter.

Charmian lowered her eyes. 'True enough.'

'She was difficult enough at first but, after all, we had a gun. Admittedly, this time I had removed the bullets before I gave it to Baby. Couldn't have Baby killing anyone. We'd never have heard the last of it. Be above herself. She's bad enough as it is.' Diana was in a good mood today.

'I don't think Baby's a killer.'

Diana said sceptically. 'Can you tell just by looking?'

'Sometimes you can. So what did you do about the bank manager?'

Diana shrugged. 'Made her an offer.'

They sat in silence for a moment, then Charmian started again.

'Which address did you ask for your bank statement to be sent to?' asked Charmian. 'Remember, I only handed over a sealed envelope from each of you.'

'Oh, the old place,' said Diana. 'It's more – private. It's a very private place. A Swiss bank, I said. Once that money's abroad I've got no more worries.'

'So that's why you keep paying such regular visits there?'

'That's right,' said Diana. 'And, of course, you're there as my guest. Mustn't neglect you.'

'But, no, it can't be just that, can it? Because I know from what Bee said, and from what you've let drop yourself, that you were in the habit of daily visits before that.'

'Always the detective,' said Diana.

'I think you hate me for that,' said Charmian.

'At least I've forced you to give it up,' said Diana with satisfaction. 'You won't go back to that trade.'

Charmian did not answer for a few minutes, then she said, 'Let's eat at your old place tonight. Where I'm staying. Fish and chips? I've had enough of Baby's coloured cooking.'

'She hasn't asked us, anyway.'

'So I noticed,' said Charmian.

Baby said to Phil: 'Did you do what I asked you to do today?' It was raining and they were alone together in their living-room.

'Sell the Merc? Yes.'

'And you got the cash?'

Phil produced a wad of notes and slapped them on the table. 'Here. I got a good price. I didn't want to do it, mind, but I did. I hope you know what you are doing. And getting me to do.'

'Oh, I know,' said Baby. 'I've watched that girl eat for two nights now. She doesn't eat like a girl who's really worried. And she ought to be worried stiff. No, it's all going terribly wrong, I'm sure of it. We must be off. Put together the things you really treasure and we'll be off.'

'And live on what I got for the car?' asked Phil sceptically.

'No.' Baby was emphatic. She bent down and dragged a cardboard box from under the table. 'Look.'

Phil looked, and then put her hand over her eyes as if she couldn't believe what she saw. 'Money.'

'Yes,' said Baby coolly. 'Money. Ten-pound notes. Unmarked and clean. I saw to that.'

'Where did you get it?'

239

'It's part of the loot from the bank. I took my own share when I was helping pack it up. No one saw me.'

'Di'll kill you,' breathed Phil.

'Yes,' said Baby coolly. 'I believe she would. But we won't be here. It's the reason we're getting out. Well, one of the reasons. Pack your things, Phil, and we'll go now.'

This conversation had been going on for some time. Baby had been saying the same thing over and over again, battering against Phil's doubts. Once Baby had heard a famous diplomat say that the essence of diplomacy was not to take no for an answer but to go on asking, and she was acting on what she had heard.

'Oh, I don't know,' said Phil wearily.

Baby scented victory. 'Yes, Phil. Yes. *Now.*'

Bee said to the man she was in love with, and with whom she had been living for the last year: 'It's time we had a talk. No, don't hold up your hand like that. I *know* I haven't said much about this business of Diana's, but I didn't want you touched by it. Old-fashioned of me, I know, but I didn't want you – well, soiled by it. I like to think of you as innocent. You *are* innocent, and I want you kept that way. It's different for me. I don't know why; it just *is.*

'What I want to say is that I think it's time we made a move. No, I don't know where – anywhere so long as it's away from Diana. Yes, I am frightened of her, always have been. She'll make a meal of me, any time she fancies to. I think she's had a bite already. But it's worse than that – it's what else she's been eating. Ferocious, that's the word for Diana.

'I've got some savings, not a fortune, but plenty for us two to make a fresh start. We'd better get married . . . . You can get a divorce, can't you? Then if anything went *really* wrong for me, you'd wait for me, wouldn't you?

240

Even "life" doesn't mean for ever, these days, you know, and we'd have each other.' She was already mourning for the child she would never bear. She was over thirty; a spell in prison would probably make it too late when she got out. Everyone knew that women in prison have amenorrhoea and that must mean infertility.

Diana and Charmian had finished their plates of cod and chips in a silence which was broken by Charmian. 'I enjoyed that. I never expected to, but it wasn't bad. A bit greasy, perhaps.'

'You want to watch your figure,' said Diana unpleasantly.

Charmian took a glance at herself in the mirror over the sink. 'Well, I know I don't look too splendid at the moment, but that'll change.'

'Splendid? That's the understatement of the year. Dear, you look a slob.'

In a level voice, Charmian said: 'I don't think that's true, but I can understand why you feel you've got to say it. You never liked me, you certainly don't trust me, and now I irritate you intensely.'

Diana pushed her plate away. 'Try not to irritate me.'

'I'm afraid I can't quite manage that at the moment,' said Charmian politely. 'It shouldn't be long now, though.'

Outside, a heavy rain was falling and a strong wind was beginning to rattle and shake the decaying joints of the old place.

'I think I'll stay the night,' decided Diana. 'There's a bed upstairs for me. The letter may come in the morning.'

'I think it may,' said Charmian.

'*Charm and Chic*'s up for sale, you know, and I had an offer this morning. My bank can handle it all. I can soon be off.'

'The best thing,' agreed Charmian.

241

Diana got up. 'I could wash your hair for you,' she offered generously.

'What, here?'

'Yes. I keep shampoo and towels here.' She added: 'And a dryer.'

Charmian considered. 'No, I don't think so; I don't fancy sitting under a dryer.'

'Oh, come on,' said Diana. 'I could do a good job, and your hair needs it.'

'Tell you what: I'll have it done tomorrow morning.'

Diana thought about it. 'That might be a good idea. I think I'll get my equipment out and ready now. Give me a hand, will you?'

Together the two women dragged out a chair with a padded head-rest, and set out towels, shampoo and several basins. A hand dryer was plugged in. Charmian could swear that Diana was enjoying herself. Charmian watched Diana give a huge yawn. 'Oh, I think I'll go to bed.'

'I'm tired myself.'

'I bet you are. See you in the morning.'

Charmian turned out all the lights, lay down on the bed, and waited. She had to wait a very long time, and the pale grey light of dawn was creeping into the room before she heard Diana moving about. She raised herself on one elbow and listened: Diana was going down the stairs; then she heard the front door open and close.

Charmian got up and watched from her window. She saw Diana turn the corner of the house and take the path towards the outbuildings and the river.

'This is it,' she said aloud. 'The moment's come.' And she felt more sick and afraid than she had thought she would.

She let herself out of the front door and slipped down the path after Diana. The latter never looked behind her once, or even paused. How confident she must be, was

242

Charmian's thought. She didn't even lock me in last night.

She caught up with Diana at the door of a low stone building, which Charmian thought had probably been a stable. Diana swung round in surprise.

'Didn't you expect me?' asked Charmian.

Diana blinked, without answering.

'What *did* you expect?'

Diana still did not answer, but her eyes went towards the door.

'Open the door, then,' said Charmian. 'I see you've got a key.'

'I was only going to have a look round in there and tidy up before I go away. I won't bother now.' Diana seemed to have difficulty in getting the words out.

'Oh, come on, Diana. You can do better than that,' said Charmian. 'Go ahead. Open up.'

'No.' Diana tried to turn away, but Charmian stopped her.

'*I* will, then,' she said. She tried the door, and it swung open easily. 'Not locked after all.' And she looked at Diana. 'You must have been mistaken.'

Diana's expression was hard to read, but she was breathing deeply and irregularly and patches of red had appeared on her cheeks. 'There's nothing in this for me,' she said. 'I'm going back to the house.'

'I think you ought to go inside,' said Charmian, maintaining her initiative, and she edged Diana to the door.

Inside was a strange and disturbing sight: a camp-bed with a tumble of soiled blankets and ropes trailing from each end as if someone had been tethered to it, head and feet. There was a bucket in one corner, and over everything a foetid stink.

But the room was quite empty.

243

Diana opened her mouth as if to say something, then shut it again, as if she'd thought better of it.

'No. There's no one there,' said Charmian, and because she now felt more confident her voice was quieter and less harsh than it had been. 'She's gone.'

'She?' said Diana.

'Yes. It's not what you expected, is it? A bit of a surprise. A shock even. You thought she'd still be here, tied up, gagged and semi-conscious. What drug did you use? Some stuff left over from your mother's illness? Phil told me she died here. I saw some tablets still in the bathroom cabinet. Or was it just violence? She had been beaten.'

'I haven't the least idea what you are talking about,' said Diana, turning away. 'If some poor vagrant has been living in there . . . .'

Charmian said: 'A better try, Diana, but not good enough. No, not a vagrant, but a bank manager. You've kept her here, and I think today you meant to send her on her way. Why didn't you kill her before?'

'None of this will do you any good,' said Diana 'You're in this as deep as any of us. And, since you ask, I didn't want to kill her. I'm not a psychopath. I don't kill for the sake of killing. Once I'd got clean out of the country I would have left her where she could be found.'

'I'm not sure that I believe that,' said Charmian. 'I think you *are* a psychopath and I think you enjoyed ill-treating her. I have some reason to think that's how you behave. Something I haven't mentioned yet. I don't think Baby and Phil knew about your prisoner,' went on Charmian appraisingly. 'But I think your sister Bee must have done. She must have helped you get the woman here. But I doubt if she knew you still had her here. I bet you spun some yarn. I feel sorry for Bee, but I suppose family feeling kept her loyal to you.'

244

'I don't care a devil's pinch what you think. You're in trouble, too, remember.'

'You're not thinking straight, Di,' said Charmian. 'Give your mind to the problem. Clearly, I found the woman here. I wasn't surprised the place was empty, was I? The fact is, I was looking for her, I found her, and I got her away yesterday, Di, and you never knew.'

Slowly Diana said: 'I never realised before what a rotten person you are. There's no loyalty in you.'

'Yes. I am rotten,' admitted Charmian. 'But it depends where your loyalty lies. Mine is to an idea. To justice, I think.' To herself she said: Although it is Alice Udell's face I see asking for justice.

'Come back into the house,' said Diana smartly. 'We'll settle this between us.'

She had the initiative again, or thought she had, and she led the way back into the house with a formidable look. 'Finish it off,' she said over her shoulder. 'It's got to be finished.'

Charmian followed Diana up the path and into the house. She could feel her heart banging in her rib-cage; she clenched her hands in her pockets.

Inside the kitchen the chair with the head-rest and all the hairdressing equipment still stood on parade. Both women saw them at the same time, and Charmian laughed.

'I don't think I'll let you wash my hair after all.'

Diana picked up a towel. 'Sure?' She was wringing the towel between her hands. 'I do a good job.'

'You know,' said Charmian, 'I don't think even now you've grasped what this is all about.'

'I know you're a rotten bloody traitor.'

'Only from where you stand.'

Diana was being slow about taking it all in, very slow for her. Charmian decided it was shock. 'But you're committed to us. I've got you tied up.'

245

'I'm afraid I fixed it all with my boss first, a man called Walter Wing, before I left,' said Charmian. 'He knew what I was up to. He didn't like it. Thought it might be dangerous. But I had my reasons for wanting to do it this way. Extend myself as a woman, you could say.'

'What's that mean?' said Diana aggressively. 'Explain yourself.'

'It's about a dead man whom we identified as a known criminal called Terry Jarvis. I saw you read the report on him. I think you even photographed it. He was put in the river, and an effort had been made to put weights on his feet; but he was dead before he got into the water. He'd been murdered and sexually assaulted. A muscular strong man like that – strange, isn't it?'

'Who is this Terry Jarvis?' said Diana. 'What's he to me?'

'He had a lot of women in his life, but he only married one: a woman called Olive Francis. But she preferred the name Diana. He called her Di.' Their eyes met. 'He didn't treat her well and eventually she left him. He was in prison at the time. But he followed her and found out her new surname, King, and her new address when he got out. I'm talking about you, Di.'

'I don't see how you can be.' She sounded puzzled.

'You think you're God, Diana, and can get away with anything. Terry Jarvis was in your hairdressing salon. He took one of your business-cards and wrote down my husband's name and address and telephone number. I suppose he had just looked it up in the telephone directory. I think he was going to visit my husband, whom he had known and whom he did not know to be dead, and tell him all about you and your plans for Deerham Hills. You killed him before he could do so, but he had that card on his body.'

Diana started to laugh. 'You mean he had one of my cards actually on him? Can you beat it? I don't know why

I'm laughing. I ought to be crying, but it is funny, you must admit.'

'In a way,' said Charmian, keeping a sharp eye on Diana. 'It didn't seem funny to Bee, though. She had read about the dead man in the papers, and reluctantly she came to the conclusion that you had killed him. She sent me a photograph of both of you taken years ago because she wanted me to know of the connection without involving herself. I couldn't identify the couple at first, so I showed the photograph around.'

'I know. You showed me.'

'Yes, and you carried it off well. But I knew it was Bee who had sent it because, of all of you, only Bee would not touch the photograph. Hardly even looked at it. So I knew then it was you, and that the man with you was probably Terry Jarvis. I was guessing, but it fitted together.'

'I don't know why he came here, but come he did, and he actually saw me in the street and followed me to *Charm and Chic*.'

'He had been to the hospital,' Charmian told her. 'He had been sent to a special clinic there.'

'What for?'

'He had a fatal illness.'

Diana frowned. 'Did he know?'

'I think so.'

'No wonder he was in such a rotten mood. I could feel it; it made me worse than I might have been, and God knows I was always bad enough with him. And he with me.'

'In the short space he had left to him, I think he wanted both the money you had taken from him (yes, I know about that) and his revenge.'

'I hated him,' said Diana. 'I'd cut free once, and there he was back again. He degraded me, all the years we were together. I was just an organism he could use. But I'd beaten him, I thought, and then suddenly here he was

247

again, full of demands and threats. He thought he'd got me right where he wanted me, too. Well, I had my own thoughts about that. He came down here with me. Sat in that chair, and told me what they'd done to his hair in the nick and asked me to wash and blow-dry it. He actually let me tie him up! He thought I was just fixing the towels and cape over his shoulders before I washed his hair. Then he tried to move. You should have seen his face! What a joke! The rest after that was pure pleasure. For me, just for once.'

'I know,' said Charmian. 'I know what you did.'

'He *almost* liked it. I could see it in his eyes. I thought to myself: If you've done nothing else in your life, Diana, you've justified your place in a woman's world. Redressed a balance or two. I was *pleased.* And now you're telling me he would have died anyway.'

'In time.'

Diana thought about it, then she said: 'Funny how things work out, isn't it? In order to hurt and abuse and humiliate him the way I did, I had to give him some pleasure. He didn't want to feel it – I hadn't always wanted to, either – but he had to experience it.'

Charmian covered her eyes; she didn't want to see Diana's face.

'Makes you think about life, doesn't it? But I honestly don't know what conclusions it brings you to. Nothing very nice, I think. His pleasure and my pain, his pain and my pleasure – which was which and where did each end?' She took down Charmian's hands. 'Look at me and answer.'

'Can't answer,' muttered Charmian. But she knew she was in for it. Diana was going to talk.

'I said to him, "Would you like to do something really freaky? Give you no end of a kick . . . ." I was talking all the time I tied him up, so he wouldn't really take in that he was being tethered. I'd got a towel over his mouth, and

248

I was sort of leaning on it, but I was talking so friendly. I saw his eyes roll at me. "Yes," he was saying. "Yes, let's do it."'

'Leave it, Diana. Leave it at that.'

'I think you ought to hear, I really do, and then you'll understand. You must have wanted to be cruel and violent yourself, too, sometimes.'

'No. Never.'

'Then you're not being honest with yourself,' said Diana contemptuously.

'Not everyone's like you, Di.'

'I cut down the front of his pants with my cutting-scissors. I saw his eyes go pop then all right. "It's all *right*," I said, "I'm not going to *cut* you." I was terribly loving then. I said, "I'll make you ready first, before we begin, ready and willing."'

Charmian was distressed. Something wild and terrible was shaking loose in Diana. If it belonged to all women, she wanted no part in it.

'To cut a long story short . . . . ' Diana stopped. 'Would you like a piece of my mind? You're *soft*. So, when he was ready, as they say, I got out one of those great plastic rollers I use for setting hair.'

'Oh, shut up, Diana.'

'A sort of plastic virgin, you might call it. Wasn't there a medieval instrument of torture called the Iron Maiden? This was a plastic one, but just as wicked . . . . I think I hit him a bit, too. I got rather wild.' Diana paused, as if considering it all. 'I suppose it was a sort of madness, really. I'm a sadist. That's what they'll say.' She paused again and summed up. 'And know what? They'll be right. Do I frighten you? I frighten myself. Bee's frightened of me, too. Not Baby. That says something for her. Good or bad, I don't know which.'

'You don't frighten me,' said Charmian steadily. 'But, by God, you appal me.'

'When I stopped and came to myself, I strangled him. Couldn't think of anything else to do. That's woman's hour over, I said. It was not exactly my best moment. When he was dead, I dragged him down the garden and rolled him into the river. I knew the current runs strongly there and that, if he didn't sink, or if he floated free, then the current would carry him further down the river, well away from here. Bee had some of that ready-mixed cement – I stuck his feet in that . . . . It didn't work very well, I think. There must be a knack to it. Bee suspected, I think; but she didn't want to think about it. Come on, now. *You* say something.'

'I'm glad I didn't let you wash my hair,' said Charmian, standing up and speaking clearly.

'So,' said Diana, and suddenly she leapt on Charmian, forcing her back against the wall, and pushing the towel into her mouth. Charmian tightened her muscles and silently thrust herself into a collision with Diana's body. For a moment, they stood braced against each other, then Charmian gave a heave and bounced Diana away from her, the towel left her mouth and she could breathe again. Diana had fallen against a table and hit her head, which dazed her for a moment, then she reared up and grabbed at Charmian, pulling her down on the floor. She had a grip on Charmian's waist; but Charmian seized her shoulders and tried to push her away. They rolled over on the floor, Charmian underneath, Diana got astride her opponent's body and began to bang Charmian's head on the floor; for a moment she spent her strength in this way, then her hands slid down to Charmian's throat and she began to press. With a tremendous effort, almost the last of which she was capable, Charmian drew her right hand up and hit Diana heavily across the face. Diana gasped as blood spurted from her nose, and her hands dropped loose.

Charmian drew herself away, panting, and sat up.

Diana had her handkerchief to her nose and was moaning. 'Stop this, Di. You don't really want to kill me.'

'No, no, you're right.' Diana was crying. 'Baby said it ages ago and it is true: women ought not to kill women.'

Charmian got to her feet and staggered to the sink, where she wiped her face. 'I'll get us a cup of tea.'

'Yes, yes. You do that.' Diana, too, stood up. Charmian threw her a wet towel and she held it to her nose. When the tea was made, both women sat down to drink it at the kitchen table.

'Don't say anything,' said Charmian. 'Don't talk at all. We'll work something out.'

Diana rested her head on one hand. 'No. I'll accept prison. I ought to be punished.'

As they sat in silence, there came a rattle at the door and the sound of something dropping through the letter-box.

'Oh, God, it's the letter,' said Diana. 'Come at last. My money in the bank.' She went out to the hall and came back carrying an envelope in her hand.

'Are you sure that's it?' said Charmian, who was more in control of herself and could see the letter clearly. 'Open it, Diana.'

Her hands awkward with bruises, Diana did so. She read, stared at Charmian as if she did not understand what she had read, then read again. Then she began to cry and laugh all at once. 'It's about the test I had for cervical cancer. It was positive; I am called to the clinic.' Her voice rose. 'I need not have worried about dying. I've got my death inside me. It's a proper woman's fate, isn't it?'

The world at Deerham Hills moved on. Gloria, alias Georgey Burdomesky (Georgey with a soft *G*), born George Beadle, on probation, got an appointment at a clinic for her operation and left town. Charmian and Tom went away for the holiday she had promised them. She was likely to get promotion because of her good secret work; she hated herself for being pleased.

'It's stupid, I know, because I went into that group to do what I did, to split it up and capture the guilty. But now *I* feel guilty. As if I were disloyal. I wonder if a man would feel like that?'

'I don't suppose so,' said Tom. 'Just a job of work. Although men are great on group loyalties. But it's usually an institution like an army or a school.'

'I don't believe women are loyal to a people or to a group, but to an idea inside them. You listen to a small note striking inside you like a bell and that's what you're loyal to if you're a woman.'

Baby and Phil were not seen again there. Diana and Bee were in different forms of custody, but Diana's time of trial had already begun: she was bad. The bank manager was making a good recovery, and it looked as though Tom would walk again. He was on the way up. Diana, on the other hand, was probably not going to be so lucky. She was on the way down. So death and life had fused into their usual amalgam, the one moving imperceptibly into the other. The crime wave in Deerham Hills was over. Diana had not achieved as much as she had hoped, for the established order had proved tougher than she. It had always been stronger than she supposed. Walter Wing on behalf of the men was firmly in charge again.

But sappers were at work under his defences.

Far away, under a warm Spanish sun, Baby rubbed oil into her skin and drew a sunshade over her head. 'I can't fry like you,' she said to Phil. 'You know what a delicate skin I've got.'

'Mmmm.' Phil, eyes closed, made a long sound of contentment. 'This is the life.'

'Well, I've been thinking about that. As I was so successful this time round, why don't we plan something

252

really big, like robbing a major bank? I know I can do it, and it's time we women really showed our power.' Delicately she rubbed the oil into her perfumed skin; Baby at her most formidable: Venus with her prey in her sights, her delicate talons outstretched. 'After all, there is more than one way of starting a revolution, isn't there?'